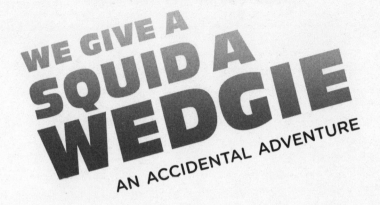

WE GIVE A
SQUID A
WEDGIE

AN ACCIDENTAL ADVENTURE

W... S.

"Dude," .... ey were climbing .... ou think you'll have to climb like this on the sailboat? Like a pirate? What if you meet pirates? Do you think they'll make you walk the plank?"

"I heard that pirates don't do that," said the other Gomez, climbing the rope on the other side of Oliver. "They just kill you and take your loot."

Oliver grunted. He had to focus on climbing the rope. Why did they make children climb ropes? It seemed like cruel and unusual punishment.

"Do you think you'll see sharks?" the Gomezes asked together.

Oliver grunted again. But he wondered, what about pirates? What about sharks? And what if they found the island of sea monsters and the map? Would they also find their mother?

"I heard that you have to go to the bathroom in a bucket off the side of the boat," one of the Gomezes told Oliver a half hour later, as they sat down in the lunchroom in front of heaping piles of Tater Tots.

"I heard you don't even get a bucket," said the other Gomez, biting into his grilled cheese sandwich. "And you have to use old gum wrappers for toilet paper."

"No way!" said his brother as he drowned his lunch in ketchup. "They're too small. Maybe you have to use, like, seaweed or something."

"Like when Corey Brandt got that rash on *The Celebrity Adventurist*?" the other one added. He gestured at Oliver with a Tater Tot. "Do you think you'll get a rash?"

The way he asked made a rash sound like a good thing.

OTHER BOOKS YOU MAY ENJOY

The Apothecary	Maile Meloy
Books of Elsewhere: The Shadows	Jacqueline West
Dragonbreath	Ursula Vernon
No Passengers Beyond This Point	Gennifer Choldenko
P.K. Pinkerton and the Deadly Desperados	Caroline Lawrence
The Secret of Platform 13	Eva Ibbotson
A Tale Dark and Grimm	Adam Gidwitz
Theodore Boone: The Abduction	John Grisham
Theodore Boone: Kid Lawyer	John Grisham
We Are Not Eaten by Yaks: An Accidental Adventure	C. Alexander London
We Dine with Cannibals: An Accidental Adventure	C. Alexander London

WE GIVE A SQUID A WEDGIE

AN ACCIDENTAL ADVENTURE

C. Alexander London

With art by Jonny Duddle

PUFFIN BOOKS
An Imprint of Penguin Group (USA) Inc.

PUFFIN BOOKS
Published by the Penguin Group
Penguin Young Readers Group, 345 Hudson Street, New York, New York 10014, U.S.A.
Penguin Group (Canada), 90 Eglinton Avenue East, Suite 700, Toronto, Ontario M4P 2Y3, Canada
(a division of Pearson Penguin Canada Inc.)
Penguin Books Ltd, 80 Strand, London WC2R 0RL, England
Penguin Ireland, 25 St Stephen's Green, Dublin 2, Ireland (a division of Penguin Books Ltd)
Penguin Group (Australia), 707 Collins Street, Melbourne, Victoria 3008, Australia
(a division of Pearson Australia Group Pty Ltd)
Penguin Books India Pvt Ltd, 11 Community Centre, Panchsheel Park, New Delhi–110 017, India
Penguin Group (NZ), 67 Apollo Drive, Rosedale, Auckland 0632, New Zealand
(a division of Pearson New Zealand Ltd)
Penguin Books, Rosebank Office Park, 181 Jan Smuts Avenue, Parktown North 2193, South Africa
Penguin China, B7 Jiaming Center, 27 East Third Ring Road North,
Chaoyang District, Beijing 100020, China

Penguin Books Ltd, Registered Offices: 80 Strand, London WC2R 0RL, England

First published in the United States of America by Puffin Books,
an imprint of Penguin Young Readers Group, 2013

1 3 5 7 9 10 8 6 4 2

London, C. Alexander.
We give a squid a wedgie / C. Alexander London ;
with art by Jonny Duddle. p. cm.—(An accidental adventure)
Summary: Eleven-year-old twins Oliver and Celia Navel are forced to give up television again,
this time for an adventure on a South Pacific island surrounded by giant killer squid.
[1. Adventure and adventurers—Fiction. 2. Explorers—Fiction.
3. Brothers and sisters—Fiction. 4. Twins—Fiction. 5. Television—Fiction.
6. South Pacific Ocean—Fiction. 7. Humorous stories.]
I. Duddle, Jonny, ill. II. Title.
PZ7.L8419Wh 2012 [Fic]—dc23 2011034404

Puffin Books ISBN: 978-0-14-242475-9

Printed in the United States of America

Design by Semadar Megged
Text set in Trump Mediaeval

ALWAYS LEARNING   PEARSON

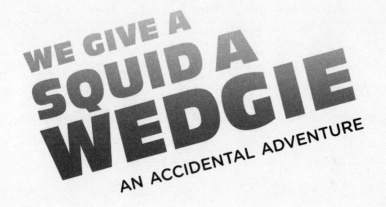

AN ACCIDENTAL ADVENTURE

CONTENTS

To Brian Jacques,
whom I never got to thank,
and to Natalie,
whom I cannot thank enough

1

WE ARE OVER ~~OCTOPUSES~~ OCTOPI

"I THINK IT'S FOOD," said Celia, studying the flaky brownish lumps on the silver tray in front of her. There were also squishy purple blobs.

"It doesn't look like food," said Oliver.

"There's a lemon," said Celia. "Why would there be a lemon if it wasn't food?"

"For decoration?" suggested Oliver.

"A lemon is not decoration," said Celia.

"What about on one of those fruit hats?" he asked.

"This is a serving tray, not a fruit hat," said Celia. "It's food. And it looks gross."

Oliver and Celia Navel were at the New Year's Eve gala for the Explorers Club, the most exclusive party of the year for the most exclusive society of explorers in the world. All of the food at this party was weird or slimy or gross, like caterpillar-stuffed quail eggs and candied shrimp heads. The party was held in the private aquarium of a famous deep-sea diver. He had a shark tank that encircled the whole room and an indoor tropical reef filled with brightly colored fish in a pillar in the center. There was a pool filled with stingrays and a dozen other tanks that Oliver and Celia hadn't even seen yet.

They were bored beyond belief.

Oliver and Celia finally had cable television at home, but instead of sitting happily on the couch watching the old year turn into the new one, they were stuck at a fancy party for fancy explorers surrounded by fancy fish, watching the new year start just like every other year. It was not their idea of fun.

Oliver poked at the brown lumps on the silver tray. They were crispy and hot. Some of them had little tentacles sticking out. The purple blobs were slimy and they glistened.

"This is calamari," said the server, who was holding the tray out to Oliver and Celia and growing quite tired of standing there while they argued.

Oliver looked at Celia with his eyebrows raised.

She was three minutes and forty-two seconds older than her twin brother, which made her the expert on things like the meanings of words and how to escape from a prison fortress in Tibet. She did not, however, know what calamari was.

Celia shrugged.

"It's fried squid," said the server, thrusting the tray toward Oliver and Celia again. "*Calamari* just means squid."

"Why not just say *squid* then?" Celia said.

"*Calamari* is the Italian word," the server told her.

"What are the purple blobs?" Oliver asked.

"Octopus," said the server.

"Aren't they the same?" wondered Celia.

"No," said Oliver, who felt good knowing something that his sister didn't for once. He liked watching nature shows. *The Squid Whisperer* was one of his favorites. "The octopus has a hard beak and the squid doesn't. They both have eight arms and squishy heads, but squids have hooks in their suckers and octopuses don't."

"Octopi," said Celia, who knew that the plural of *octopus* was *octopi*.

"*Octopuses* is right too," said Oliver.

"It is not," said Celia.

"It is too," said Oliver.

"It is not," said Celia.

"It is too," said Oliver.

"Look, kids, do you want some of this or not?" the server interrupted. "There are a lot of guests who want to eat."

"What's the lemon for?" Oliver asked.

"That's for decoration," said the server.

"Aha!" Oliver gloated. "I was right! Lemons for decoration!"

"Whatever," said Celia.

"Ahem," coughed the server, trying to get their attention back on his tray of brownish and purple lumps.

Celia shook her head at him. "We don't eat squid or octopi," she said.

"-puses," added Oliver.

Celia glared at him.

"We don't eat anything weird or slimy or gross," she said.

"Whatever," sneered the server. He trotted back into the party, weaving between the guests dressed in ball gowns and tuxedos, eating their squid and their octopi. Octopuses. Whatever.

Tiger sharks and bull sharks and sleek silver reef sharks swam in never-ending circles around the edge of the room.

"I can't believe we're missing *Velma Sue's Snack Cake Times Square New Year's Eve Spectacular* for this," Oliver grumbled.

"It's called VSSCTSNYES," Celia corrected her brother. "*Vuss-Cat's-Knees*," she emphasized. It was the television event of the year, but Oliver couldn't even get the name right.

"Whatever it's called, I can't believe we're missing it," he complained, picking at the bow tie on his neck, which was too tight. The rest of the tuxedo was too short. His father, the world-famous explorer Dr. Ogden Navel, hadn't even noticed that Oliver had outgrown it.

"We miss everything good," agreed Celia, slouching against the glass of the tank behind her. She didn't so much as glance at the grimacing tiger shark as it swam above her head.

Now, if we were lucky enough to receive an invitation to the Explorers Club gala at the private aquarium of a famous deep-sea diver on New Year's Eve, we would most likely thrill to find ourselves in the rarefied company of astronauts, explorers, motocross champions, ichthyologists, and deputy editors of assorted discount travel websites. We would, however, have to look up exactly what an ichthyologist or a deputy editor actually does.

And while we, like Oliver and Celia Navel, would avoid eating the caterpillar-stuffed quail eggs, candied shrimp heads, and fried calamari being passed about on silver trays, we would certainly not linger on the edges without exploring any of the wonderful undersea creatures on display.

But for Oliver and Celia, exploration had long ago lost its charm. It had cost them no end of hardship and heartache over the years. Even though they lived on the 4½th floor of the Explorers Club, and even though their parents held the prestigious title of Explorers-in-Residence, Oliver and Celia hated exploring.

Their mother and father, however, loved exploring. Their mother loved it so much that she had gone off to search for the Lost Library of Alexandria over three years ago, and after three years without hearing from her, she suddenly returned to drag her children into a dangerous race to help her find it.

Their father, determined to make their lives

interesting, always made them go to his lectures on things like "Ancient Polynesian Navigation" or "Rites of Passage in Seventeenth-Century Samoan Culture," and he regularly put them in mortal danger with trips to places like Tibet and the Amazon jungle. To make matters worse, they still had to get through the second half of sixth grade.

"Corey Brandt hasn't even talked to us all night," Oliver observed, pointing across the room where the teen heartthrob and star of *Agent Zero*, *Sunset High*, and *The Celebrity Adventurist* was surrounded by a group of crazed fans, who also happened to be professional sumo wrestlers. Every time he tried to get away from them, they blocked his path and asked him about his newest show or his last Christmas special or his hair gel.

He looked toward the Navel twins and gave them an apologetic shrug.

"We save his life from an evil Corey Brandt impersonator," Oliver said, scowling, "and all he gives us is a shrug."

"He's trying to join the Explorers Club," explained Celia. "He can't be rude to anyone here. They all get to vote on his application."

"Why would anyone want to join the Explorers

Club?" wondered Oliver. "All you do is listen to boring lectures and get bitten by exotic lizards."

Oliver spoke from experience. He had listened to a lot of lectures and been bitten by a lot of lizards.

"Beats me," said Celia. "But Corey said he'd hang out with us. We just have to wait a minute."

"Oliver, Celia!" Their father strode across the room to where the twins were standing. His own tuxedo was too small for him, just like Oliver's, but his beard was neatly trimmed and his glasses had slid down his nose like they always did when he was excited or being attacked by a yeti. "Isn't this a wonderful party? Did you try the octopus? Or the fried squid?"

"They called it calamari," said Oliver.

"Yes, of course, the Italian word." Dr. Navel pushed his glasses back up his nose.

"We don't eat squid," said Celia. "Or octopi."

Oliver was going to correct her, but she gave him a look that told him something terrible would happen if he did. He bit his lip and didn't say a word.

Dr. Navel shrugged and looked out at the collection of explorers, adventurers, daredevils, and website editors who had gathered to celebrate New Year's Eve.

Professor Rasmali-Greenberg, the president of the Explorers Club, buzzed from explorer to explorer, laughing and telling the same joke about a jaguar and Dr. Livingstone in a hot tub. He pulled Corey Brandt away from the sumo wrestlers and dragged him over to meet a group of Rajasthani fire dancers and their escort from the Indian Embassy.

"It's, like, mad tight meeting you nice folks," Oliver and Celia heard the sixteen-year-old superstar tell the ambassador from India. He had pulled out his cell phone to take a picture with them. The ambassador smiled widely. Like everyone else in the world, he couldn't get enough of Corey Brandt.

"Corey is certainly kibitzing with all the right people tonight," Dr. Navel said.

"What's kibitzing?" asked Oliver, who was tired of waiting around for the celebrity.

"It's something people do at fancy parties," his father explained. "It's like chatting."

"Why not just say *chatting* then?" Oliver asked.

"Because"—Celia rolled her eyes—"Dad's an explorer. He can't talk like a normal person."

"I didn't make up the word *kibitz*," his father said. "It's from the noble language of Yiddish."

"That sounds made up too," Oliver said.

"Well, it's not," his father answered.

"Well, I don't want to do any kibitzing with anyone tonight," said Oliver. "So can we go?"

"We can't go yet," Celia told him. "We haven't talked to Corey!"

"Ugh," Oliver groaned.

Celia had decided that she was Corey Brandt's number one fan, but she hadn't seen him since they'd saved his life after their adventure in the Amazon. The girls at school were starting to think she didn't really know him. Sixth-graders could be so suspicious.

Tonight she was going to ask Corey to visit her class. That'd wipe the smug grin off Stephanie Sabol's face.

"Whose face?" Oliver asked, startling Celia.

"What?" she said.

"You were muttering about a face," he said. "And somebody named Smug."

"What? No I wasn't."

"Yes," said Oliver. "You were. You were muttering. You said *smug*."

"Did not."

"Did too."

"Did n—"

"You did say *smug*, Celia," her father agreed with Oliver.

"Whatever," said Celia.

"Anyway, I don't want to be at this party," Oliver said. "I want to go home to watch Vuss-Cat's-whatever."

"*Velma Sue's Snack Cake Times Square New Year's Eve Spectacular.*" Celia rolled her eyes. "VSSCTSNYES. At least get the name right."

"Madam Mumu is going to perform 'Cheese Arcade Magic,'" Oliver explained to his father. "It's historic."

"That's true," Celia added.

Their father shook his head at his children.

He was a world-famous explorer. He had discovered the royal tombs of the ancient Pyu kingdom in Burma. He had paddled a kayak across the Atlantic Ocean. He'd been to Dayton, Ohio. Twice!

Yet Oliver and Celia were world-class couch potatoes. He simply couldn't understand how that had happened.

"Your show will be there after the banquet." Dr. Navel sighed. "We have cable now. It's recording."

"But it's live TV!" Oliver had a way of crossing his arms and pouting that got right under his father's skin.

"But you won't miss anything."

"But it'll be in the past when we watch it!" Oliver complained. "It'll have already happened."

"So it'll be like time travel!"

"Dad, it's not the same," Oliver said. Explaining culture to his father was impossible. He had too many college degrees in anthropology.

"Just be patient, Oliver," said Celia. Her brother could be so annoying.

Oliver turned to his sister, shocked. Why was she suddenly on their dad's side? She was supposed to be on *his* side. They were twins! She was supposed to want to go home and watch TV and complain about explorers. She was not supposed to stay at some fancy party and make googly eyes at Corey Brandt.

"What was that?" Celia snapped at her brother.

"What?" said Oliver.

"You just muttered the word *googly* out loud," said Celia.

"I did not," said Oliver.

"You did too," said Celia.

"Did not."

"Did too."

"Did n—"

"You did mutter the word *googly*," his father said.

Celia crossed her arms in triumph.

Oliver looked from his father to his sister, back to his father, and then back to his sister.

"Whatever," he said, and stomped away to be on his own.

If they wanted to gang up on him to make him stay at some stupid party just so she could make googly eyes at some stupid teenager, then they could do it without him. He didn't need his sister on his side anyway. She always made him watch that dumb soap opera, *Love at 30,000 Feet*. Without her, he could watch whatever he wanted. She wasn't his boss. She didn't get to tell him what to do.

He glanced over his shoulder to make sure she was watching him storm off. He had an idea that would really get on her nerves.

Just then, the server with the tray of octopus and calamari passed by. Oliver grabbed a big handful of the purplish blobs and brownish lumps and smiled at his sister. Then he shoved the blobs and the lumps into his mouth.

"No!" yelled Celia across the room. Everyone fell silent. She couldn't believe what her brother had just done.

"You don't tell me what to do!" Oliver yelled back across the room at her, spitting bits of calamari out of his mouth.

"It's not that," said Celia. "It's . . . you're . . ." She pointed behind him.

"Dude," Corey Brandt said loudly. "Like, D-U-D-E, dude."

"What?" Oliver asked. "What's going on? Why is everyone looking at me like that?"

No one was moving. The entire room just stared at Oliver.

"Ollie," his father said. "Don't move."

"What? Why not?" Oliver peered over his shoulder where his sister was pointing, and saw that he had just put a fistful of octopus in his mouth right in front of an octopus tank.

And the octopus did not seem happy about his friends being eaten.

Also, the octopus had just escaped.

2

WE ARE NONPLUSSED

OLIVER FELT A TENTACLE wrap around his left ankle. And then another wrap around his right ankle. And then another around his waist. They were sticky and harder than he expected, and much, much stronger.

"Ah!" he yelled as Celia and Dr. Navel raced across the room to help him. The octopus was already climbing up his back and onto his head with its sharp beak ready to snap his ears off.

"Don't panic!" yelled his father, which was his advice for everything.

"There's an octopus on my head!" Oliver yelled.

"It's your own fault," said Celia.

Oliver wanted to stick his tongue out at her, but he was afraid of what the creature would do if it caught his tongue.

"Dude!" Corey Brandt rushed over to his side.

He took out his phone and snapped a picture. "Oliver, you've got an octopus on your head! That is E-P-I-C, epic!"

"Uh," said Oliver, not sure why the teen star was spelling everything. It must be a Hollywood thing.

"Help," he said quietly.

"Zat ees mai octo-pous!" their deep-sea-diving host shouted from a balcony above the shark tank. He had a thick French accent that made it very hard to take him seriously, especially when he was shouting about an octopus.

"Apologies, Jacques," Dr. Navel shouted. "We'll be out of your hair in no time. Well, we'll get that octopus out of Oliver's hair first."

"Quickly, please," said Oliver.

"Don't worry, we'll help you, bro," said Corey, putting his phone away.

"Yeah . . . um . . . bro," said Celia, smiling at Corey. "I'll help you."

She started pulling tentacles off of Oliver, making sure Corey was watching her.

Oliver rolled his eyes. She was happy just to make fun of him until Corey came over.

"Ow, be careful!" Oliver said.

"We're trying," said Celia.

For those of you who have never practiced the sport of octopus wrestling, one can imagine it is something like trying to wrestle a bag of Jell-O, if that bag of Jell-O was also trying to strangle you. As soon as Celia, Corey, and Dr. Navel had pried one tentacle from Oliver's neck, another would wrap around his waist.

"Ow!" Oliver shouted again as Celia, Corey, and Dr. Navel tugged him most of the way free. "I think it's still got a grip with one of its tentacles."

"Where?" asked his father. "I can't see it."

"On my . . ." Oliver looked around the room. Everyone was watching him. He swallowed hard. "On my underwear," he said. "It's giving me a wedgie."

"O-U-C-H, ouch," said Corey Brandt.

"This is going to hurt," said Dr. Navel, and yanked Oliver one more time, extremely hard.

"Ow!" yelled Oliver.

Dr. Navel fell backward and Oliver fell onto him. The octopus still held a scrap of Oliver's underpants, and its tentacles flailed in the air with it, as if it were waving a white flag of surrender.

Corey grabbed the octopus by two of its tentacles

and swung it up through the air to toss it back into its tank.

However, he overestimated the distance and the octopus flew right over its tank and hit the current Sumo Wrestling Champion of the World right in the chest with a loud wet slap. The octopus wrapped its tentacles around the Sumo Wrestling Champion of the World in a hug, and the Sumo Wrestling Champion of the World looked back at the teen superstar with an expression that could only be described as *nonplussed. Nonplussed* was a word that Oliver and Celia had learned by living at the Explorers Club and having famous explorers for parents.

It meant confused to the point of bewilderment.

Oliver and Celia spent a lot of their time nonplussed.

They were nonplussed when their mother showed up on a mountaintop in Tibet, after being missing for three years, to tell them that she was part of an ancient secret society and that the twins were destined to discover the Lost Library of Alexandria. Then she ran off again.

They were nonplussed when she appeared another time in the Amazon to help them find the city of El Dorado, where the Lost Library had been hidden, and they were nonplussed when they discovered that some mysterious explorer named P.F. had moved the whole Lost Library before they even got to El Dorado.

They were really, really, really nonplussed when their mother sent them a copy of the complete works of Plato and two wet suits.

They had to look up Plato using their universal remote control, which, aside from controlling the television, gave them access to the complete catalog of the Lost Library of Alexandria on any TV screen.

That too had been a present from their mother.

She never just got them a gift certificate to the mall.

When they'd looked up Plato with the remote control, they saw that he was an ancient Greek philosopher, that he had once been kidnapped by pirates, and that he had written the earliest descriptions anyone had ever seen of the lost civilization of Atlantis.

Plato said that Atlantis was a ten-thousand-year-old island kingdom that had become the center of wealth and power in ancient times. When the Atlanteans—that's what the citizens of Atlantis were called—grew too wealthy and too powerful and tried to conquer the whole world, they were punished. Their entire civilization was swallowed by the ocean in a single terrible day. At least, that's what Plato said he'd heard. Scholars, mystics, and explorers had been searching for Atlantis ever since Plato told that story.

Knowing all this made Oliver and Celia even more nervous about those wet suits their mother had sent. They preferred not to get wet.

At this moment, however, they were very wet, although it was the Sumo Wrestling Champion of the World who was nonplussed. The octopus trying to wrap itself around his giant chest might have been a little confused and bewildered too.

"Out!" cried the deep-sea diver whose party had been ruined. "All uf you, out uf my house! *Vite!* Quickly! Go! Out!"

Within minutes, Corey Brandt, Oliver, Celia, and their father were in a taxi on their way back to the Explorers Club, wet and smelling like fish. As they left, no one noticed one of the fire dancers slip away from his group to hail a cab and follow them. In most places, a Rajasthani fire dancer hailing a cab would be a strange sight, but in New York City, even that wasn't strange.

"You got your wish," said Celia as they climbed the stairs to their apartment on the 4½th floor of the Explorers Club. "We got to leave the party early."

"Yeah," said Oliver, still blushing from his very public octopus wedgie.

"Don't worry about it, dude," Corey told him. "That party was L-A-M-E, lame. We'll have a lot more fun watching VSSCTSNYES up here, chillin'."

"We will!" Celia said. "C-H-I-L-L . . ." She stopped spelling when she saw her father and Oliver raising their eyebrows at her. "It'll be fun," she said. This time she blushed a little.

"Dr. Navel?" Corey asked. "Do you think this will hurt my chances of getting into the Explorers Club? I kind of threw an octopus at a sumo wrestler during the New Year's Eve party."

"Oh, don't worry about it," said Dr. Navel. "All you have to do is discover something fantastic before you turn seventeen and they'll certainly let you in."

"Something fantastic? Like what?"

"Oh, there are all kinds of things to discover," said Dr. Navel. "We'll think of something."

"Corey?" Oliver was about to ask why he wanted to be in the Explorers Club so badly, but his sister had stopped in her tracks on the landing outside their apartment. Something was wrong. The moon rock, which was usually perched on a shelf above the doorway, had fallen, and the door itself was partway open. The lock was broken clean off.

From inside the dark apartment they heard a loud hiss, followed by a piercing shriek. There was a yelp and then a thunderous crashing noise.

"That sounded a lot like—" Oliver started.

"Our television falling off the wall!" Celia finished his sentence as they rushed past their father and Corey Brandt to confront the intruder, who had just done the unthinkable.

3

WE ARE AWARE OF OUR DESTINY

WE MIGHT FIND IT UNUSUAL for two children, who admittedly have no taste for excitement, to storm in on an intruder, but one must understand their situation.

You see, not only was their television in danger, the one thing they truly cared about in this world, they also knew themselves to be perfectly safe.

The hiss that they heard belonged to Beverly, a large venomous lizard of the species *Heloderma horridum*, who was fiercely loyal to a particular armchair in their apartment and would fight anyone to protect it. She also enjoyed strawberry snack cakes.

The screech that they had heard belonged to Patrick, a small gray howler monkey whom their mother had befriended in the Amazon rain forest. He considered himself their guardian rather than their pet, and he lived with the Navels only because he felt a duty to protect them while their mother was away. He also had no idea how to get back to the Amazon from their apartment.

As for the crashing sound, it had indeed been their television falling off the wall and smashing to the floor, and the tiny yelp just before it fell belonged to the man who was now sprawled on his face with Beverly the lizard sitting on the back of his head and Patrick the monkey pinning his arms to the floor. In spite of the cold weather, he wore only a short-sleeved Hawaiian print shirt, shorts, and flip-flops.

"Excuse me?" the man called from under Beverly, his face smushing into the floor. "Is anyone there? Did I hear someone come in? Help. Please help."

"Who are you?" Celia demanded. "What are you doing in our apartment?"

"And why did you break our television?" added Oliver.

"I . . . I . . . I . . . ," the man spluttered. "Dr. Navel. Squid. Island. Map."

"The dude is, like, C-R-A-Z-Y, crazy," Corey said, stepping up behind the twins.

"I'm Dr. Navel," Dr. Navel told the man.

"No, no. Dr. Navel. Dr. Claire Navel," the man said. "Your wife is in peril!"

Oliver and Celia raised their eyebrows at each other.

Corey sucked his breath through his teeth.

Dr. Navel nodded at Oliver and gestured to the lizard.

"But—" Oliver started, not wanting to lift the lizard off the intruder's face but knowing he was the only one who could. If anyone else tried to handle Beverly, that poor soul would get a nasty bite that would knock him out for days.

Reluctantly, he lifted Beverly off the man's head and set her back on her armchair. Patrick scampered onto the couch. They helped the man up and sat him next to the monkey, realizing immediately that they knew him.

"You!" Celia pointed. The man had a bright red nose, like he spent too much time blowing it. They had seen him before, when he had them thrown out of an airplane over Tibet. He was part of their mother's secret society, the Mnemones (which was pronounced "knee-moans"), which had been try-ing to find the Lost Library of Alexandria for al-most two thousand years.

"Good to see you again, children," he said.

Celia frowned at him. Oliver scrunched his face at the man in what he thought was a threatening look.

Celia elbowed him so he'd stop.

"You look like you have stomachache," she whispered.

"Chris!" Dr. Navel said. "What are you doing here? Why were you lying on the floor?"

"You *know* this guy?" Celia turned to her father.

"Of course," said Dr. Navel. "This is Chris Stickles. We've known each other since graduate school. He's a noted ichthyologist."

Oliver looked at Celia.

"Fish scientist," she said.

"I specialize in cephalopods," he said.

Oliver looked at Celia again. She shook her head.

"Like octopi and squid," Chris Stickles told them.

"Octopi! Ha!" said Celia. Oliver grunted.

"He had us thrown out of an airplane in Tibet," Oliver complained.

The man smiled sheepishly.

"That was you?" Dr. Navel asked.

"I was traveling incognito," he answered.

"Wonderful!" said Dr. Navel. "I had no idea. You really are a master of disguises."

"It was nothing," said the man. "Just a new suit, and some makeup, and—"

"We nearly died!" interrupted Oliver. "And now he broke our television!"

"Sorry about that, but look—" He stopped himself and looked at the teenager next to Dr. Navel. "Are you really Corey Brandt?" His face lit up.

"Yes," Corey answered.

"I loved you on *Sunset High*," he said. "Although you should have ended up with Lauren, I think. Annabel was no good for you, even if she was willing to become a vampire."

"Annabel was his destiny," Celia said. "And that's not important right now. Why did you smash our TV?"

"My specialty is in giant squid," he said.

"That's no excuse for breaking our TV," Celia repeated.

"The television is not really important right now," Chris Stickles replied.

The children gasped. Beverly hissed.

"I mean, it's important, I guess . . . but what I meant . . . ," he stammered.

"Why don't you explain why you came here," Dr. Navel asked his old friend.

Chris Stickles nodded. He looked the children up and down. "I am sorry to tell you that you are in grave danger. I fear your mother is lost."

"We know," said Oliver.

"We're always in grave danger." Celia shrugged. "And our mother has been lost for years. She'll show up eventually."

"Um." Chris Stickles looked at Dr. Navel. This was not the reaction he was expecting.

"Look," Celia explained. "I know whatever you've got going on seems, like, really, really important. But we've heard it all. There's even a prophecy about us."

"*The greatest explorers shall be the least,*" Oliver said in his best oracle-type voice. "*The old ways shall come to nothing, while new visions reveal everything. All that is known will be unknown and what was lost will be found.*"

"Cryptic, right?" his sister said. "Oracles are impossible to understand. We met this one in Tibet."

"I talked to a yak," said Oliver.

"They don't just say what they mean," added Celia.

"Yaks?" Chris Stickles asked.

"Oracles," said Celia. "So you can't expect us to get excited when you come in here being all cryptic too."

"And breaking the TV," added Oliver.

"Right," said Celia.

"The TV was an accident! I'm here because of your mother." He looked at Dr. Navel. "Your wife, I was with her. We were together, but she left me to seek"—he dropped his voice to a whisper—"the kraken. She never returned."

"Oh, whatever," Celia groaned in disbelief.

"No way," whispered Oliver.

"What's a kraken?" asked Corey.

"It's a giant squid with claws in its suckers and massive fangs," said Oliver. "But *Beast Busters* did a whole episode about how it doesn't exist."

"It does exist," said the man. "I have seen it. And I'm an ichthyologist."

"Malcolm from *Beast Busters* is a retired science teacher," Oliver replied.

"I have a PhD in marine biology!"

"Well, why don't you have a TV show then?"

"Please, go on," said Dr. Navel.

"I was with your mother just a few weeks ago," Chris Stickles said. "We were searching for the man we believe found Plato's map to Atlantis. The man who knows the location of the Lost Library of Alexandria."

"P.F.," said Oliver.

"Yes," said Chris Stickles. "We believe that P.F. was none other than Colonel Percy Fawcett. We believe he sailed in secret from South America, across the Pacific Ocean, heading through Indonesia toward India, with the entire library aboard a ship."

"Dude," said Corey. "Percy Fawcett was murdered by cannibals in the jungle."

"There are no cannibals in the jungle," said Oliver.

"I auditioned to play Percy Fawcett's son in a movie," said Corey. "And the script said he was eaten by, like, cannibals."

"I'm telling you," said Oliver. "We met them and they don't really eat people."

"Chris," said Dr. Navel. "Everyone knows that Percy Fawcett vanished in the Amazon over a hundred years ago. He was looking for the remains of a lost civilization, a new Atlantis."

"Yeah, yeah," Celia interrupted. "We've heard this story a million times. He went to find this lost city, but instead he and his son and his son's friend all vanished forever. The same thing almost happened to us in the Amazon last summer."

"Well," said Chris Stickles. "To make a long story short—"

"Too late," said Celia.

"We believe that Percy Fawcett did not perish in the Amazon. We believe he found El Dorado just like you did, loaded its contents onto a ship in secret and sailed away across the ocean, with Plato's map as his guide, to hide the Lost Library at Atlantis."

"Why would he want to hide it if he, like, discovered it?" wondered Corey.

"In his day, there were many people who would have used the vast store of ancient knowledge for evil purposes. Those people still seek it today."

"Like Sir Edmund," said Dr. Navel.

Oliver and Celia shuddered at the mention of

their nemesis, which was another word they had learned this year. It meant a horrible enemy bent on their destruction. They actually had a whole collection of such enemies, but they didn't know the plural of the word *nemesis*.

Sir Edmund S. Titheltorpe-Schmidt III was the worst of them. He used to be a member of the Explorers Club before he left to start a club of his own, the Gentlemen's Adventuring Society. He was rich and powerful. He had sent an abominable snowman to attack them in Tibet, had enslaved them in Peru, and had tried to kill them in the Amazon. He also used a lot of wax in his giant red mustache and his breath could make professional sewage treatment engineers gag. He wanted to find the Lost Library before the Mnemones did.

"Your mother and I were trying to retrace the journey of Percy Fawcett's ship," Chris Stickles explained. "We interviewed elders in the islands of Malaysia who might have heard stories about him. An old fisherman told us about an island, far out at sea, where the ancients feared to sail. They said that monsters lived there, giant squid with claws and eyes of fire. He said that a generation ago these creatures had dragged a ship to the bottom of the sea. For weeks wreckage washed up on their shores, and among the wreckage they found this."

He pulled a small brass plaque from his pocket, the kind that was used to label old luggage. On the back it was engraved with two letters: *P.F.*

"You think Percy Fawcett was attacked by the kraken?" asked Corey.

"Yes," said the man. "Your mother simply had to know where this place was. She left me behind to sail with a small group of fishermen to find this place, and she never came back. I fear the monsters took her too."

"Why come to us?" asked Oliver.

"Because," said Chris Stickles, "if she is gone, it is your destiny to complete her quest. You must find P.F. You must find Plato's map. Sir Edmund cannot be allowed to—" Suddenly, a loud buzzing sound zipped past Oliver's ear.

"Ahh!" Chris Stickles screamed and fell back against the couch, clutching his neck.

Corey rushed forward and pulled the man's hand away to reveal a large dart sticking out of his throat.

They all turned to see a Rajasthani fire dancer

standing in the doorway to the apartment, holding a blowgun.

Except he wasn't a Rajasthani fire dancer at all.

He was the celebrity impersonator who had tried to kill them in the Amazon while impersonating Corey Brandt. His real name was Ernest, and now he was impersonating a Rajasthani fire dancer. He made the whole idea of playing dress-up quite sinister.

Ernest gave a cruel wave and ran back down the stairs.

"That's my impersonator!" said Corey.

"He didn't look like you anymore," said Oliver.

"The kraken. The island . . . the map," Chris Stickles groaned. "Seek your mother . . . seek the Orange Lords."

He passed out.

His hands flopped to his sides and the twins saw his gold ring, inscribed with the symbol of the Mnemones, a picture of an old key with ancient Greek writing below it. It made them think of their mother, who wore the same ring.

Oliver and Celia feared she might be gone forever this time.

4

WE ARE DEFINITELY DAUNTED

DR. NAVEL RAN INTO THE HALL, chasing the man dressed as a fire dancer. He looked to the left and looked to the right, but no one was there.

"Dad!" Celia called. "Help!"

Chris Stickles had started shaking and shivering and foaming at the mouth. It was quite terrifying and quite disgusting at the same time. His face was pale. Even his nose had lost its bright red shine.

Dr. Navel rushed back into the apartment. He slid the dart out of his old friend's neck and sniffed it. "A distillation of psilocybin and arsenic," he said. "This is quite toxic. Corey, call an ambulance."

Corey pulled out his fancy phone and dialed.

"The Orange Lords," Chris Stickles muttered again, turning his bleary eyes to Dr. Navel. "Seek out the Orange Lords."

"What's he saying?" Oliver asked.

"The Orange Lords," Dr. Navel answered. "He might mean the Orang Laut, a people who live in the Malacca Strait between Malaysia and Indonesia. They are a sea-dwelling people, fishermen and pirates. They live most of their lives on their boats. They must be the people your mother went off with to find this Squid Island where P.F. was shipwrecked."

"You think that Mom went off with pirates?" Oliver was worried.

"Your mother is a very trusting person," said Dr. Navel. "And the Orang Laut are a complex and misunderstood people."

"What happened here?" Professor Rasmali-Greenberg burst into the apartment. He scowled at Corey Brandt. "It is not even midnight and you have thrown an octopus at the Sumo Wrestling Champion of the World and knocked a man unconscious in the Navels' living room. I should have known teenage celebrities were trouble."

"It's not my fault," said Corey Brandt. "That me-impersonator, like, shot this fish scientist with poison!"

"Oh dear," said the professor. He turned and shouted to a group of motocross racers who had given him a ride back from the New Year's Eve gala. "You all! Search the building! Find this impersonator. He is an enemy of the Explorers Club, and does an impressive Corey Brandt impression!"

"Found him!" one of the motocross racers shouted, running into the Navels' apartment.

"That's the *real* Corey Brandt," Celia said. "The evil one is dressed like a fire dancer. His name is Ernest."

"Right," said the motocross racer, and ran back into the hall.

"I fear that Sir Edmund and his Gentlemen's Adventuring Society are growing bolder in their attacks on our work," the professor said. "What was this all about?"

"This guy broke into our apartment," said Oliver. "He smashed our television and told us that Mom ran off with some Orange Lords to find an island surrounded by giant monster squid where a long-lost explorer hid Plato's map to Atlantis and that we had to go help her or else Sir Edmund would find it first and then he got shot with a poison dart and then you came in and now we'll never see Madam Mumu perform 'Cheese Arcade Magic.'"

"Oh," said the professor, as if that made perfect sense.

"This would explain the wet suits my wife sent to Oliver and Celia," said Dr. Navel. "I think she wants us to follow her."

"No way," said Celia.

"No way," said Oliver.

"Cool," said Corey Brandt. "I'd like to help. I'm, like, *The Celebrity Adventurist*, right? And I need to discover something to prove I'm a real explorer so I can, like, join the Explorers Club, right?"

"That is true," said Professor Rasmali-Greenberg, tapping his finger on his chin as he thought.

"Well," said Corey, "I've got a sailboat. We could all go together to meet the Orang Laut and follow Mrs. Navel's path to this Squid Island."

"It's *Dr.* Navel," Oliver corrected. "My mom has her PhD. And it's not a Squid Island. That scientist said it was surrounded by kraken, demon-monster squid things. Which makes it a Kraken Island."

"Corey," said Dr. Navel. "You are only sixteen. I'm not sure it would be right to bring you along on this expedition."

"Oliver and Celia are only eleven, and they are two of the best explorers in the world," Corey said.

"Are not!" objected Oliver.

"Eleven and a half," said Celia. She was not about to let her brother make her sound like a child in front of Corey Brandt. They would turn twelve in the spring.

"We are so not going," said Oliver.

"Well." Celia blushed and looked at Corey. "We could maybe . . . you know, tag along."

"What?" Oliver's mouth dropped open.

"Oh, Celia!" Professor Rasmali-Greenberg clapped. "I am so glad to see you are undaunted!"

"Undaunted?" Oliver asked.

"Fearless," said Celia. She smiled at Corey.

"Oh," said Oliver. "Well, I am definitely daunted. Way, way daunted."

"You know," Dr. Navel thought out loud, "finding Plato's map and rescuing my wife from an island surrounded by giant killer squid would be . . ."

"Insane," said Oliver.

"Educational," said Dr. Navel. "It would be the discovery of a lifetime, in fact."

"You say that about every discovery," complained Oliver.

"I think Corey is right." Dr. Navel ignored Oliver. "I think we should all go together."

"But Daaad," Oliver whined as loud as he could. "We can't go sailing in kraken-infested waters looking for a lost explorer's stolen map! We're eleven!"

"And a half!" corrected Celia.

"I can call your teachers," their father said. "They'll understand that you have to miss school. It's for your mother. And for science! You'll meet the Orang Laut. You'll learn about marine biology! You'll become expert mariners!"

"I don't even want to know what a mariner is," said Oliver.

"It's a navigator of the sea," said Celia.

"I said I didn't want to know!"

"We'll start training right away," said Dr. Navel.

"You have to be kidding me," said Oliver.

"No," he answered. "I have to be teaching you how to sail!"

"But—" Oliver looked to his sister for help.

They heard a clattering in the hallway. A chorus of shouts erupted. They rushed out to see Ernest, the celebrity impersonator, throwing the helmet off the suit of armor where he had been hiding. He headed for a window at the end of the hall with a loud clatter.

"Catch him!" Professor Rasmali-Greenberg shouted.

Ernest threw off the top of his armor, breaking the window. He was dressed like a Rajasthani fire dancer from the waist up and like a medieval knight from the waist down. The explorers chased after him, but he leaped out the window and crashed into the street with a grunt, sprinting as fast as his armored legs could carry him.

Just then, the New Year struck and fireworks lit the city sky.

"The Orange Lords," muttered Chris Stickles as they waited for the ambulance to come. "Seek the Orange Lords."

5

WE GET GAS

THE NEW YEAR'S EVE party at the Gentlemen's Adventuring Society had been a smashing success.

Edmund S. Titheltorpe-Schmidt III—or Sir Edmund, as he insisted everyone call him—could not have been more pleased. The last guests had stumbled out into limousines waiting to take them home. Servants scurried about cleaning up champagne glasses and vacuuming up spilled whale fritters off the Persian carpets. The exotic animals Sir Edmund had displayed all evening for his guests' enjoyment—white tigers, bald eagles, and even a rare Congolese okapi, sometimes called the African unicorn—were packed back into shipping crates to be returned to his private zoo in Fiji.

His guests had been some of the wealthiest and most powerful people in the world—industrialists, politicians, dictators, warlords, and a few dozen explorers who had remained loyal to Sir Edmund when he left the Explorers Club. They had all donated generously to his new society, and they supported his work without question. Even if most of them didn't know what his work really was.

He smoothed his extravagant red mustache with his fingers and rested his feet on the back of a stuffed warthog he used as an ottoman. He had poached it himself in East Africa some years ago. Sir Edmund took great pride in his hunting abilities, although some in the press criticized him for using automatic weapons and hunting from a helicopter. They just didn't understand sportsmen such as himself.

He set his cell phone on the ivory table next to him and waited for it to ring. He was expecting important news from his spies in the field.

It had been months since he'd last seen Dr. Claire Navel in the Amazon rain forest, when she and her brats had yet again ruined his plans for the Lost Library. It had always been that way with her. She was an itch that he just couldn't scratch.

When she first vanished all those years ago to search for the library, Sir Edmund knew it was trouble. Claire Navel wasn't merely an explorer like her husband, pursuing science and wisdom and all that nonsense. She was one of the Mnemones, descendants of the ancient scribes of Alexandria.

Sir Edmund really hated the Mnemones. What a stupid name for a secret society! How was a person even supposed to pronounce it? Knee-moan? It sounded more like pneumonia to him.

The Mnemones had destroyed the Great Library back in ancient times, framing Caesar for the job. They wanted to keep the collection out of the Roman general's hands after he sacked ancient Alexandria, so they secreted its contents away and burned it to the ground. Unfortunately, they hid the collection too well. They lost it.

Someone really should have kept better track of where they had put it.

Ever since the library had gone missing, the heirs of the Mnemones had been trying to find it again, a mission now led by Dr. Claire Navel.

Well, Sir Edmund was determined to find it too. His Council, made up of some the most powerful people in the world, would stop at nothing to find it. Where Caesar had failed, Edmund S. Titheltorpe-Schmidt III would succeed. There was power in that library beyond the imagining of simple scribes.

Claire Navel was a great explorer, that was undeniable. In fact, she was far better at it than Sir Edmund would ever be. He had decided to use that to his advantage. When Claire Navel did find the library, he intended to be there. It would be the last thing she ever discovered.

Of course, first he had to find her. And that had proved difficult.

He rolled a large gold coin between his knuckles as he waited for his phone to ring. The coin was inscribed with the symbol of the Council, a scroll wrapped in chains. It was an elegant symbol, he thought, free from all the clutter of the Mnemones and their silly key with their silly writing: *Mega Biblion, Mega Kakon* was their motto. Big Book, Big Evil.

He snorted a laugh. They were so afraid of the very library they were after. Big Evil? They had no idea!

But Claire Navel had more allies than Sir Edmund had expected. She had escaped his clutches in Tibet, vanquished his henchman in Fez, and vanished from under his nose in the Malacca Strait.

But he had allies too. Even now he had Ernest as his spy, dressed like a Rajasthani fire dancer, gathering information on the Navels' next move. It wouldn't be long. Claire Navel would make contact with her family again soon, somehow, somewhere. She needed her children as badly as Sir Edmund did. It had been prophesied.

The greatest explorers shall be the least, the sacred Oracle in Tibet had said. *The old ways shall come to nothing, while new visions reveal everything. All that is known will be unknown and what was lost will be found.*

Sir Edmund ground his teeth. It was so cryptic. Oracles never could just speak clearly.

The greatest explorers shall be the least.

Well, if anyone was the least of anything, it was Oliver and Celia Navel. They were the least interesting, least curious, least adventurous, least likable children he had ever known. Not that he had known a lot of children. He preferred the company of warlords or wild animals to the company of kids. They had a smell that disturbed him.

"Has he called?" a woman asked, entering the room.

Sir Edmund didn't stand when she walked in, which would have been the polite thing to do. He didn't feel the need to be polite to this particular person. She was a grave robber. She had once been an explorer—in fact, she was known, along with her partner, for discovering the Jade Toothpicks— but the Navel twins had exposed her as a fraud and a thief. They'd fed her partner, Frank, to a yeti in Tibet. They'd nearly drowned her and Ernest in the Amazon.

She probably deserved it, thought Sir Edmund, who had never been very fond of her or either of her partners. But she wanted nothing more than revenge on the Navels, and that suited Edmund's purposes perfectly.

"Janice," he said. "Where have you been skulking about?"

"I stayed upstairs like you told me to," she said, running her hand through her short dark hair. "It was a dull way to spend New Year's Eve. I watched some stupid variety show. *Vuss-Cat's-Knees*, they called it. Madam Mumu sang some song about a cheese arcade. I think my IQ dropped twenty points by the time it was over."

"Well, I couldn't have you wandering around down here. You've been disgraced out of polite society."

Janice snorted back at Sir Edmund. But she didn't deny it.

"Anyway," Sir Edmund said. "Your new partner hasn't called. He better not have messed this up."

"Ernest is a first-rate spy," Janice said.

"He's a terrible celebrity impersonator."

"He fooled you in the Amazon, didn't he?"

"As I remember it, I had to pull both of you from a sinkhole in El Dorado. And now that you are working for me, I think a little more respect is in order."

"We are working *with* you now," Janice snapped. "Not for you."

"If it suits you to think of it that way, fine," said Sir Edmund. "But if Ernest messes this up, I will make sure you both are eaten by yaks."

"How many times do I have to tell you that yaks don't eat meat?" said Janice.

Sir Edmund ignored her. He poured himself a glass of crystal-clear plum brandy from a bottle labeled with a skull and crossbones. He savored a sip.

Suddenly there was loud knocking on the door.

Sir Edmund heard his butler open it and object loudly as someone clattered into the mansion.

Janice pulled a switchblade from her pocket. Sir Edmund pulled out a silver revolver and set it on his lap. The doors to the lounge burst open and in came Ernest, dressed as a fire dancer from the waist up and a knight from the waist down. He was being chased by the butler, and was trying to catch his breath.

"What are you doing here, you fool?" Sir Edmund demanded. "Why are you dressed like that?"

"Stuck . . ." Ernest panted. "Underpants stuck. Terrible armor wedgie. Had to hide. Had to run . . . they . . . saw . . . me." He put his head between his legs, trying to catch his breath.

"They saw you?" Sir Edmund sighed, setting down his glass. "I knew you would mess this up."

"Stickles . . ." he panted. "He told them . . . about the map and the . . . the kraken. He told them about the Orang Laut."

"Of course he did." Sir Edmund nodded.

"I silenced him . . . before he could say . . . too much." Ernest grabbed the glass that Sir Edmund had set on the side table. He gulped it, thinking it was water.

"BWAH!" He gasped, spitting the burning brandy all over Sir Edmund's face.

Sir Edmund's nostrils flared.

"Sorry," Ernest choked out.

Sir Edmund's butler rushed over and began wiping the little man's face. Sir Edmund waved his servant off and squeezed the liquid out of his mustache himself. "You should not have silenced him," he said. "We want them to know about that place!"

"We do?" Janice asked.

"We do?" Ernest asked.

"As for you two"—he gave them both a withering look, ignoring their questions—"you will continue to keep an eye on the Navels. Track their every move, wherever they go."

"Explain yourself," Janice demanded. "Why do we want them to know about the kraken? What if they find the island before we do? What if they get their hands on Plato's map?"

"If?" Sir Edmund laughed. "There is no if. I'm counting on it. The question is when."

6

WE DISAGREE, DISAGREEABLY

AFTER THE AMBULANCE took Chris Stickles away, the Navels gathered back in the great hall to discuss their plans for the expedition to find the island of the kraken and, hopefully, their mother.

Oliver and Celia sat on a hard sofa just underneath the glowering portrait of Colonel Percy Fawcett himself. They were too anxious to fall asleep and now that their television was broken, they had nothing else to do but watch Corey Brandt plan an expedition with their father.

"*Beast Busters* says the kraken doesn't exist," Oliver muttered. "And we're going to believe some crazy explorer over *Beast Busters*?"

"I guess so," said Celia.

"But the kraken is just made up! *Beast Busters* uses science!"

"Oliver." Dr. Navel sighed. He had heard every word of Oliver's complaint. "You should know that a myth comes from somewhere. It might not be a kraken that took your mother, but it could be something that made people believe in the kraken. The monster behind the myth. Understand?"

"Whatever," muttered Oliver.

"We'll need a crew." Dr. Navel turned back to Corey and Professor Rasmali-Greenberg. Oliver pouted.

"I'll start hiring the crew as soon as I get back to Los Angeles," Corey said.

"If we take a small boat through the Malacca Strait, we should be able to avoid attracting the attention of pirates," said Dr. Navel. "We can find an Orang Laut flotilla and see if they can tell us about this island where fishermen fear to go. If my wife—" He glanced back at Oliver and Celia and dropped his voice. "If my wife is alive, she'll no doubt be there, looking for Plato's map."

"Celia," Oliver whispered to his sister. "Do you think this is another one of Mom's plots to get us to find the Lost Library?"

"Probably." Celia yawned. She was getting very tired. It was almost one o'clock in the morning.

"So, why . . . you know . . . why did you tell Corey we would go?" Oliver asked. "Every time we go on one of these adventures, it's horrible."

"It's like the prophecy said," Celia told him. "Maybe it's our destiny. We'll end up having an adventure even if we try to avoid it."

"It's like changing the channel from commercials, but every other channel's on commercials too," said Oliver.

"Right," said Celia.

"But you don't believe in destiny," Oliver told her.

Celia pursed her lips. He was right of course. She didn't believe in that destiny nonsense. She didn't want to tell Oliver that she was just trying to impress Corey Brandt. Oliver would make fun of her. And after their last adventure in the Amazon with the fake Corey Brandt, he wasn't likely to go happily on another adventure.

So she told a lie, a terrible lie that not even she believed.

"Maybe if we find Plato's map," she said, "Mom will come home."

She knew it wasn't true. Even if they rescued their mother from Squid Island and found Plato's map or even the Lost Library itself, there would be new things to discover and new places to explore. People who like adventure are just like people who like cheese puffs. One was never enough. You had to eat the next one and the one after that and just one more after that and then another. So what if your fingers got all orange from the fake cheese powder or if your children ended up thrown out of an airplane or lost in the jungle?

But she knew that Oliver wanted nothing more than for their mom to come home. His eyes widened. Celia felt bad already.

"You think so?" he asked. "You think she really will?"

They would be twelve years old in a few months, but Oliver still thought like a little kid. She felt bad for him. He wanted to believe so badly that their mom would stop being an explorer one day. She couldn't lie to him.

"No," she admitted. "I don't really think so."

"So why'd you say it?"

"Because."

"Because what?"

"Just because."

"You're trying to make Corey Brandt think

you're cool," Oliver said. He had suspected this for a while.

"I am not," Celia snapped back at him, but of course Oliver knew the truth. They were twins, after all.

"You would never go on an adventure if it was just to save Mom," Oliver said. "But for Corey Brandt you'd lie right to my face. You like a weird teenager from TV more than our own mom!"

"Well, that weird teenager from TV never tried to get me killed!"

"Mom never tried to get us killed," said Oliver. Celia tilted her head and frowned at him. "Okay, well, she never tried to get us killed on purpose. She thought she was helping."

"She left us," said Celia. "She likes adventures more than she likes her own children. At least Corey's my friend."

"Corey doesn't think you're his friend," said Oliver. "You're just a little kid."

"You're just a whiny brat," said Celia.

"You're just a mean jerk," said Oliver. "Maybe I'll stay home. You can go without me."

"Good," said Celia. "Who needs a little brother anyway?"

"I am not your little brother," said Oliver. "We're twins."

"Well, I wish we weren't!"

"Well, so do I!" It wasn't much of a comeback, but Oliver was tired.

Both of them felt like they'd been hit in the stomach with a dodgeball. They weren't sure how they had gotten so mad at each other, and they both felt like they'd just crossed some line, gone too far. But neither one of them wanted to apologize first.

They sat next to each other beneath Percy Fawcett's portrait, looking in opposite directions, their arms crossed, wearing matching scowls. They were like angry mirror reflections of each other, and that was how Corey found them when he came back over.

"Celia, Oliver, so glad you guys stayed up late." He squatted down in front of them to talk at their level. "Your father and I think we'll spend next week practicing on the river. You guys can go to school and get your assignments and you'll have time to get your sea legs before we head out."

"I'll keep my own legs, thanks," Oliver huffed.

"'Get your sea legs' means get used to the sea," Celia corrected him.

"Well, I won't need sea legs," Oliver told Corey. "I'm not going."

"Oliver's worried that it will be dangerous," said Celia.

"It *will* be dangerous!" said Oliver, glaring at his sister. "But that's not why I'm not going." He didn't want Corey to think he was a wimp. "I eat danger for breakfast," he added.

"You eat Tooth Blaster cereal for breakfast," said Celia. "And you won't even do that if it's too soggy."

"It's gross when it's soggy!" Oliver said.

"It's okay." Corey put his hand on Oliver's shoulder. "I know it's scary, but I would, like, totally not let anything bad happen to you on the open seas. And you'll have your dad and Celia there too."

"Yeah," said Celia. "I can protect you." She smiled an exaggerated smile.

"I'm not scared!" Oliver hollered. "Celia's just being a jerk because she has a crush on you!"

"Oliver's joking around," said Celia, grabbing Oliver's hand and squeezing it until his fingers turned red. "Aren't you?"

"Whatever," said Oliver, gritting his teeth and

pulling his hand out of his sister's grip. He stood up.

Corey acted like he hadn't heard any of what they just said to him. He put his hand up for a high five. "This is gonna be the coolest trip E-V-E-R, ever. You get to miss school and we're gonna make history! Ollie, don't leave me hanging! Gimme a fiver!"

Oliver's arms hung limp at his sides. He did not give Corey Brandt a fiver.

"Don't call me Ollie," he said as he turned and stomped up the stairs toward the broken door of their apartment.

"Happy New Year!" he heard his father call from below. "Good night!"

He grunted and kept going. He didn't even look back at his sister. She wanted to say she was sorry, that she'd gone too far, but the words caught in her throat. He was the one who started it. He was the one being a jerk. Why should she apologize?

Her eyes were fixed on the stairs as the untied laces of her brother's sneakers dragged away behind him. Corey's high five hung abandoned in the air beside her.

7

WE'RE NOT GETTING ALONG

OLIVER AND CELIA SPENT the last two days of their winter vacation watching their broken television. They made their father remount it on the wall, and if they tilted their heads at the right angle and didn't move, they could kind of see most of the picture. The sound crackled with static, like they were watching television on the beach during a storm at sea, but if they listened through the ocean noises they could make out most of what was being said. They had barely spoken to each other in the new year.

They watched hours and hours of *Sharkapalooza* and *The Squid Whisperer* and *KidSwap*, where families traded one of their children so they could try out a different brother or sister for a week. All of the shows were Oliver's choice. He kept telling Celia how much he liked *KidSwap*. She got the message loud and clear. She was tired of her brother being mad at her.

"Can we watch *Valerie-at-Large*?" Celia asked. It was a new show, the biggest hit on TweenTV, and she hadn't seen a single episode. The thought made her feel sick. Everyone at school would be talking about it.

"Humph," Oliver grunted without looking at her. *The Squid Whisperer* was demonstrating something on a bagpipe. Or maybe it was an octopus wearing a kilt. The show was really stupid.

"Please? Anything but this." Celia groaned. "Oliver, fine. I'm sorry."

"For what?" Oliver asked. His sister had chosen Corey Brandt over him and he wanted her to admit it.

"For . . ." Celia didn't want to admit that she actually wanted to go sailing with Corey Brandt. She had to think of something else to apologize for.

"Too late." Oliver dropped the remote on the couch and went to his room, slamming the door. He didn't really feel like watching *The Squid Whisperer* anyway.

Celia watched him go. He was being such a baby.

She changed the channel. She tried to watch *Valerie-at-Large*, but she had trouble paying attention. Valerie was a reporter for the school paper and she wanted to know what happened at Addison Garrity's birthday party, but only the girls in the Six Sisters Club were invited. To join, Valerie had to do all these crazy stunts. She spent a night in a graveyard and she stole a towel from the boys' locker room. Then there was a ceremony with candles and a chant about being friends forever. She promised to keep their secrets, even though they weren't nice girls. But she needed to write her article. It was a moral dilemma. Break her vow or break her duties as a reporter for the school paper?

Celia turned it off. She didn't like all the double-crossing and the moral dilemmas on the show. There were enough of those in real life.

She tried to get Oliver to come out of his room, but he just shouted for her to go away.

"Go call your new best friend, Corey!" he yelled through the door.

Celia slouched into her room and flopped onto the bed, staring at the ceiling until she fell asleep.

Just as their father had promised, they began training the next day. They had to learn about the laws of the sea and how to read navigational charts and what to do if they fell overboard during a monsoon. Dr. Navel taught them the five "points of sail" and how to launch a dinghy—a smaller motorized boat—from a moving sailboat, while holding supplies on your back and a knife in your teeth. They used a wooden spoon for practice.

"Aye ill ee eed u oh dat?" said Oliver with the spoon gripped in his mouth.

His father looked puzzled.

"Why will we need to know that?" Celia translated. Oliver glared at her.

"Oh," said Dr. Navel with a shrug. "These are just basic skills that every mariner should have. Pop quiz! Question one: which sail is the mizzen sail on a sailboat?"

The children groaned and spent the next hour answering their dad's questions, never once speaking directly to each other.

Afterward they watched television side by side in silence. *Beast Busters*, *The Squid Whisperer*, and *Sharkapalooza* reruns. Oliver refused to watch anything with Corey Brandt in it—Celia's betrayal was that teenager's fault—and he wouldn't let her watch *Valerie-at-Large*, mostly because it was boring. When she tried to grab the remote, he pulled it away. When she tried again, he shoved it down the back of his pants and sat on it.

"Gross," Celia said.

"Whatever," said Oliver. "It's safe there."

It was the closest thing they had to a conversation that day.

8

WE FACE OUR FRIENDS

AFTER WINTER VACATION, school started again for Oliver and Celia Navel the way it starts for everyone: too soon.

The first few days back in sixth grade were a jumble of kids comparing the presents they got and the video games they played and the vacations they took or didn't take. The teachers spent those first cold days desperately trying to remind their students of everything they had learned in the first half of the year and somehow totally forgotten during two weeks of winter break.

"OMG!" Stephanie Sabol squealed at Celia in the hallway, before she could even put her books in her locker. "I read on Brandtblog.com that you're going to sail across the ocean with Corey Brandt! Is that, like, for real?"

"Like R-E-A-L, real?" Annie Hurwitz spelled loudly behind her.

A gaggle of girls gathered around, asking questions and making suggestions and wondering if she'd get to be on TV. Celia tried to see where her brother had gone, but she couldn't find him through the forest of friends that had sprouted around her.

Their teachers agreed to let the twins make up their missed classwork after they got back, as long as they promised to give a report to the whole school about what they learned on their trip. Celia didn't think it was fair that they were getting more homework. Oliver thought it was the greatest injustice in history. Although Celia didn't see him, he glared at her down the hallway.

In the gym locker room, Greg Angstura snuck up behind Oliver, grabbed the waistband of his underpants, and performed the universal ritual of the bully: he yanked upward, hard, and gave Oliver a wedgie almost as bad as the one that octopus had given him.

"Don't drown on your trip, weirdo." Greg laughed. He didn't care that Oliver knew Corey Brandt or had famous explorers for parents. He just liked being mean.

The rest of the boys, however, were eager to hear about the trip.

"Will you be the first mate? Or the bosun?" asked one of the Gomez brothers.

"What's a bosun?" asked the other Gomez brother.

They were identical twins. Oliver didn't know which was which. Talking to them reminded him that he missed talking to his sister.

He just shrugged.

"Dude," one of the Gomezes said to Oliver as they were climbing neighboring ropes in gym class. "Do you think you'll have to climb like this on the sailboat? Like a pirate? What if you meet pirates? Do you think they'll make you walk the plank?"

"I heard that pirates don't do that," said the other Gomez, climbing the rope on the other side of Oliver. "They just kill you and take your loot."

Oliver grunted. He had to focus on climbing the rope. Why did they make children climb ropes? It seemed like cruel and unusual punishment.

"Do you think you'll see sharks?" the Gomezes asked together.

Oliver grunted again. But he wondered, what

about pirates? What about sharks? And what if they found the island of sea monsters and the map? Would they also find their mother?

The other kids were so excited about the voyage that Celia never even got a chance to talk to Oliver.

"OMG!" Stephanie squealed. "I read on Brandtblog.com that Corey Brandt is hiring the entire crew for your trip from fans on his website!"

"Do you think he'll hire us?" asked Annie. "We could totally go with you!"

Celia didn't answer.

This was an unsettling idea.

"I heard that you have to go to the bathroom in a bucket off the side of the boat," one of the Gomezes told Oliver a half hour later, as they sat down in the lunchroom in front of heaping piles of Tater Tots.

"I heard you don't even get a bucket," said the other Gomez, biting into his grilled cheese sandwich. "And you have to use old gum wrappers for toilet paper."

"No way!" said his brother as he drowned his lunch in ketchup. "They're too small. Maybe you have to use, like, seaweed or something."

"Like when Corey Brandt got that rash on *The Celebrity Adventurist*?" the other one added. He gestured at Oliver with a Tater Tot. "Do you think you'll get a rash?"

The way he asked made a rash sound like a good thing.

"Oliver is a rash," Greg Angstura butted in, smashing his fist down on Oliver's plate and squashing Oliver's Tater Tots into a potatoey mush.

"You're just jealous because Oliver's going somewhere cool and exciting and the only place you ever go is baseball camp!" the other boys objected.

"You all go to baseball camp with me!" Greg yelled back at them and the whole group fell into an argument about baseball camp and the relative coolness of Oliver Navel over Greg Angstura.

Oliver finished his lunch silently while they argued about him. It wasn't really important that he speak. Anything he said would probably just undermine their point about him being cool. He didn't feel cool. He just felt lonely.

And it was all Corey Brandt's fault.

While the boys argued about Oliver, he decided that he would get back at Corey and Celia. Then she could see what life would be like without her twin brother. Then she'd be in trouble. He had a great idea.

"What'd you say, loser?" Greg Angstura was suddenly in his face.

"What?" said Oliver.

"You were muttering to yourself, weirdo."

"Was not," said Oliver.

"Leave him alone," said the Gomez brothers.

Greg shook his head and stomped away to find somebody else to bully.

"Hey, Oliver." One of the Gomezes turned to him. "You really were muttering, you know?"

"Really?" Oliver said. "What'd I say?"

"Just one word, and you kinda smiled all creepylike when you said it," said the other Gomez.

"What word did I say?" Oliver asked.

"Sabotage," they told him.

"Yeah," said Oliver, nodding. "I guess I did."

9

WE CAN'T STAND SABOTAGE

THE DAY OF THEIR DEPARTURE had arrived and the fight between Oliver and Celia had taken on a life of its own. Removed from the original cause, the argument turned into a game of wills— whoever apologized first was the loser.

Oliver didn't want to admit that he missed his sister and that, really, sailing around the ocean with Corey Brandt was going to be kind of cool, if only Celia would stop acting weird around him. And he really wanted to find their mother.

Celia didn't want to admit that she had been a jerk, betraying her brother just to impress Corey Brandt.

Also, the television was still broken. It was almost impossible to watch, the static was so loud.

Dr. Navel arranged for Professor Rasmali-Greenberg to look after Beverly the lizard and

Patrick the monkey while they were gone. It was kind of a relief not to have to take care of two wild animals. Oliver and Celia were not really animal people. They liked them better on TV. In real life, wild animals smelled.

They flew to Hawaii to meet Corey, where he was preparing his boat for their voyage. He greeted them at the dock, dressed for the sea with a striped shirt and a captain's hat and flared white pants with all kinds of zippered pockets.

"You like 'em?" he asked. "These are from my new line of clothing, Corey Brandt's Pocketed Pants! They're made right here in Honolulu!"

"Great," said Celia. She was pretty sure that giant white pants were not the best look for TweenTV's "Coolest Teen in the World," but he looked so excited about them.

"I brought you all a pair in different colors!" He tossed a pair of pants—in impossibly bright orange and red and green—to each of them.

"The crew won't fly in from Los Angeles until tomorrow morning," Corey explained. "There were some problems picking the fans through my website. Like, hackers and stuff. I don't know about computers, but I think it's all sorted out now, and it means we have an extra day to practice sailing before we head out."

"Excellent," their father cheered. "Let's get to it!"

Oliver made sure to complain loudly as the boat eased out of the boat slip. Vacationers in plush bathrobes and supermodels in little swimsuits gathered on the decks of their yachts to look down on the Navels and the famous teenager as they set out.

"Okay, trim the mizzen sail!" their father called out to Oliver. They had studied all the parts of the boat, and Oliver knew that the mizzen sail was the one at the back of the boat.

He quickly rushed to the front of the boat and started tugging on the line that held the Explorers Club flag.

"That's not even a sail!" Dr. Navel shouted. He slapped his forehead in exasperation. "You knew this yesterday! Aft! Aft!"

Oliver knew that *aft* was what sailors called the back of the boat. Why they couldn't just say "the back of the boat" was anyone's guess. Sailors, like explorers, doctors, and librarians, liked to have their own words for things. It helped them tell who was really a sailor and who was just pretending to be.

"What's aft?" Oliver pretended not to know.

"Let me help him, Dad," said Celia, pulling the rope that tightened the mizzen sail. The boat picked up speed.

"Good job, Celia!" said their father.

"Good job, Celia," Oliver muttered under his breath mockingly.

"Why don't you take the helm, Oliver?" suggested Dr. Navel.

"Sure!" Oliver rushed to the steering wheel, grabbed hold, and smiled widely at his sister. "Like this?" Oliver asked, and gave the wheel a big spin with all his strength.

The boat heaved around, the sails snapped and billowed in the wind; the lines tangled and whipped around the deck and the boat spun out of control—heading straight for a Russian billionaire's luxury yacht.

The ruddy-faced billionaire on deck started waving his arms and shouting in a frantic tone. His overdressed girlfriend shrieked. We don't need to speak Russian to understand that their admonishments were not particularly polite.

"Wait! Not like that!" Dr. Navel leaped across the deck to catch the wheel and turn them away from the yacht before they crashed. Once he got the boat pointed in the right direction, Corey and Celia had to struggle to get all the ropes untangled again.

"You're doing this on purpose," Celia whispered to her brother.

"Who says?" Oliver snapped back at her.

"I do!" said Celia. "You know all this stuff. I know you do."

Oliver stuck out his tongue at her and turned away.

"Okay," Dr. Navel called out. "Oliver, you'll get the hang of it! Let's review! What do you do when you're on watch?"

"Um." Oliver made a big show of thinking hard. "You watch."

"Yes," their father prompted. "But what do you watch?"

"*Agent Zero*?" he suggested.

Corey gave him a thumbs-up.

"Be serious," their father scolded. "Our safety at sea counts on you. What do you look out for when it's your turn on the watch?"

"Um . . . ," Oliver tried again. He knew the right answer, of course. He couldn't forget it after all the episodes of *Porpoise Pirates* he'd seen. The watch had to look out for big ships in the distance. A tanker ship could go from a speck on the horizon to right on top of them in less than twenty minutes and they wouldn't even see a small sailboat as they ran over it.

Plus there were whales to worry about. You wouldn't want to crash into a whale in a little fiberglass sailboat. You'd be split to pieces and shipwrecked for certain.

Oliver looked over at Corey, who nodded encouragingly. Celia, standing next to him, was shooting laser beams at Oliver with her eyes.

"When it's your turn on the watch, you look out for . . . ?" Dr. Navel prompted Oliver again.

"The time?" said Oliver.

"What? The time? No!" Their father slapped his forehead again. It was red from all the slapping. "Not that kind of watch!"

It went like that for hours as they sailed up and down the coast. Oliver ran from end to end on the boat, tangling ropes and dropping sails and steering them in the wrong direction, all while answering every question he was asked as wrong as he could think of, even when the right answer was obvious.

It was hard work making sure nothing worked at all. Sabotage turned out to be even harder than sailing the right way.

"Dude," Corey whispered to Oliver as he was catching his breath. He patted Oliver on the shoulder. "Don't worry about it. It's hard to remember all these different sailing words. You'll get the hang of it soon, just like your sister."

Celia gave Oliver an exaggerated smile.

"Bro," Corey added. "You're kinda green."

Oliver wasn't feeling well. The rocking and rising and falling of the boat was turning his stomach inside out.

"Don't you dare," whispered his sister.

"I'm not doing it on purpose," said Oliver.

"That reminds me of this episode of *The Celebrity Adventurist* where I was in Madagascar," said Corey. "I had to eat these cookies with grasshoppers in them. It was G-R-O-S-S, gross!"

"Oh no," said Oliver. "I remember those— chocolate chirp cookies!"

His face went from kinda green to dark slime green, his stomach heaved, and he leaned over the side of the boat. The sound of Oliver hurling up his lunch carried all the way back to the yachts docked at the marina.

"I think we'll call it a day," said Dr. Navel.

Celia and Corey agreed.

As they tied up the boat, Dr. Navel took Oliver aside and knelt down to talk to him.

"Listen, son," he said. "You have nothing to be ashamed of. Some people are natural-born sailors— like your sister—and some just aren't." Oliver clenched his fists and tensed his jaw. "But as long as you do your best, we'll be just fine. I believe in you, okay?"

"Sure," Oliver grumbled.

"No," said his father. "Look me in the eyes. I. Believe. In. You."

Oliver realized that his dad was never going to give up on him, no matter what he did. Oliver couldn't let his father down and he couldn't let Corey think that he was a doofus and Celia was, like, a genius. He used to think Corey Brandt was the most awesome guy in the world. He was a superspy and an action hero and a reality TV star all in one. But around Corey, Celia turned into an alien.

How could someone that cool make his sister so uncool?

He had to accept that sabotage would never work. And anyway, it was way too hard.

"All right, Dad," he said. "I'll try harder. I promise."

Dr. Navel rubbed Oliver's hair and finished tying up the boat. Oliver came up next to Celia as they walked down the pier.

"You win," he said.

"I do?" said Celia.

"Yeah." Oliver grunted. "I'll go on this stupid adventure to find this stupid Squid Island. I won't try to mess it up anymore."

"See?" said Celia. "It wasn't so hard to realize I was right, was it? I heard that girls mature faster than boys, so you know, I knew you'd come around eventually."

"It's not for you," said Oliver. "It's for Mom."

"Well, whatever it is, I'm glad you're not being stupid anymore."

"You still owe me an apology."

"For what?"

"If you don't know, then I'm not telling you."

"Oliver." Celia groaned. "Don't be such a baby."

"Humph," he said, and sped up.

Celia sped up behind him.

"Hey, guys, why are you walking so fast?" Corey called, but he was mobbed by a group of fans who recognized the teardrop freckle under his eye and the famous swoop of his hair.

"See you later." Dr. Navel smiled, running to catch up with the twins, who were almost racing each other now.

As the Navel family ran along, wrapped up in their personal dramas, a young woman followed them at a discreet distance, making notes in a small notebook. If they had paid any attention to her, they might have noticed that she looked a lot like a young Vivian St. Claire, a classic actress from the 1950s who had played sassy reporters and fast-talking society dames. They would have also noticed that the young woman had a light layer of prickly beard stubble on her face.

It wasn't his favorite disguise, but Ernest the celebrity impersonator had to make due with what he had. He couldn't very well be the Rajasthani fire dancer again and his Corey Brandt getup was no good anymore. He'd sworn never to wear it again anyway, out of spite for the teen star.

Sir Edmund and his Council wanted to know everything the Navels were up to, and Ernest took diligent notes. He didn't know what the Council's plan was, but they had promised him the perfect reward for his efforts: revenge.

10

WE'RE IN SHIP SHAPE

THE *GET IT OVER WITH* sliced across the waves heading from Hawaii toward Indonesia. Corey's boat was a forty-eight-foot ketch, which meant that it had two masts—a mainmast and mizzenmast—and another sail at the front called a jib.

There was enough cabin space for six private bunks, a small lounge, and a galley, which is what sailors call the kitchen. In the galley, there was a couch and, much to Oliver and Celia's relief, a working television set.

Corey had allowed the twins to name the boat when they set off, and they had chosen *Get It Over With*. Corey liked the name because he thought the twins were being ironic.

They weren't.

They really did want to get this whole adventure over with. They set sail early on the morning after their training day, as soon as the deckhands arrived.

There were three deckhands, and they had applied for the job through Corey Brandt's fan website. That struck both the twins as pretty odd, because none of them looked much like Corey Brandt fans.

There was a twitchy little guy named Bart. He spent most of his time climbing up and down the tall mainmast, adjusting lines, and looking out to the horizon.

"Watching for pirate ships," he said. "They come up on you fast."

There was the cook, also named Bart, who was the size of two normal grown-ups combined. They called the cook Big Bart and the other one Twitchy Bart.

Big Bart had tattoos of all kinds of birds covering both his arms and he'd brought a chicken on board with him.

"Why do you have a chicken?" wondered Oliver.

"He's a rooster," the cook explained. "And don't

get any ideas. He's not for eating. This guy's my friend. His name's Dennis, but don't bother calling him that. He doesn't know he has a name. He's just a rooster after all."

"Does he do anything? Like tricks?" Oliver asked.

"Nope," he said. "That's why I like him. He doesn't fly, he doesn't talk, he doesn't do anything at all."

Oliver had to admit he kind of liked Dennis too. That was his idea of the perfect life.

The last deckhand was a young woman. She didn't say much, except that her name was Bonnie and that she came from a long line of sailors and she'd seen everything Corey had ever done, even the Tooth Blaster cereal commercial he'd made when he was little.

"What'd you think of the *Sunset High* reunion?" Celia asked.

"It was okay," said Bonnie. She went back to coiling ropes without another word.

"How about *The Celebrity Adventurist* last season?" Celia tried.

"Uh-uh," said Bonnie without looking up.

Celia wondered what good it was to have Corey Brandt fans on the crew if none of them would talk about it. Normally she would have talked to her brother about Corey Brandt, but he was still being grumpy with her.

"This must be what they call smooth sailing," their father said with a contented sigh.

They had fair weather their first day at sea, with plenty of sunshine and even-tempered winds. A pod of dolphins danced in the water, jumping and splashing and diving below the surface again. Even Oliver and Celia, who had never been fans of live entertainment, were impressed. But the dolphins left them as they got farther out to sea, and they quickly found themselves alone on the rolling swells of the Pacific Ocean.

"You turning green, Oliver?" Dr. Navel asked his son.

The deckhands snickered.

"I'm fine, Dad." Oliver blushed, even though he was feeling a little queasy. His father handed him a steaming mug of bitter tea.

"Is this made out of something gross?" Oliver asked, sniffing it suspiciously.

"It's neem tea." Dr. Navel smiled. "For your stomach."

"Oh," said Oliver, who didn't know what neem tea was.

"Tea made from the leaves of the neem tree is considered very effective in treating upset stomachs, agitated nerves, and malaria," Dr. Navel explained. "It's also quite effective for killing termites."

Oliver poured it over the side of the boat when his father wasn't looking.

"Isn't this great?" Corey strolled over to Celia, watching the deckhands work. "I never knew my fans could be such good sailors."

"Aren't you a little suspicious of them?" Celia asked.

"No. Why should I be?" He turned away from Celia and shouted down the length of the boat. "Hey, guys! I almost forgot! I brought a pair of Corey Brandt's Pocketed Pants for everyone!"

He rushed along the deck handing out colorful pocketed pants.

Celia went to the front of the boat, where Oliver was dangling his legs over the side, and sat quietly next to him. She didn't say anything. They just watched the ocean together in silence, like it was a really boring TV show on a really big screen. It felt almost normal.

"Don't look so glum, guys," Dr. Navel told the twins. "With a good wind, we'll reach the Malacca Strait in about a week and then we'll find the Orang Laut!"

"A week?" Oliver muttered.

"A week?" Celia groaned.

The small crew shared all the responsibilities on the *Get It Over With*, but it became obvious almost immediately that Oliver and Celia couldn't be left alone for the overnight watch.

On the first night, they both fell asleep and sent the boat wildly off course, right into an international shipping lane.

The whole crew woke to the sirens of a massive ship's collision alarm.

Corey rushed onto the deck wearing Corey Brandt's Pocketed Pink Pajamas and spun the wheel hard to port—which is what sailors call left. The boat turned very slowly and the tanker ship moved toward them very fast.

It towered over them, blotting out the sky.

....

Corey flailed his arms in the air at the crew of the tanker on deck, making the universal sign for panic.

The crew on the deck of the tanker waved their arms back at him, making the universal sign for "we're your biggest fans."

If they didn't turn faster, their boat would be crushed and they would surely be swallowed by the unforgiving sea. Oliver had always thought it would be a lizard bite that did him in. Celia was still looking forward to dying of a broken heart at 102 years old, like Elaine Deveaux on her favorite soap opera, *Love at 30,000 Feet*.

The sailboat kept turning and the tanker honked its horn as their small vessel brushed right past the giant steel hull. They missed it by just a few feet, rising high on its wake in the water and settling back down as the ship passed. Within minutes, the tanker had vanished over the horizon. Dr. Navel offered to stay awake with his children for the rest of the night watch, and the twins quickly fell asleep against his chest.

It became obvious the next day that Corey Brandt could not be given responsibility for an early morning shift, because, being a teenager, he was completely incapable of waking up before noon.

The deckhands refused to take any of the shifts on watch, as they claimed they were not officers on this expedition and it wouldn't be right.

"I thought you came from a long line of sailors," Celia said to Bonnie.

"Uh-huh," said Bonnie, and went back to cleaning the deck.

After the drama of the first night, however, sailing across the Pacific Ocean didn't seem particularly dangerous or particularly hard.

It was, like a lot of exploring, quite a bit more boring than an outsider would imagine.

As the first days went by on their way toward the Malacca Strait, Oliver and Celia found themselves without much to do. The TV on board could only play the shows that Corey had brought with him, and they were all Corey's shows. They rewatched every episode of *Sunset High* and *Agent Zero* that he had, but that only lasted the first few days. They saw Corey as a sad-eyed vampire who broke the heart of his best friend and they saw him as a high-school superspy who broke the arm of a terrorist posing as a math teacher.

Once those episodes were over, they didn't know what to do. The real-life Corey Brandt was on deck working. Everyone was on deck working.

"We could use the remote control," Oliver suggested, reaching into his backpack for their universal remote control. "You know, to see in the catalog of the Lost Library if it says anything about kraken or Plato's map to Atlantis . . . anything that could help us find Mom. And, you know," he added, "Corey would probably be happy if we helped him make this discovery."

"I guess we could help," said Celia, happy that Oliver had made a peace offering.

Oliver hit a few buttons on the remote, but nothing happened.

"Let me try," said Celia.

"I got it," said Oliver.

"You don't," said Celia.

"I do too," said Oliver, hitting more buttons. Suddenly the image on the screen changed to the symbol of the Mnemones, a key with ancient Greek writing below it. "See?"

The peace didn't last long.

"Okay, now let me see it," said Celia.

"This was my idea," said Oliver.

"Yeah, but you can't even spell *kraken*," said Celia, lunging for the remote.

Oliver yanked it away and shoved it into the back of his pants.

"Why do you keep doing that?" Celia demanded. "It's gross."

"Because you won't grab it from there," said Oliver.

"Oh yeah?" Celia moved toward him.

"What are you . . . what are you doing?" Oliver's eyes widened. Celia dove at him and grabbed onto the waistband of his Pocketed Pants. She yanked up.

"Ow!" said Oliver. "That's a wedgie! No fair! Ow!" He reached around to the back of her pants and yanked, giving his sister a wedgie.

"Ow!" said Celia. "You can't give a girl a wedgie!"

"You're not a girl," said Oliver. "You're my sister!"

"What's going on?" Corey said, coming into the galley.

"Nothing," said Oliver, letting go of his sister and rushing to turn off the TV before Corey saw the symbol on the screen.

"Nothing," said Celia.

Oliver pulled the remote out of his pants and set it on the couch. Celia wrinkled her nose at it. She had lost the desire to watch TV, or at least to watch TV using that remote control.

"Looked like a wedgie war," said Corey.

The twins shrugged.

"Well, it's no use," he said. "Corey Brandt's Pocketed Pants are wedgie proof. Look."

He reached around to his back, like he was giving himself a wedgie. He made an uncomfortable face and then the waistband of the pants broke away and he was holding it in his hands. "See?"

"It didn't work for me," said Oliver, picking at the back of his pants.

"I guess it only works for a really bad wedgie. Like a life-or-death wedgie."

"I guess so," said Oliver.

"You know, you guys shouldn't fight," Corey told them. "You're family and you need to work together. We're all alone out here at sea."

"That's not totally true," said Celia.

"It's not?" Corey asked.

"Have you seen that sail in the distance?" Celia asked.

Corey looked confused. The twins led him onto the deck and pointed to the horizon, where a tiny sailboat appeared and disappeared as the sea rose and fell. It had been behind them since they'd left almost a week ago.

"Do you think they're following us?" Corey wondered.

"Of course they are," said Celia. "Someone's always following us."

"I didn't know you saw them too," Oliver told Celia.

"Of course I did," she said. "I didn't know you saw them."

"Yeah, I did," said Oliver. "Who do you think it is? Pirates?"

"Or Sir Edmund and his Council," said Celia. "Or the Mnemones."

"Or crazed Corey Brandt fans," said Oliver.

Corey laughed. So did Celia.

She smirked at her brother and he smirked back. Things were getting back to normal.

All three of them kept their eyes fixed on the sailboat in the distance, wondering who was following them and also wondering why.

• • •

On board the tiny sailboat on the horizon, Ernest, dressed like a pirate in an old movie with a sash and a hat and even a plastic parrot on his shoulder, steered. Janice stood at the bow with her binoculars raised.

"The chase is on," she said.

"What?" said Ernest, who couldn't hear her over the wind.

"I said the chase is on!"

"What?" He still couldn't hear her.

"The! Chase! Is! On!"

"The chaise? What's a piece of furniture got to do with anything?"

"I said chase! The chase is on!" she yelled back at him. "Oh, never mind. Just steer."

Janice couldn't believe she had to spend the next several weeks on this tiny boat with Ernest. She hoped they would meet up with Sir Edmund soon so she could take a shower and get some distance between herself and the celebrity impersonator. He was not an ideal partner in crime, but he would have to do until she got what she wanted. Luckily, he didn't know how much Sir Edmund was really paying them to follow the Navels.

She did not intend to share it.

11

WE SORT OF SWIM
WITH SHARKS

ON THE NEXT AFTERNOON, the seas grew rougher, and the ocean swells grew larger. The *Get It Over With* rose to the top of each swell and then surfed down again into the deep trench between the waves.

For hours they followed their course, rising and falling, rising and falling through the swelling sea.

"Now you're, like, really starting to turn green, dude," Corey told Oliver, who was watching the first season of *Agent Zero* for the fifth time. "G-R-E-E-N, green. You gonna lose your lunch?"

"Shh . . . I'm trying to watch you on TV," Oliver told him. "I'm fine. F-I-N—" But he couldn't finish spelling back at Corey because he felt his stomach do a somersault. He rushed from the cabin to the front of the boat. He knelt on the hot fiberglass deck, getting ready to return his lunch to the ocean, when he looked up to see a most bizarre sight.

The boat had slid down into one of the trenches between the waves, so there were walls of water on either side like an aquarium, except there was no glass. Oliver was looking straight into the face of a shark as it swam peacefully in the waves.

He forgot all about his upset stomach and nearly fell backward from the boat's edge. Suddenly, the boat lifted onto the back of the next wave and the wall of water sank below them again.

Oliver stayed where he was so he could see into the ocean when they slid down into the next trench. It was like he was watching a nature show on television, except he could reach out through the screen of water if he wanted. All sorts of sea life floated in the swells—schools of large silver fish and small undulating squid, the long blobby tails of jellyfish, the doofus grin of a sea turtle, and the zombie-eyed stare of sharks.

"You've got to see this!" Oliver called out.

Corey and Celia came over and watched with Oliver as the live sea show sank again below them and the horizon rose up in the distance.

"I am, like, awed by the majesty of the sea," Corey said.

"Yeah," Celia agreed. She settled down next to her brother. They spent the entire afternoon watching the walls of water filled with sea life rise and fall. The twins forgot they had ever been mad at each other. They even forgot about the television down in the cabin.

Dr. Navel happily watched his children. It was nice to see them enjoying nature instead of television and even nicer to see them getting along again. He let them skip their turn at the watch so they could keep watching the ocean.

As the sun began to set, Big Bart came over to where they sat. Dennis the rooster clucked happily beside him.

"I thought you might like to eat out here," he said, handing them each a steaming plate of rice and beans. "Just don't eat too close to the edge of the boat."

"Why's that?" Oliver wondered.

"Well, it's dusk," said Big Bart. "They call this

the sharking hour. It's when sharks hunt. Wouldn't want one coming on board to snatch your dinner."

"Sharks don't eat rice and beans," said Oliver.

"Oh, I suppose not." Big Bart laughed. "But what about little children?"

"We're not little children," Celia explained with a sideways glance at Corey. "We're almost twelve. That makes us tweens."

"Tweens, huh?" Big Bart said. "Well, in that case I'm sure the sharks won't bother you!" He chuckled and bid them good evening, lumbering his way back belowdecks, with Dennis hopping along after him.

"He's weird," said Celia.

"I kind of like him," said Oliver.

"I think he's pretty cool," said Corey.

"I guess he's okay," Celia conceded. Oliver rolled his eyes a tiny bit when his sister wasn't looking. They ate quietly and watched the sleek silver bodies of sharks slice through the water.

That night, the twins were sound asleep inside their bunks in the cabin when they heard a loud bang that shook the entire boat. The walls of the cabin flexed, like they had been hit with something really big. They heard a terrible sound from outside, thrashing and scraping. It was as if a fight had broken out on deck.

They rushed outside to see what was going on and stopped short in the doorway.

Just in front of them, a large octopus was engaged in a violent battle with the ropes that Bonnie had spent so much of the afternoon coiling. Its tentacles were tangled and it was squirming and sliding, trying to get itself back to the water.

"Is that the kraken?" Corey wondered.

"It's an octopus," said Big Bart, standing beside him. "The kraken is a squid."

"If the kraken's real," Oliver added, "it would have giant fangs and be about as big as this whole boat. But *Beast Busters* says it's not real, so it doesn't matter."

"*Beast Busters*?" asked Big Bart.

"Don't ask," said Celia.

As they stood watching the octopus struggle in the ropes, a large tiger shark darted along the wall of water alongside the boat. It gave no warning, but in a flash it turned its whole body around and shot toward the deck, slicing right through the wall of water, and, much to its surprise, plummeting through the air and landing right beside its prey.

The shark's eyes glistened in the moonlight. Its rows of razor-sharp teeth shined.

As the *Get It Over With* rose to the top of the swell, the octopus and the shark found themselves thoroughly out of the water. The octopus's eyes scanned the shark beside it and the shark did what came naturally to a fish out of water: it panicked.

Ropes and tools went flying. A heavy steel winch handle, used for raising the sails, plopped overboard and disappeared into the ocean. The shark tried to snap its jaws around the octopus. The octopus tried to wrap itself around the shark to sink its sharp beak into the shark's head. Black ink sprayed from its belly, smearing all over the deck. The humans dove for cover.

"Dude!" Corey Brandt shouted, not very help-fully.

"We've got a shark on board," Dr. Navel an-nounced from the steering wheel at the back of the boat. "And an octopus."

"We noticed!" Celia yelled.

"Don't panic!" yelled their father.

"Keep it down, down there!" yelled Twitchy Bart from high above in the mast. "I'm trying to sleep."

"I don't get paid enough for this," said Bonnie.

She turned around and went back to her bunk to sleep.

"Don't worry, kids," said Big Bart, putting his massive arms around Corey, Oliver, and Celia. "I'm here to help. Just tell me what to do."

"How should we know?" objected Oliver. "We're eleven!"

"And a half!" Celia added.

"Well." Big Bart turned to Corey. "You're the Celebrity Adventurist. What do we do?"

"I, like, never did an episode about this," said Corey.

"Oliver." Celia turned to her brother. "You watch *Sharkapalooza*! What have you learned?"

"Sharks live in the water!" Oliver yelled.

"Well duh, professor," Celia scoffed at him.

Oliver hated when his sister made fun of him for not knowing something when she didn't know it either. And he didn't like looking like an idiot in front of Corey Brandt or Big Bart.

"Dad!" he yelled. "What do we do?"

"Don't panic!" their father added again. That seemed to be as much advice as he could offer.

"Well . . ." Oliver racked his brain to remember something useful, anything useful. "They say that if you rub a shark's nose and flip it upside down, it sort of falls asleep."

"Rub its nose?" Celia repeated in disbelief.

"And then we can push it overboard," Oliver said miserably.

"What about the octopus?" Corey wondered.

"I guess we'll just have to grab it and toss it overboard," said Oliver.

"Like we did with the octopus at the New Year's Eve party," said Corey.

This time Oliver blushed. He didn't like to be reminded about the killer wedgie he'd received.

We should note that, much to their dismay, Oliver and Celia were no longer awed by the majesty of the sea.

"No time to lose." Big Bart stepped forward. "The shark will die if we don't help it."

"Yeah," said Celia. "But we might die if we do help!"

"Come on, Celia." Corey Brandt smiled. "I'll make sure you don't get hurt."

Celia nodded, and she and the teen star moved carefully after Big Bart toward the thrashing shark. Oliver let out a low groan and stepped up behind them. He almost wished he had just let his sister watch her soap operas and never seen *Sharka-palooza* at all. A little knowledge was a terrible thing.

But it was too late for regret; it was time for action.

"I hate to rush you all," Dr. Navel called from the stern of the boat, "but we seem to be heading into rough weather. We'll want to throw those animals back in the water somewhat quickly! A storm's a-comin', as they say!"

Oliver and Celia could swear they heard a bit of glee in their father's voice. Shark and octopus wrestling reminded him of their mother.

That's how they had spent their honeymoon.

"Oliver." Celia looked back at her brother. "I'm really sorry I got us into this. I know it was my fault."

"It's cool," sighed Oliver. "It was, you know . . ."

"Destiny," said Celia.

Oliver nodded. "Now let's get this sharktopus wrestling over with."

12

WE WON'T JUMP THE SHARK

"WE'VE GOT TO JUMP THE SHARK," said
Big Bart, rubbing his hands together and preparing
to leap. The shark and the octopus were battling
each other, thrashing all over the deck.

Big Bart timed his leap over the fish fracas—
which is just another way of saying fight—with
great care. One swipe with the shark's muscular
tail would send even a man of his size overboard
and, in the growing sea swells in the dark of night,
it would be impossible to rescue him.

"You two wait here," Corey said to Oliver and
Celia, although it didn't really seem necessary.
They had no plans to jump the shark.

"Corey! Be careful!" Celia exclaimed way too
dramatically. She blushed. Oliver didn't even
bother to roll his eyes. His sister knew.

Corey blew a strand of hair off his forehead,

gave the kids his trademark wink and smile, and took his own running jump over the fracas. He overestimated and nearly jumped clear off the front of the boat. Big Bart caught him by one of the pockets on his Pocketed Pajamas and pulled him back on board.

"Those are some good pajamas," said Big Bart.

"Double stitched," Corey said. "I wouldn't endorse a bad product. You know, I get offers all the time, for energy drinks and adventure gear and hair gel. But these Pocketed Pants products are the first ones ever to earn the Corey Brandt seal of—"

"Guys!" Celia called out. "Shark? Octopus?"

"Right," Corey called back to her. "Sorry, Celia."

"It's no problem," Celia said. "I just, you know, thought I'd remind you."

"It's no problem, Corey . . . you're so dreamy . . . ," Oliver muttered, mimicking his sister under his breath. She frowned at him and flicked his ear. "Ouch," he said.

"Okay!" Corey said. "Big Bart, you can take the . . . uh . . . shark, and I'll handle the octopus."

"Sure." Big Bart grunted. He called to Oliver and Celia. "When the shark is docile, you two start untangling it!"

"Docile?" Oliver asked.

"Easy to control," said Celia. "You should know that one."

"Hey," he objected, but just then Big Bart pounced onto the shark, pressing it down with the full weight of his body. He was trying to roll it onto its back with one hand while rubbing its nose with his other hand. Corey hesitated; a flicker of doubt crossed his face. Then the shark snapped at him and he dodged it. The jaw slammed into the deck of the boat with a *crunch*. Corey leaped out of the way and dove forward to catch the octopus. As soon as he landed on it, it slipped out from under him and slithered onto his back. He turned to catch it, but he found himself lifted into the air.

"Ow!" he yelled as his feet left the deck. The octopus wrapped one tentacle around his waist, while another pulled at his legs.

"This thing is giving me a killer wedgie!" Corey yelled. "K-I-L-L—ow!"

"See?" Oliver pointed.

"My pants!" Corey cried. "The wedgie-proofing doesn't work! The wedgie! It's terrible!"

"What should we do?" Celia shouted.

"I dunno," said Oliver. "I never watched a show about octopuses giving wedgies!"

"Octopi!" Celia yelled. "What about *Squid Whisperer*?"

"That's about squid! They're different!"

"Corey," Celia yelled at him. "Rub the nose!"

"Where's the nose?" Corey shouted back.

Oliver and Celia looked at each other and shrugged.

The octopus had wrapped another arm around Corey's head. Every time he tried to grab its body, the octopus slipped out of his grasp.

The shark, meanwhile, was resting calmly as Big Bart rubbed its nose. Corey wished he'd chosen the shark.

"Watch out!" Celia shouted as a tentacle whipped around at Oliver. He jumped just in time.

"Help," Corey croaked as the octopus started to move toward the edge of the boat, dragging the teen heartthrob with it.

Celia and Oliver sprang into action. Without a word to each other, they both leaped at the octopus. Sometimes it was nice having a twin. Oliver was glad to have his sister back on his side.

Celia was glad her brother wasn't being a jerk anymore.

They grabbed at the creature's arms, trying to pull Corey free. Every time they grabbed onto it, the octopus seemed to change shape and slip free.

"Ow!" Oliver yelled as the octopus hoisted him into the air by his pants. "Not again!"

"Oliver, you've got to—" Celia started, but the octopus caught her too. Its sharp beak was chewing on her hair and it started to pull all three of them off the boat.

They heard a splash as Big Bart rolled the shark back into the water.

"Help!" Celia yelled.

Suddenly the octopus dropped her. She hit the deck with a thud. Oliver and Corey fell after her. They looked up to see Dennis pecking at the octopus's head.

"Bwak! Bwak!" Dennis clucked and squawked as all eight arms of the sea creature flailed around him.

"Dennis!" Big Bart yelled, charging forward and landing one hard kick right at the octopus. It flew through the air, arcing high into the night, and splashing back into the inky-black ocean. They saw its dark shape dart away under the water, probably just as relieved to be off the boat as they were to have it gone.

"I played kicker in high school football." Big Bart smiled. "Kicking an octopus isn't much harder than kicking a football."

Celia slumped back against the railing of the boat, exhausted. Oliver and Corey slumped next to her.

"That's twice we've almost been killed by a normal octopus," said Celia. "I really don't want to meet the kraken."

"How many times do I have to explain that the kraken is a squid?" Oliver muttered. "If it's even . . . oh, never mind." He dropped his head to his chest, too tired to argue.

Celia nodded, too tired to win an argument. She looked at the deck of the boat next to her foot. There was a large sharp tooth stuck into the fiberglass. She yanked it out.

"Shark tooth," said Big Bart. "They say it's good luck."

"Yeah," said Celia. "Good luck it didn't eat us." She put it in her pocket anyway, just in case.

The whole ordeal had lasted only minutes, but

it felt like a lifetime. It was only after they caught their breath that they noticed the boat was pitching wildly from side to side.

They looked up and saw the last of the stars blotted out by heavy black clouds. The boat lurched sickeningly upward and crashed back down again with a blast of salt water.

Oliver and Celia were already soaked and they smelled like fish. They were scraped and bruised from the octopus's suckers. Aching, they ran to the cabin, swaying from side to side like Professor Rasmali-Greenberg after too much sherry.

"I don't feel so good," said Oliver.

Corey began barking out instructions to ready the ship for the worst of the storm, although by that point it was almost impossible to hear him over the howling wind. Walls of water crashed around them, leaving entire schools of fish flopping on the decks, only to be washed away again by the next crashing wave. Inside the cabin, a soup of seawater and stray fish sloshed along the floor.

"Bonnie!" The twins knocked on the door to her bunk. "Bonnie, there's a storm. Wake up!"

"Is it time yet?" she called through the doorway.

"Time for what?" called Celia.

"Nothing," groaned Bonnie. "Wake me in the morning."

Oliver and Celia knocked for a few more minutes and then gave up.

They poked their heads back outside.

They saw their father at the wheel, struggling to keep the boat pointed in the right direction and to keep himself from being knocked overboard by the raging water. Corey was further forward, trying to tie the sails down so the heavy winds didn't tear them to shreds. He had tied a rope around the mast and looped it around his waist so he didn't get washed away.

Big Bart was racing this way and that, falling over with every crashing wave that hit, trying to get himself to the cabin.

Oliver and Celia took one more look around the battered deck and one look at each other and quickly ducked back inside.

"I bet we'd just be in the way out there," said Oliver.

"And we wouldn't want to distract them from their work," said Celia.

"And Dad would probably worry about us going overboard," said Oliver.

"Right," said Celia. "He'd be worried for our . . . um . . . safety."

Neither of the twins believed it. They could hear their father's whoops of excitement even through the sound of the howling wind. He loved a duel with nature.

"Blow, winds, and crack your cheeks! Rage! Blow!" they heard him yelling.

Oliver looked questioningly at Celia. She shrugged.

"I mean, we did wrestle an octopus," she said.

"Yeah," Oliver agreed.

"And someone will need to be rested for the morning watch," she said.

"Yeah," Oliver agreed again.

"So I think," said Celia, "that we should get some sleep."

"Yeah," agreed Oliver a third time. It felt really good to agree with Celia again.

They had their hammocks strung up in the corner of the cabin like bunk beds, one above the other. Celia put her foot right on Oliver's face on the way up to the top bunk.

Yep, he thought. His sister was back to herself again. Oliver flipped on the TV so they could watch *Sunset High* reruns while they slept. If they weren't sailing through a storm in the middle of the Pacific Ocean on their way to meet a mysterious sea people who would lead them to an island guarded by mythic squid where their mother may or may not have discovered Plato's map to Atlantis, things would be almost normal.

"Bwak," said Dennis, racing into the cabin. He settled comfortably down below the hammocks.

"I hope chickens don't snore," said Celia.

"He's a rooster," said Oliver.

In the galley, pots and pans crashed from side to side with wild seas. As the boat rolled and swayed, the hammocks hung smartly, rocked gently on their hooks. Dennis didn't snore. Neither did Oliver and Celia. Outside, however, the wind howled.

13

WE SLEPT WITH THE FISHES

WHEN THE TWINS WOKE UP, rested and re-laxed, the sun was high in the sky; the seas were calm, and the deck of the *Get It Over With* looked as if it had been redecorated by a stampeding herd of yaks. They stretched and rubbed their eyes.

"I guess the storm was pretty bad," Oliver observed.

"Guess so," said Celia, taking in the scene on deck.

Coils of rope were tossed every which way. Containers of supplies had spilled open, their contents no doubt washed away. The boat bobbed slightly on the water. All was quiet.

Dr. Navel and Big Bart were sound asleep, leaning on each other, both of them lashed to the wheel with a thick rope. Corey Brandt had somehow tangled himself into the mainsail. He was lying flat out on the boom of the mast a few feet above the deck, snoring lightly, with the sailcloth pulled around him like a blanket. One arm hung limply out of the tangle and a thin stream of drool dangled from his mouth almost to the deck of the boat. He looked quite unlike a world-famous teen heartthrob. His hair, however, was still perfect.

Bonnie hadn't come out of her bunk and Twitchy Bart was still high up on the mast, snoring and sopping wet.

"Should we wake them?" asked Oliver.

"Well," said Celia, "we'll need breakfast."

They went to their father and poked him with a paddle that was lying on the deck.

"Is that all you've got, you thunderbolts of Zeus!" Dr. Navel yelled as he snapped awake. Oliver and Celia jumped backward. "Oh, children. Hi. Good morning."

He smiled and knocked some water out of his ear. Suddenly he squirmed and made a strange face. He pulled a large silver fish out of his shirt. He studied it curiously for a moment and tossed it back into the sea, where it darted away under the waves.

Big Bart stretched upright and cracked his neck, slowly untying himself from the wheel.

They worked together to wake up Corey. He didn't respond to shouting or poking or jostling. They eventually had to raise the sail so he flopped onto the deck of the boat in a puddle of seawater and dozens of those silver fish. He clutched one of the fish to his chest like a teddy bear. It was only when it flopped onto his face that he stirred, muttering about not being in the mood for sushi.

"Oh, guys, hey," he said when he finally opened his eyes and saw the Navels and Big Bart standing over him. "Morning."

"Land ho!" Twitchy Bart shouted from above. "Land ho!"

They squinted at the horizon and saw, barely higher than the gentlest of waves, a colorful patch of huts.

"That's not land," said Big Bart. "Those are rafts and boats. Dozens of them tied together."

"The Orange Lords?" Oliver wondered.

"Orang Laut," said Dr. Navel. "They tie their boats together to trade and socialize. We'll take the dinghy over to them." He pointed at the small inflatable motorboat tied to the back of their sailboat. "Corey, why don't you stay with the crew and keep us in ship shape. Kids, you want to come with me to meet one of the last of the nomadic sea peoples on earth?"

"Not really," said Celia.

"Nope," agreed Oliver.

Dr. Navel shook his head and sighed. He had thought he was making progress, but Oliver and Celia were just as incurious as ever.

"Well," he said, "I need someone to come with me."

"I'll go," said Corey. "Meeting the Orang Laut would be M-E-G-A, mega!"

"Mega," Oliver mouthed to Celia and rolled his eyes, but she was gazing at Corey and didn't notice.

"All right," said Dr. Navel. "Oliver and Celia can take command of the ship until we're back."

"I'll go too," said Celia.

"Wait a second," said Oliver.

"I mean, you know. It could be not totally terrible." Celia smiled at Corey. "They spend their whole lives on the ocean . . . that's, um, mega?"

Corey nodded and the three of them climbed into the dinghy. Celia saw that Oliver was giving her that look of his with the wrinkled eyebrows and the frown.

"Sorry," she mouthed to him. She hoped he'd understand. How often was it that she got to ride in a dinghy with Corey Brandt? The girls at school would go crazy.

"I can't command the ship!" Oliver complained. "I'm eleven!"

"Eleven and a half!" Celia corrected him again.

"I believe in you!" Dr. Navel smiled as he tossed off the rope, tugged the engine to life, and sped off toward the collection of boats, taking Corey and Celia with him.

His sister hadn't changed at all, Oliver thought. Just after they'd finally made up, she was ready to abandon him for Corey again. She was just like their mother, always leaving Oliver behind. She didn't even look back as they sped away, just watched Corey laugh at something that was probably dumb.

"D-U-M-B," Oliver spelled out loud.

"Don't worry, little bro." Big Bart came up beside him. "Command ain't nothin' to be afraid of. You got us crew here and we're at anchor. All you have to do is make sure we stay at anchor."

"Whatever," Oliver grunted and went to sit in the captain's chair behind the wheel. The deckhands all came together for lunch, but Oliver didn't feel like being sociable. He watched the dinghy arrive at the rafts and watched Corey and his sister wave at the fishermen.

"Stupid teen heartthrob," Oliver muttered. "Thinks he's so cool."

While Oliver watched Corey and his sister and his father, he didn't notice the deckhands signaling to each other with their eyes, and one by one disappearing into Bonnie's bunk, where they shut and locked the door.

14

WE COME IN PEACE

AS THEIR DINGHY PULLED AWAY from the *Get It Over With*, Celia started to feel bad about leaving Oliver behind with the weird deckhands and that chicken. She was going to turn around and at least wave to him as they sped off toward the Orang Laut, but just then Corey turned to her.

"Did you hear the joke about the two squid?" Corey asked.

Celia shook her head.

"There were two squid swimming side by side in the ocean," he said. "One squid turns to the other one and says, 'The water is pretty cold today.' The other squid looks at his friend and shouts, 'AHHH—A TALKING SQUID!'"

Celia stared back at Corey. He slapped his knee and nearly fell off the boat laughing.

"I guess that's funny," she said, her expression blank.

"A talking squid," Corey repeated, still laughing. "I love that joke."

Celia glanced back at their sailboat, getting smaller and smaller in the distance. She wondered if Oliver would have thought the joke was funny. Probably not. He didn't seem to like Corey Brandt in real life very much.

"Hello!" Dr. Navel called out as they approached the flotilla of small wooden boats. "These boats are called *lepa-lepa*," he said to Corey and Celia. "They are a traditional boat that the sea nomads have used for centuries, perfectly designed for their lives on the oceans . . . most of them have been forced to settle on land, but this community is one of the last that still calls the ocean home." He waved as their boat approached. "*Selamat datang!*" he said, greeting them in the Malay language and hoping they understood.

The Orang Laut didn't look like an ancient fishing people. They were dark skinned and dressed in normal clothes, chatting and eating and repairing fishing lines. Their little wooden boats were all tied together and bobbing gently on the water. They had little covered canvas huts at the back of each boat, which must be where they slept, and clotheslines hung between the boats. They had made their own little island.

They all stopped talking as Dr. Navel cut the engine and drifted up alongside them.

"Hello." He smiled and reached into one of his many pants pockets and started pulling out gifts for the fishermen—steel fishhooks and string. He tossed them like he was tossing beads from a parade float. People ducked and yelled at him, dodging hooks. No one dared pick them up.

"They will not take your gifts," said a boy who had popped up from the water holding a net filled with fish and shells. He had been underneath the surface when they arrived. He didn't have an air tank on, just goggles and a swimsuit.

"How did he stay down so long?" Celia wondered aloud.

"Their children learn to dive very deep on a single breath from a very young age," Dr. Navel said.

The boy climbed on board the Navels' boat, dripping wet.

"The spirit of the giver is in every gift, and they do not know your spirit yet," he said. "You could mean to put on a curse on all of us with these gifts."

"We come in peace," Corey announced loudly. The boy cocked his head at the celebrity. The old men wrinkled their brows and spat again. "That's, like, what they say in movies," Corey explained.

"We need your help," said Dr. Navel. "These gifts are given in friendship. I do not speak the language of the Orang Laut. Would you translate for me?"

"Yes, I will help," said the boy. "My name is Jabir."

"Hello, Jabir," said Dr. Navel. "This is my daughter, Celia, and this is—"

"Corey Brandt!" The boy smiled at Corey. "I learn English from *Agent Zero! Sunset High!*" He shook Corey's hand eagerly. Then he frowned and added, "You should have been with Lauren."

"Yes, of course," Dr. Navel said, before Celia could object with her opinions about Annabel and destiny and all that TV trivia. He had really hoped to get away from television gossip in the middle of the Pacific Ocean.

We should not be surprised that some products of

the human imagination cross all distances. No matter where our adventures take us in life, whether to Kuala Lumpur or Dayton, Ohio, we will find that most strangers can become friends by sharing a soda, most arguments can be resolved over a friendly meal, and most people will have strong opinions about vampire romances on television.

"We are trying to learn if anyone has seen this woman." Dr. Navel held up a photograph of his wife. Before the boy could even translate the question, the older fishermen shook their heads and spat into the sea.

"No one knows," said Jabir.

"She perhaps traveled with some of your people to a terrible place. An island of giant squid? Kraken? There was a shipwreck there long ago."

The boy translated into his language. The fishermen shook their heads, made clicking noises with their teeth, and spat some more into the sea.

"They will not tell you," said the boy. He glanced around nervously and leaned closer. "They know this place, and they know this woman, but say that it is not for you to know. They do not tell secrets to outsiders."

"I understand, and I promise to respect your

ways," said Dr. Navel. "I will not reveal your secrets, but I must find this place. My wife—her mother"—he pointed at Celia—"is in danger!"

"Others have come here in the past to learn from us," said the boy. "There was once a group of outsiders who came to make a 'documentary film,' they called it. We taught them many things: how to dive deep with a single breath, the names of the spirits in our canoes, in the currents, in the birth of a shark. Our legends of this island of the giant squid. They made their documentary movie and we, who have shared our secrets with them, we did not ever see any—what do you call it?—royalty payments from this movie. They put it onto television, I think. We do not share with outsiders anymore. Television contracts are simply too unfair."

"Television." Dr. Navel sighed. "Always television," he repeated, shaking his head. Corey slumped, disappointed. He knew exactly how unfair television contracts could be. Celia couldn't believe they were giving up so easily. She had an idea.

"Have you ever seen *Valerie-at-Large*?" she asked the boy.

"Celia," said her father. "This is hardly the

time to talk about television. The Orang Laut are a wise and learned people. They live their lives on the—"

"I love that show!" The boy smiled and pointed to a satellite dish on one of the boats. "TweenTV!"

"Right," said Celia.

Dr. Navel slapped his palm on his forehead.

Celia ignored him. "Did you see that episode where Valerie was writing a story for the school paper and she wanted to know what happened at Addison Garrity's birthday party, but only the popular girls were invited and Valerie wasn't popular, so she had to find a way to get invited? She offered to do Madison Graham's biology paper for her if she could come, but Madison said, well, you have to be in the Six Sisters Club, which is a secret club that the popular girls had, though I don't know why it was called the Six Sisters because there were a lot more than six of them, but Valerie said, 'Okay, I'll do it.' So she had to do all this stuff to join the club, like spend the night in a graveyard and steal a towel from the boys' locker room, because that was her initiation, and then she got to go to the party, but it was really boring and the girls were actually mean to each other, but she was one of them now, so she kept her promise and never told anyone their secrets, because she'd been made part of the group?"

"Um, yes?" said the boy, unsure what Celia was saying. Dr. Navel and Corey looked questioningly at her too.

"So is there anything like that, like an initiation that we can do to become one of the Orang Laut?" she asked.

"You want to sneak into the boys' locker room?" asked Jabir, scratching his head.

"No." Celia rolled her eyes. "We want to do whatever it takes to become one of you."

The boy turned and translated for the elders. They laughed and he talked some more. They laughed again and he turned back to Celia.

"They say there is one thing you can do, and then they will tell you where to find this island where the monsters live," he said. "You must prove you are true people of the sea."

"How do we do that?" Corey asked.

"I am sorry, Mr. Corey," said Jabir. "Not you. But the girl"—he smiled at her—"she must go through our . . . what was the word?"

"Initiation," said Celia.

"Yes," said Jabir.

"Why me?" groaned Celia. Jabir blushed and wouldn't look at her.

"Celia," her father scolded her. "It is not polite to question their ways. Please, Jabir, continue."

"Okay," said Jabir, looking back at Celia. "First, you must complete a task of great danger and bring us the tooth of a tiger shark."

Celia smirked. Maybe this wouldn't be so bad after all. She reached into her pocket and pulled out the shark tooth she'd pulled out of the deck of their boat the night before.

"Done," she said, like it was the most normal thing in the world. The boy took it from her, wide-eyed. "From shark wrestling." She shrugged.

Jabir turned and showed the tooth to the others. There was another round of murmuring and muttering. Some nodding. No one spat.

"Okay," said Jabir. "This last thing you must do alone. You will show that the sea accepts your spirit." He glanced back at the elders and wrinkled his eyebrows. "Or something."

"Is this for real?" Celia demanded.

The boy nodded, but Celia wasn't sure she believed him.

"What do I have to do?" she asked. "Like medi-
tate and hum or something?"

When Jabir told her what she had to do, she really wished she had stayed aboard the *Get It Over
With* like her brother.

15

WE DON'T LIKE WHAT WE HEAR

THE SUN BEAT DOWN on Oliver all morning. Seabirds circled the mast, squawking and searching for food. He knew Bonnie would be mad if they pooped on the deck she spent so much time cleaning. The boat rocked gently in the water, and pretty soon Oliver found himself drifting off to sleep.

Hunger woke him up some time later. The sun had moved past the high point in the sky, so it was afternoon and his father and sister and Corey were still over on the rafts of the Orang Laut. Oliver couldn't hear any of the deckhands talking, so he figured they were napping or something. He remembered seeing a box of snack cakes in the galley and he decided that he had earned one or two by being in command of the boat all morning. He hopped up to get one.

He was just turning to go back out on deck with the whole box of snack cakes shoved into his backpack—in case he needed more than one—when he heard loud whispers coming from behind the closed door of Bonnie's bunk.

"They don't suspect a thing," he heard Twitchy Bart say. "Don't worry about it. We hacked into Corey's website perfectly. He thinks we're just regular contest winners. If any of them was suspicious, I'd see 'em conspirin' an' such from my perch up the mast."

"I don't like the way that little girl asks me so many questions about Corey Brandt," said Bonnie. "She needs to mind her own business."

Oliver nodded in quiet agreement but kept listening.

"I say we wait," Big Bart said. "If the Orang Laut help them, they'll take us right to this island of the sea monsters. If that place is worth all this trouble, there must be something valuable there. Treasure and the like."

"You believe this stuff?" Bonnie sneered. "You're crazy, Big Bart. There's no such thing as a kraken and no mysterious island. This is a wild-goose chase. I say we stick to the plan."

"I don't think these explorers would go through all this trouble on a wild-goose chase," Big Bart tried to reason with her. "They seem pretty smart to me."

"They're just kids," Bonnie spat.

"They're tweens," corrected Big Bart. "They handled that shark and octopus nicely. I didn't see you helping out." Bonnie sniffed the air loudly. "And their father has lots of fancy degrees."

"Even more reason not to go along with him," said Bonnie. "Two brats, a teenage heartthrob, and an overeducated fool. We'd be wasting our time."

"We'll get a nice ransom for Corey Brandt, no matter what," Twitchy Bart said. "I bet the television studio will pay up. That was the plan, and I want to stick to it."

"We could sell the Navels off as shark bait," said Bonnie. "Like my great-great-great-great-grandmother Anne used to do."

Oliver's blood ran cold.

"Corey Brandt is not the big prize here," said Big Bart. "The real money's in that island they're looking for! We should let the Navels do all the work of finding it for us, I say. Then we take 'em hostage afterward!"

"I'm tired of sailing," Twitchy Bart complained. "It's dull and it's hard and I want to get back to our ship to put my feet up and watch TV. I'm sick of being stuck on this sailboat taking orders from that teenager. I don't care how good his hair is. I say we take these dumb saps prisoner the moment we're clear of these sea people, forget all about some fairy-tale monster island, and make a bit of Hollywood ransom money, just like we always planned to do."

"Twitchy Bart's right," said Bonnie. "And I'm tired of listening to that Celia going all googly for him. It'll be nice to shut her up for good at the bottom of the sea."

Oliver couldn't believe what he was hearing. He didn't actually disagree that his sister was annoying, but she shouldn't get sent to the bottom of the sea for it!

"You're being penny-wise and pound-foolish, I tell you," Big Bart snapped at Bonnie.

"Now what's that supposed to mean?" Twitchy Bart moaned.

"I think Bonnie knows."

"What if I don't?" snarled Bonnie.

"Well, find out then."

"Well, maybe I don't wanna."

"Well, maybe you're an idiot."

"Well, maybe I'll cut that big face of yours off if you talk like that again."

"Well, maybe you should try it."

"Well, maybe I—"

"Hey!" Twitchy Bart whisper-shouted. "Keep your voices down or the boy will hear all yer jabbering."

Oliver sucked in his breath and tried to be as still and silent as possible. No sound came from inside Bonnie's bunk. An eternity passed. Oliver didn't dare so much as shift his weight on his feet, lest it make a noise. He was getting pretty uncomfortable. He really needed to use the bathroom after his nap.

"Okay," he heard Bonnie say; her tone meant business. "By the articles of piracy, as laid down at the dawn of the Barbary Corsairs, we'll take a vote."

"Fine," said Big Bart.

"Suits me," said Twitchy Bart.

"By show of hands, who votes we take control of this vessel as soon as we are clear of the Orange Lords or whatever they're called, take the hostages back to the Princess and get what we can get for ransom, and forget all about some sea monster island."

There was a moment of silence. Oliver wondered who the Princess was.

"That settles it, captain," sneered Bonnie. "Two votes to one. Your crew has spoken."

"So be it," said Big Bart. "I swore an oath to our articles of piracy and I'll abide by them. Although I think you're being fools."

"Think what ya like," said Twitchy Bart. "Just make sure you knock out that Dr. Navel first. You never know what a father will do to protect his young."

"He seems kind of harmless to me," said Big Bart.

"You never know with fathers and children," said Bonnie. "I'll take care of the bossy little girl and her mopey brother."

"That leaves Corey Brandt for me," said Twitchy Bart. "It'll be nice to take that Hollywood type down a notch. I hated *Sunset High*. He should have ended up with Lauren at the end."

"Annabel was his destiny," said Big Bart. "You can't run from destiny."

"Whatever," said Bonnie.

"His other stuff's pretty good," Big Bart added. "You can't argue with that."

"I liked *Agent Zero* the best," Twitchy Bart chimed in. "And these Pocketed Pants are great. They're breezy and warm at the same time. And the pockets . . . you can never have too many pockets."

"The color selection's nice too," Big Bart agreed.

"I'm still gonna wallop him," added Twitchy Bart. "I wanna see if anything can mess up that hair."

They all guffawed and Oliver heard the sound of backslapping, their arguments forgotten in favor of their brutal mischief.

Oliver didn't know which was worse, that the crew of their ship was planning a mutiny or that he agreed with their taste in television.

Just then he heard the whine of the dinghy's motor as it came back to the ship. A knot formed in his stomach and his skin prickled with nerves. He closed his eyes for a second to think. They were in danger and he was the only one who knew. He asked himself, what would Agent Zero do?

The engine grew louder. They were almost back. He'd have to warn them. Corey *was* Agent Zero after all. And their father had certainly faced worse dangers than this.

He just had to figure out how to keep the *Get It Over With* close to the little fishermen until he could tell them the treachery that was afoot.

The door to Bonnie's bunk burst open and Oliver fell backward onto the floor, scattering plastic-wrapped snack cakes everywhere and spilling the remote control out of his bag. He slipped it into his pocket as fast as he could.

"Oh, sorry . . . sorry," he muttered. "I just woke up and thought I'd get something to eat."

Bonnie and Twitchy Bart watched him, their eyes narrowing to slits. Big Bart crossed his arms and took a deep breath, looking down at Oliver with watery blue eyes.

"Ahoy!" Dr. Navel called from outside. "We're back! Somebody want to help us aboard?"

"Oliver, I have to ask you something important." Big Bart bent down and looked Oliver right in the eyes. Oliver gulped.

Big Bart reached down and snatched up a snack cake in his giant hand and held it right in front of Oliver's face. "May I?" he asked with a smile.

"Sure," squeaked Oliver.

"I love these things." Big Bart shook his head, standing. "I know they're mostly rubber and industrial waste, but they're just so delicious. You eat up. We'll go help your dad and them. You are now relieved of command, sir!" He saluted.

"Um," said Oliver. "What?"

"You know." Big Bart smiled. "Because your dad and Corey are back! You don't have to be in charge anymore." He patted Oliver on the back. "Well done, kiddo! You kept us in ship shape!"

He led the other treacherous deckhands out into the glaring sun while Oliver started shoving snack cakes into his backpack, along with the wet suits he hoped never to have to use.

"Hey, Oliver," Big Bart called back. Oliver froze. "Thanks for the snack cake!"

"You're welcome," said Oliver, too frightened to move.

"Where's Celia?" he heard Big Bart ask.

"She'll be back shortly," his father said. "She had to find a cucumber."

Oliver didn't know what that meant or why his sister needed to find a cucumber, but at least it bought him some time to come up with a plan.

16

WE CAN'T CATCH
A CUCUMBER

"YOU MUST EMPTY YOUR LUNGS of air and then take a big breath," Jabir explained as he handed Celia some homemade wooden goggles with scratched glass lenses. "You want to get as much new air as you can before you dive down." Celia wrinkled her brow at him. "It would also help if you burst your eardrums," he added.

"I am not bursting my eardrums," said Celia.

"Suit yourself." Jabir shrugged. "You will not be able to dive as deep. The pressure will hurt too much."

Celia really wished she had kept her mouth shut about the whole *Valerie-at-Large* initiation thing. She knew that if she wanted to find out where her mother had gone, get back to the *Get It Over With*, and get home again, then she had to complete this challenge. She had to dive down deep into the ocean with no air tank or anything, and come back up to the surface with a sea cucumber. She didn't even know what a sea cucumber was.

"It looks just like a big cucumber on the bottom of the ocean," Jabir told her. "Its skin feels like leather and when you pick it up, it will throw up all its guts."

"That's disgusting," said Celia.

"They are a delicacy," he answered her.

"So people, like, eat it?" asked Celia.

"They are very good for you." He smiled. "You might like them."

"Do I really have to do this?" Celia looked over the edge of the small fishing boat, straight down into the sea. Dark shapes moved in the depths. The old men of the Orang Laut watched her from their boats and chuckled. "I don't even like to swim in the swimming pool," she whispered to Jabir.

"The elders will not tell you where your mother has gone unless you first show them that you respect our ways," he whispered back to her. "Don't worry. I will help you."

"But why me?" she asked. "Why not Corey or my father? Or my brother, Oliver? He's back on our boat. He could dive with you. It'd make him feel special if you asked for him."

She shaded her eyes from the sun and looked over the water toward the sailboat, where her father and Corey were just climbing on board again. Big Bart had come out of the cabin to greet them. It looked like he was eating a Velma Sue's Snack Cake. Celia wished she were over there eating one too.

"Do you know the story of our people?" Jabir asked.

"No," said Celia. "How would I?"

"A long time ago, there was an unhappy princess who liked to watch the sea for hours and hours. One day, a great flood rose up and swept her away," Jabir said. "Her father, the king, sent a fleet of boats out to find his daughter and ordered them not to return until she was found. And so we remain at sea, waiting for a princess to return." Jabir smiled.

"That's the dumbest thing I've ever heard," said Celia. "You live on these boats because some ancient princess got lost in a flood? You know she's not coming back, right?"

"That's just the story," said Jabir. "It's the myth that we tell about how we came to live at sea. It doesn't have to be true to be, you know, true. Maybe you are the princess?"

Celia wrinkled her brow at him. He blushed.

"Let's get this over with." She sighed. Then she took a deep breath and jumped into the water.

It felt good to swim in the cool ocean, rising and falling with the gentle swells. Jabir tossed a net down to Celia and then he jumped in, treading water while he held two bags of stones.

"These . . . will help you . . . get to the bottom . . . faster." He kept having to spit water out of his mouth as he struggled with both bags of stones. Celia wondered why he was being so helpful.

"Okay," she said, taking one of the bags of stones from him. "Let's—" Before she could finish her sentence she sank straight down like a . . . well, like a stone.

Underneath the surface, another world blossomed. Celia looked up and saw the waves above from their undersides; she saw the sun high above, bent and shimmering like seeing it through a stained-glass window. She looked down and saw the sandy bottom racing up toward her. Coral reefs

burst from the ocean floor. Some were round and grooved and looked like pictures she had seen of human brains; others were like giant leaves, waving in an underwater breeze. Colorful fish swamped between the clusters of coral, nibbling at the sand or vanishing between the spongy fingers of colorful sea anemones.

She looked at Jabir, who was sinking right beside her. He smiled widely and shook his head back and forth so his hair waved just like the sea anemones. That made Celia laugh in a hail of bubbles. She'd lost a lot of air with that laugh.

Jabir grabbed her hand and pulled her to the ocean floor. They began scouring through the sand, kicking and swimming. As Celia approached one large beige rock, it suddenly turned purple, unfurled eight legs from its underside and swam away as fast as lightning. She hadn't realized that an octopus could camouflage itself so well. That made her think again of the kraken, the giant squid with razor-sharp fangs.

She turned her head around in a panic, imagining squid tentacles reaching for her, pulling her deeper into the endless blue of the ocean. She looked up to the surface, feeling a tightness in her lungs. She was running out of breath and hadn't really even looked for a sea cucumber. On a reef not even twenty feet away, a sleek shark cruised by, eyeing her with steely calm.

She looked around her and saw nothing but the sandy ocean floor. Jabir was gone. Celia was alone on the bottom of the ocean.

She did, of course, what came naturally to a tween alone on the seafloor without so much as an air tank or spear gun as hungry sharks circled.

She freaked.

She dropped her bag of stones and kicked madly toward the surface. As she rose, she felt a tug on her leg. Something had her, gripping her tightly, pulling her down. The kraken! The kraken was taking her! She let out a scream of bubbles, the last of her air, when suddenly she was face-to-face with Jabir. He shook her to make her calm down. It was he who had grabbed her leg, he who slowed her mad dash to the surface, and he was now putting a large, spiny, slimy tube into her hands. He'd gotten the sea cucumber for her. He looked at her and smiled.

Celia blushed. The moment was almost like something out of one of her soap operas and Celia felt her heart racing. That, of course, had more to do with the fact that she was about to drown than with Jabir's kindness. As she squeezed the sea cucumber in her grip, it let out of splurt of blackish, greenish gritty liquid all over her hands.

"Blech!" she cried as she broke the surface of the water, gasping for air, and dropping the sea cucumber by accident. "Its guts!" she cried out. "It spat its guts on me!"

"You . . ." Jabir panted. "You dropped it?"

"Oops," said Celia.

She looked up at the sun and breathed in deep. It felt wonderful to be back on the surface again, alive, even if she had totally failed to bring back a sea cucumber. One of the *lepa lepa*, the small fishing boats, eased up beside them. The old woman on board wagged her finger and yelled at Jabir. He said something back, but the woman wouldn't let him finish.

Celia couldn't understand the words, but scolding sounded the same in any language.

Jabir climbed aboard the boat and helped Celia out of the water.

"My mother says I have to take you back to your boat now." Jabir sighed.

"But can't I try again?" Celia felt like a failure. What were they supposed to do now? "I just dropped the cucumber straight down. It's right below us. We can go get it!"

"I'm sorry," said Jabir. "I lied to you. There is no initiation with shark teeth and sea cucumbers. I made that up so you would stay a little longer."

"You made that up?" Celia's face turned red with rage.

"It gets so boring out here," said Jabir. "And I thought, maybe if you stayed longer, we'd be friends. You'd be my very own princess." Jabir looked down at his feet. His mother was still scolding him as she rowed back toward the *Get It Over With*. "Don't tell Mr. Corey Brandt, please? I don't want him to think I'm a liar."

Celia felt bad for Jabir. She knew what it was like to be bored; she knew what it was like to want to make a new friend.

"I won't tell," she said. "And we can still be friends."

"We can?" Jabir looked up at her.

"Yeah, I mean, you never know. We're always

going on all these stupid adventures. Maybe we'll be back again."

"I hope you will," said Jabir. "I hope you find this island and your mother and come back to see me!"

"I guess I hope so too," said Celia as they reached the sailboat.

"Ahoy!" Dr. Navel called. "How was your first dive in the ocean?"

Celia didn't have a chance to answer because Jabir's mother started yelling at Dr. Navel right away.

Celia reached for the ladder to climb back aboard her boat.

"You take this." Jabir grabbed her hand while his mother was still shouting. He pressed a small brass compass into her hand. He smiled at her. The compass needle didn't point to the *N* for north. It pointed to a symbol, one Celia knew all too well: an old key—the symbol of the Mnemones. "You follow." Jabir winked at her, then turned away to try to calm his mother down.

Celia climbed aboard the *Get It Over With* and watched as Jabir's mother rowed back toward the other boats, still scolding her son.

Celia looked down at the compass in her hand and saw that it was engraved with two initials, *P.F.*

She slipped it into her pocket just as Oliver rushed over to her, looking very, very alarmed.

"We're in trouble," he whispered. "Big trouble."

17

WE ARE HARDLY SERENE

THE RESEARCH VESSEL *SERENITY* was neither a research vessel nor was it serene. It had been, until recently, one of three harpoon ships in a whaling fleet. Sir Edmund had purchased it on behalf of the Gentlemen's Adventuring Society and quickly renamed and renovated it.

He painted the word RESEARCH on the side in bright yellow paint, although he left the large harpoon gun on the bow just in case. A harpoon gun could come in handy when chasing sea monsters. Or the Navel family.

He appointed the officers' quarters in dark wood and soft leather, working to make his time on the ocean as comfortable as possible. He filled the bookshelves with rare manuscripts by the world's greatest Atlantologists—which is what experts in the lost civilization of Atlantis are called.

Atlantology is an obscure field of study, filled with crackpots and lunatics and nonsense theories. In the seventeenth century, a Swedish count was convinced that Atlantis lay somewhere near the Arctic Circle—in Swedish territory, of course. Others had proposed islands in the Mediterranean or the Azores off the Atlantic coast of Africa. One of the experts even believed that Atlantis was somewhere in the deserts of Egypt. Another claimed to have found it off the coast of Spain. Sir Edmund found the books useless, as he found most books. He was not what one might consider "a reader."

Sir Edmund had come to realize that his only hope of finding Atlantis—and with it, the Lost Library of Alexandria—would be to follow the Navel twins and to find their mother. And then they would all be his prisoners. Then, Sir Edmund would find Atlantis and Sir Edmund would control the Lost Library. Well, Sir Edmund and his Council would control the Lost Library . . . if he told them about it at all.

He smirked at the thought.

He twirled his fingers through his mustache and looked at the large painting behind his desk. He kept a surprise hidden in a chamber behind that painting, a nasty surprise for anyone who tried to stop him. He listened closely, pressing his ear against the wall to try to hear any noises coming through. He wouldn't want the prize to get out too early. That would be a disaster. Just capturing it had cost the lives of three of his ichthyologists. Zookeepers is what they really were, even if they liked to call themselves scientists.

Well, he chuckled, they weren't even zookeepers anymore. Squid food. That's what they were now.

He heard a bang and nearly fell backward off his chair.

"Ah!" he yelled, afraid his surprise was escaping.

"Sir!" Someone knocked on his cabin door. Sir Edmund caught his breath and glanced around, glad no one was in his office to see him startle. It wouldn't do to show fear in front of his crew. They were afraid enough of the cargo they were carrying.

"What?" he bellowed, angry to be interrupted.

"We have a report from your spies following the Navels."

"Yes? What is it?"

"Are you going to let me in, sir?"

"No, I am not!" Sir Edmund said. "There is

nothing you need to say that you can't say through a door."

"Yes, sir," said the sailor on the other side of the door. "Janice and Ernest continue to follow them, sir. They report that the Navels and Corey Brandt spent the afternoon with the Orang Laut and that the daughter, Celia, went for a swim. They have now all returned to their vessel."

"And what is their course? Give me coordinates, you fool! They will lead us right to Plato's map!"

"Your spies say that the ship is behaving oddly, sir."

"Oddly?"

"They are sailing around in tiny circles," said the sailor. "They don't appear to be going anywhere."

Sir Edmund leaned back in his chair and twirled his mustache absentmindedly. "What new devilry are the Navels up to?" he said to himself.

"And they are all fighting with each other," the man called. "Even the children. They say it has gotten . . . well, rather violent on board the *Get It Over With*."

18

WE DO NOT SAY ARRR

OLIVER STILL HADN'T COME UP with a plan to stop Big Bart and the others from hijacking the *Get It Over With* when his sister got back from her swim with the Orang Laut. Celia was the one who was good at plans. She never should have gone off to the Orang Laut to begin with.

The moment she set foot on board, Oliver raced over to her, giving her a big hug just so he could whisper in her ear. She was soaking wet, so it was kind of gross to hug her, but he needed her help right away.

"We're in trouble," he whispered. "Big trouble."

"Oliver." Celia shoved him away. "What's wrong with you?"

"Shh," he snapped, glancing quickly at Big Bart, who was helping the other two deckhands raise the anchor. The mutineers had said they would take over the boat once they were away from the Orang Laut. The anchor was up and the Orang Laut were already paddling off in the opposite direction. There wasn't even time to tell his sister what was going on.

"Why did you take so long to find a cucumber?" He complained and decided he would do the only thing he could think of. They had to stay close to the fishermen. He turned his back on Celia and rushed to the big captain's wheel. He nearly knocked his father over diving for it.

"Wow, Oliver." Dr. Navel smiled. "I've never seen you so eager to do anything! You've found your sea legs, I guess?"

"These are my normal legs," said Oliver. "I'm just, you know, um, bored. I want to steer, okay?"

"All right, but be careful," his father told him. He dropped his voice. "We don't want any repeats of our practice run, do we?"

"I learned how to sail, Dad, jeez," Oliver groaned.

"Celia," Dr. Navel called out to her. She was still looking very puzzled. "Did the Orang Laut give you a direction we should follow? I couldn't tell from what that lady was yelling."

"Um, yeah, Dad." Celia reached into her pocket for the compass, but before she could even pull it out, Oliver grabbed the big steering wheel with both hands and spun it with all his strength, letting it twirl free. The boat heaved to the left and the boom—the heavy pole that holds the bottom of the mainsail—swung across the deck with ferocious speed.

Celia and Dr. Navel were knocked off their feet.

"Coming about!" Corey yelled, so Bonnie hit the deck just in time as the boom swept above her.

"Darn," Oliver muttered under his breath.

"Oliver!" Dr. Navel shouted. "Catch the wheel! Try to straighten us out! You could have knocked Bonnie overboard!"

Oliver caught the wheel, but only long enough to give it another spin to keep them going in circles. In the distance, the Orang Laut had stopped to watch the strange sailboat spinning around, going nowhere. Oliver didn't have much more of a plan than circles.

"Whoa!" Twitchy Bart nearly lost his grip climbing up the mast, but he clung tightly and didn't fall.

"Coming back about!" Corey warned as the boom swung across the deck the other way. Everyone ducked again as it swept over them. The sails flared and fluttered and ropes slashed about in the air like live wires, pinning everyone where they'd ducked.

"He's trying to sabotage us again!" Celia yelled. "Just because I went to meet the Orang Laut with Corey!"

"Dude," Corey called out. "Just be cool, Oliver. You don't need to get jealous. I think you're R-A-D, rad!"

"I'm not jealous!" yelled Oliver.

"Stop being a baby then!" Celia yelled back at him. She couldn't believe her brother was acting like this. Just because she was three minutes and forty-two seconds older than he was did not give him the right to be so childish, not after she dove underwater and had a sea cucumber puke on her.

"I am not being a baby!" Oliver yelled, giving the wheel a spin in the other direction, which knocked everyone off their feet once more as the boat heaved to the other side and the boom raced back across the deck. "I'm trying to help!"

"Some help!" yelled Celia. "You're more dangerous behind that wheel than a giant squid!"

"Celia!" yelled Dr. Navel. "That's not nice! You cannot insult your brother just because he's not as good of a sailor as you."

"I am as good a sailor!" Oliver yelled. "I was trying to save you!"

"Save us?" said Dr. Navel. "What are you talking about? Save us from what? Don't be silly."

"I'm not being silly!" he yelled. "But fine! If you don't believe me, I won't save you!"

He caught the wheel and stopped it spinning, straightening the sailboat out away from the fishing boats of the Orang Laut.

"It's okay," Oliver called to Big Bart, who was crouched in the entrance to the cabin trying to protect Dennis the rooster from all the ropes slashing to and fro. "I've had enough of them. They think I'm a baby. I want to join you guys, like on *KidSwap*. I'm a good sailor. I can be one of you."

"What are you talking about?" Big Bart played innocent.

"I heard everything," said Oliver. "How you want to take us hostage and ransom Corey Brandt and all that. It's fine with me. I want to join you. I need a new family anyway. Mine doesn't appreciate me."

"Oliver," asked Celia. "Did you fall asleep in the sun and bake your brains?"

"You doing all right, pal?" Corey asked sympathetically. "You're talking kind of C-R-A-Z-Y, crazy."

"Stop spelling!" Oliver yelled. "It's bad enough you stole my sister from me. I don't want to get a spelling lesson from you too!"

"That's not nice, Oliver," said Dr. Navel. "No one is stealing your sister. No one is stealing anything."

"I'm afraid that's not entirely true," said Big Bart, standing up to his full height and setting Dennis down on the deck. "Someone is stealing this boat."

"Who?" asked Dr. Navel, looking urgently toward the horizon.

Dennis the rooster clucked and cocked his head from side to side. Bonnie stepped up behind Celia and grabbed her, pinning her arms behind her back.

"Us," said Big Bart. "Just like Oliver said."

Twitchy Bart slid down the mast and stood face-to-face with Corey Brandt, holding up a big bowie knife and touching its point gently to the teardrop freckle under Corey's eye.

"You should have ended up with Lauren on *Sunset High*," he said.

"Don't hurt him!" said Oliver. "I'll join you and help . . . but just don't hurt anybody."

"Oliver." Dr. Navel slumped back against the railing. "What are you doing?"

"I'm doing what I have to do to keep you safe," said Oliver.

"Oliver, son, listen. You can't trust—"

Big Bart walked over to Dr. Navel, towering above him with his fist raised.

"No!" Oliver shouted, and stood between Big Bart and his father. He was too small to actually block an attack, but he puffed his chest up and tried to look brave. Big Bart stopped and smiled.

"Brave kid," he said.

"Oliver, let me handle this," said Dr. Navel. He stepped around Oliver toward Big Bart, but his foot slipped on the wet deck and he knocked into the wheel. The boat spun to the side and the boom swung again. Everyone ducked, just as Dr. Navel stood up straight. "Now, Bart, surely we can negotiate some—"

The boom knocked him right on the side of the head, sending him sprawling flat on his back, unconscious.

"That was easier than I thought it'd be," said Big Bart.

"Yeah." Oliver sighed. "Dad gets knocked out a lot. But now you don't need to hurt anyone."

"You can't join them, Oliver," Celia yelled as she struggled against Bonnie's grip. "They're pirates!"

"Not really," said Oliver. "Pirates have peg legs and eye patches and parrots."

"I have Dennis," said Big Bart. "He's a bird."

"He's a chicken!" Oliver objected.

"He's a pirate chicken," Big Bart corrected. "And, technically, he is a rooster. That's a male chicken. So he's a pirate rooster. And I am a pirate captain."

"But real pirates say *arrr*!" Oliver said.

"No," said Big Bart. "They don't."

"I think Oliver's right," said Celia. "They say *arrr*!"

"No," said Bonnie. "We don't."

"You do," said Celia.

"We don't," said Bonnie.

"You do," said Celia.

"We don't," said Bonnie.

"Do you say ouch?" said Celia.

"What?" said Bonnie, confused.

"Ouch," Celia repeated, and stomped on Bonnie's foot. She wriggled out of Bonnie's grip.

"Ouch!" Bonnie yelled as Celia slipped away. But Bonnie was quick. She snapped her wrist and her knife whistled through the air and caught the waistband of Celia's pants before sticking into the mast, pinning her in place by the cloth and yanking her back.

"Ouch," said Celia. "You're not supposed to give a girl a wedgie!"

"Who says?" Bonnie laughed.

"Everyone! It's a rule!" Celia struggled to pull away. "I thought these pants were wedgie proof!"

"Me too." Corey's shoulders slumped. He was very disappointed in his Pocketed Pants' wedgie-proofing performance.

"I could have sliced you in half if I'd wanted," said Bonnie as she pulled the knife out of the

waistband and grabbed Celia by the arms again. "So be happy it was just a wedgie."

"Bonnie is a bit touchy about the whole '*arrr*' thing," said Big Bart. "She comes from a long line of pirates and she's very sensitive about their embarrassing history."

"I am not sensitive!" Bonnie waved her knife around, far too close to Celia's face for comfort. "Great-great-great-great-grandmother Anne was one of the greatest buccaneers in history and she should not be mocked with peg legs and parrots and all those nasty *arrr*s."

"Anne Bonny was your grandmother?" Celia was shocked.

"My great-great-great-great-grandmother," said Bonnie.

"How do you know about Anne Bonny?" asked Oliver.

"*John and Anne in Love*, the made-for-TV movie about Anne Bonny and her pirate lover, Captain John Rackham."

Oliver wrinkled his nose. He hated when his sister watched movies where people used the word *lover*. All that kissing. It could even ruin a pirate story.

"Everybody hold on a second!" Corey yelled at the top of his lungs, stepping back from the point of Twitchy Bart's knife. He looked from Bart to Bart to Bonnie to Dr. Navel crumpled on the deck of the boat. He lowered his voice. "Does this mean that you three aren't really Corey Brandt fans either? Did you"—he gulped—"lie on my fan website?"

They all laughed loudly, which was answer enough for Corey. He slumped against the mast, surrendering. "I can't believe I gave you free Pocketed Pants."

"They are quite comfortable, if it makes you feel better," said Big Bart.

"Enough talking," said Bonnie. "Let's throw these Navels overboard and take Mr. Brandt back for ransom, like we voted."

"Wait!" said Oliver. "I want to join you! You can't throw us overboard."

"Well, you can't join us," Bonnie snapped at him. "We don't take on kids. Especially not brats like you."

"I am not a brat." Oliver pouted.

"No, son, you're not." Big Bart patted him on the shoulder. "The problem is, you see, it'll cost us more than you're worth in ransom to give you food and water. Piracy is our business. It's not a hobby. We're in it for the money."

"If I was with you, though, I could help!"

"But your sister and your father would still be a problem, Oliver," Big Bart said. "You see?"

"We could both join," Celia suggested. "And we can help you find this island . . . that's worth a lot! Sir Edmund would pay a fortune to know where it is!"

"Sir Edmund?" Big Bart asked.

"He's this, like, evil billionaire," Oliver explained.

Big Bart tapped his finger on his lips, considering.

"We took a vote," Bonnie said. "We voted to take Corey Brandt hostage. You are bound by that vote. It's the Pirates' Code. If the captain starts breaking the rules, then where will we be? Chaos! Anarchy!"

"That's right." Twitchy Bart nodded. "Without our code, we'd be no better than common criminals!"

"All right, I hear you two," said Big Bart. "But I won't be throwing these Navels overboard either. They may yet prove their worth."

Celia exhaled with relief. She and Oliver made eye contact, but neither one of them could tell what the other was thinking. So much had happened between them and they'd never felt farther apart.

"So what now?" Corey asked.

"Well," said Big Bart, "we'll tie you up in the cabin and take you back to the Princess."

"The Princess?" Celia wondered, thinking about the myth of the Orang Laut.

"Oh, you'll see." Big Bart laughed.

Although they couldn't tell each other, both Oliver and Celia had the same feeling that if this were a television show, now was the moment ominous music would start.

None of the pirates noticed the tiny sail still following them on the horizon.

19

WE PRACTICE PIRACY

"I CAN'T BELIEVE YOU got us into this!" whispered Celia, lying on the bunk next to her brother. Her arms were tied to her sides and her legs were tied to each other with thick rope, so she felt more like a sea cucumber than a girl.

"Bwak," said Dennis, who was perched on a shelf just above her head, keeping a beady little bird eye on the twins.

"*I* got us into this?" said Oliver, lying next to his sister and looking up at the business end of the chicken's behind. He was tied up the same way as Celia, unable to move, and he was hoping that the chicken had eaten a light lunch. "I tried to save us from the pirates!"

"By turning the boat in circles?"

"Yes!"

"That was your entire plan?"

"Well, I didn't have any help coming up with it."

"I was busy almost drowning because of a sea cucumber!"

"That never would have happened if you weren't trying to impress Corey!"

"Hey, guys," said Corey from the floor, where he was tied back-to-back with Dr. Navel. "Don't argue, okay? You're, like, brother and sister. You shouldn't be fighting about me."

"I'd love to dance, grandmother, but not with that bear," their father mumbled, still unconscious.

The door in front of him that led to the galley was closed and locked.

"We have to get out of here," Corey said. "Pirates are not good news. It's not like in the movies where they sing and dance."

"What movie is that supposed to be?" Oliver scoffed.

Corey ignored him. "Are you guys wearing the Corey Brandt's Pocketed Pants I gave you?"

"Yeah," said Celia.

"Yeah," said Oliver.

"Great," he said. "They're designed with a special feature just for situations like this."

"I hope it works better than the wedgie-proof waistband," said Oliver.

"It does," he said. The twins heard a zipping sound and a rustling of fabric and then some more zipping and suddenly Corey was standing up, free of the ropes. "Swiss Army zippers." He smiled. "They double as cutting knives along the edges, tiny magnifying glasses in the hole, and data storage if you plug them into a computer."

"Wow," said Oliver. "These are nice pants."

Corey showed the twins how to use the pants to escape, and soon they were all free, standing up in the little cabin. Dr. Navel was still out cold.

"So what do we do now?" said Oliver. "How are we going to retake our ship?"

They all thought for a little while, as the boat splashed through the waves.

"Don't you know martial arts from *Agent Zero*?" asked Oliver.

"It's all choreographed on TV," said Corey. "Like a dance."

"And real pirates don't dance," Oliver thought.

"We could pretend to have stomachaches," Celia suggested.

"And then what?" Corey asked.

"I dunno," said Celia. "On TV, prisoners always pretend to have stomachaches so they can escape."

They thought some more.

"Bwak," said Dennis quietly. "Bwak-bwak-bwak."

"I've got it!" said Celia. "We can beat them at their own game."

"We can?" asked Oliver.

"You wanted to be a pirate?" Celia looked at her brother. "Well, now's your chance. We're taking a hostage on the high seas!"

"We are?" asked Oliver.

"Bwak!" said Dennis.

All eyes turned to the pudgy, flightless bird. "Bwak-bwak," it said again and then cocked its head from side to side.

Sometimes even a chicken knows when it's in trouble.

20

WE PLAY CHICKEN

BIG BART RESTED HIS FEET on the transom of the boat and was steering with one hand. Bonnie adjusted the winches to tighten the sails, getting a few extra knots of speed. Twitchy Bart was nowhere to be seen, which meant he was probably up the mast again. It turned out that the pirates were actually very good sailors, better than Corey and the Navels had been.

"How do we do this?" Celia whispered, peering out the crack of the door to their bunk.

"We need to make demands," said Corey.

"Why do I have to hold the chicken?" said Oliver, who was struggling to keep Dennis quiet under his arm. He didn't think it was fair that he always got stuck with the animals on their adventures, but Celia said he had the most talent for it and Corey needed to keep his hands free in case the pirates tried anything sneaky.

Oliver had thought about tying up the chicken just like they had been tied up, but it was way too hard to do. The octopus and the tiger shark were easier to wrangle than the chicken.

"Bwa . . . bwa . . . bwak," the chicken squawked.

"Hush," Oliver commanded it, and, much to his surprise, the chicken hushed.

"So what'll you tell the others when we get back to the Princess?" Bonnie asked Big Bart.

"Tell the others about what, Bonnie?" he answered.

"About our extra hostages, the Navels."

"I'll tell them there's a billionaire who might pay ransom for 'em," said Big Bart.

"You believe that?" Bonnie asked. "Some snot-nosed kids say they know an evil billionaire, and you believe it? I think they were just mouthing off to save their own skin."

"You're not the motherly type, are you, Bonnie?"

She snorted.

"Well," said Big Bart, "I theorize that this young lad and that young lass have a mother. Perhaps she'll be interested in paying their ransom."

Oliver and Celia glanced at each other at the mention of their mother.

Usually, when things got dangerous, their mother had a way of showing up to help out, or to explain things, or to save the day, like the whole adventure was her idea all along.

But this was the open ocean and these were vicious pirates. Who knew where their mother even was? Oliver wondered if they'd find her disguised as a pirate, ready to rescue them the moment they showed up.

"We're on our own," Celia whispered, as if she could read his mind.

"How did you know what I was thinking?" Oliver wondered.

"I'm your sister. I just know," said Celia.

"You guys ready?" Corey asked. He looked over at Oliver and Celia, gave them his famous wink and smile, kicked the door to their bunk wide open, and strode out onto the deck of the boat. "Nobody move!" he shouted. "Or the chicken gets it!"

"Bwak!" squawked Dennis, squeezed snugly in Oliver's grip.

"Go ahead!" Oliver said, lifting the frantic chicken in the air. "Make my day!"

He'd always wanted to say that.

Dennis's little clawed feet ran in the air, as if he might just fly away if only he could get a running start.

"Don't you hurt Dennis," yelled Big Bart. "Or I'll cut you from your gizzard to your gullet."

The threat would have been terrifying if any of them had the slightest idea what it meant.

"We'll give you your chicken back," said Corey. "If you surrender control of this vessel back to us, like, now."

"Look around, kid." Big Bart laughed. "We're on the ocean. There's no one here to help you. Give up and no one will get hurt."

"Your friends want to throw my friends overboard," Corey said. "I can't let that happen."

"Bwak," said Dennis.

"Okay, kids, you got the jump on Big Bart, that's true." Big Bart sighed. He looked at Oliver. "If you still want to join us, you can. Just bring Dennis over to me. Back on our ship, we've got satellite television and all the movies and TV shows you could ever watch. We even have the *Agent Zero* Christmas special."

"Hey!" Corey objected. "That was never supposed to be released!"

"What can I say?" Big Bart shrugged. "We downloaded it illegally."

"But that's piracy!" Corey yelled.

The pirates laughed at him.

Out of the corner of her eye, Celia saw Twitchy Bart high up on the mast, unsheathing his big knife again. Bonnie was shifting her weight to her back foot, like she was about to pounce on them. Celia glanced at her brother. A trickle of sweat was running down Oliver's cheek as he struggled to keep the chicken still. He was whispering for it to calm down. Oliver could never hurt a chicken, not one with a name anyway. Big Bart had probably guessed that already.

"There must be a way we can join you," said Celia. "Like on *Valerie-at-Large.*"

"What?" Big Bart wondered.

"What?" Corey wondered.

"What?" the other pirates wondered.

"I hate that show," said Oliver.

Celia sighed and, for the second time that day, talked through the whole episode about Valerie's story for the school paper and the Six Sisters Club, and spending the night in a graveyard and stealing a towel from the boys' locker room and the initiation.

"You want to steal a towel from the boys' locker room?" Bonnie asked.

"No." Celia rolled her eyes. "We want to do what it takes to become real pirates."

"Interesting." Big Bart drummed his fingers on the wheel of the boat.

"Big Bart," said Bonnie. "You can't go making decisions on your own. We've got a say in whatever you're thinking."

"I think you're getting a bit too bossy for your own good," said Big Bart, standing to his full, gigantic height. Celia took a step backward.

"I think your days as captain might be numbered," said Bonnie, stepping toward Big Bart and glaring up into his eyes.

"Do you?" said Big Bart.

"I do," said Bonnie. "I think, perhaps, we should settle this the old-fashioned way."

"You challenging me to a fight, Bonnie?"

"I think I am, Big Bart."

Celia, Corey, and Oliver all took nervous steps backward. Oliver stumbled a moment to get his footing on the wet deck, and suddenly Dennis broke free in a riot of squawking and feathers. His little wings flapped in the air, but in spite of his best efforts he made it no more than a foot before landing on the deck and running to peck at Bonnie's feet.

"Ow, you dumb chicken!" she yelled, kicking at the bird.

"He's technically a rooster!" Big Bart roared, and while Bonnie was distracted, he grabbed her in one quick motion around the waist and tossed her overboard.

"Ahh!" she yelled as she splashed into the sea.

"We're about four miles due south of land!" Big Bart called back as the *Get It Over With* sailed on. He tossed a flotation ring into the ocean toward her and laughed loudly as he shouted, "Good luck with your new boat, Bonnie! Watch out for sharks!"

Bonnie was still shouting when her voice faded on the wind behind them.

Big Bart turned to face a shocked Oliver, Celia, and Corey Brandt.

"You . . . you threw her . . . you . . . ," Corey stammered.

"Pirate justice," said Big Bart. "She challenged me and she lost."

"Bwak," said Dennis, strutting around the deck.

"Stupid chicken," Oliver muttered, trying to catch the chicken again. Big Bart glared at him. "Rooster . . . I mean rooster," Oliver corrected himself.

Big Bart smirked. Dennis ran to safety behind his leg and Oliver didn't go after him.

"Twitch!" he called. "Come over here and tie up our star of stage and screen."

"Aye-aye, cap'n," said Twitchy Bart, putting the knife between his teeth to tie Corey up.

"You'll never get away with this," said Corey as Twitchy Bart led him below. "I have people in Hollywood. Powerful people! They've canceled television shows tougher than you are!"

Twitchy Bart didn't reply. He just pulled his knife out of his teeth and put it against Corey's cheek. Corey swallowed hard as he disappeared into the cabin.

"As for you two," Big Bart told the twins. They

stepped closer to each other. "If you still want your initiation, we'll get right to that as soon as we're back to my ship."

"Do we have a choice?" Oliver gulped.

Big Bart smiled widely. "Of course, my lad!" He laughed. "You always have a choice. We're pirates, not schoolteachers."

Oliver and Celia looked at each other, relieved.

"You can both join Bonnie's crew at the bottom of the sea," said Big Bart. "Or one of you can join my crew."

"Just one of us?" It was Celia's turn to gulp.

"Oh yes, young lady," said Big Bart. "Once we get to my ship, we'll do just like on your television show and have our initiation."

"Are we going to steal towels from the boys' locker room?" Oliver suggested.

"Oh no." Big Bart chuckled, sitting back down in the captain's chair. Oliver and Celia took another step away from him.

"We're going to have a duel," he said. "Brother versus sister! The winner joins the great and honorable tradition of Blackbeard and Captain Kidd, raiding the high seas for fun and profit, lounging the days away in comfort and luxury, and watching as much television as he or she likes."

"And the loser?" squeaked Oliver.

Big Bart didn't answer; he just smiled his toothy grin and fed one of their snack cakes to Dennis, who clucked happily, devouring his plunder.

21

WE WILL NOT BE CHUMS

TWITCHY BART TIED COREY UP and threw him in with Dr. Navel, who was just waking up. He put Oliver and Celia in another bunk.

"Don't try anything fishy," he warned, and waved his big knife in the air to make sure they understood what he meant. Then he locked them in.

The boat rocked and rolled as it cut through the waves. Oliver's complexion started to turn the color of an unripe banana.

"Don't puke in here," said Celia.

"I won't," said Oliver. He looked over at her and grunted.

"What?" she said.

"Nothing," said Oliver. He was still upset she had called him a baby when he was trying to save them.

"Fine," said Celia. She was still annoyed that he'd told Corey she was trying to impress him. "We have to think of a new plan, or they'll turn you, me, and Dad into shark food, and who knows what they'll do with Corey."

"Oh no, poor Corey," Oliver grumbled.

"You used to like him."

"That was before he turned you into my evil twin."

"I'm not your evil twin."

"Whatever you say."

"Yes, whatever I say, and I say I'm not your evil twin. You're just too sensitive."

"Whatever," said Oliver, crossing his arms.

They stewed in their own silent anger for a while.

"You're wrong, by the way." Oliver broke the silence. "Sharks don't eat people. That's a myth."

"No it's not."

"Yes it is," said Oliver. "On *Sharkapalooza* they said that even when sharks bite people, they usually spit them back out, because we aren't their natural diet."

"Why are you telling me this?"

"Because the pirates can't turn us into shark

food," said Oliver. "They'd just chew us up and spit us out. They were going to turn us into shark bait, you know, to lure sharks. It's called chum."

"Hmm," said Celia. "Chum. I thought that meant friend."

"Well, I guess there's a word I know that you don't. Chum is shark bait."

"I'm not sure that's better. I don't want to be chum."

"Me neither," said Oliver. "Even if it means friend."

"Whatever," said Celia. And they fell silent again.

There was a small porthole in their bunk, through which Oliver and Celia could occasionally catch a glimpse above the waterline. All they saw was deep blue ocean stretching out forever. The hours passed. We should not be surprised that they eventually fell into their favorite pastime, the one that they could always share, even in the midst of their most heated arguments: complaining.

"I hate this," said Celia. "This is the worst."

"I'd rather be stuck in a cave in Tibet," said Oliver.

"I'd rather be lost in the Amazon," said Celia.

"I'd rather be watching the news," said Oliver.

Celia shuddered. "It's not that bad," she said.

"But what are we gonna do? We can't fight the pirates and we can't, you know, duel each other."

"I don't know," Celia said. "After the way you've been acting . . ."

"Hey!" Oliver exclaimed. "You *are* my evil twin!"

"I'm just kidding," said Celia. "We'll figure something out. We sort of have to."

"Maybe Dad or Corey will have an idea."

"If we ever see them again."

"Maybe Mom will show up to save us," suggested Oliver.

"When she shows up, things usually get worse for us," said Celia.

"Well, I don't see how things could get worse for us now," said Oliver.

"Don't say that," said Celia.

"Why not?"

"Because whenever someone on TV says that, that's when things get worse!"

Just then, they heard the sound of a ship's horn blaring and they pressed their faces to the porthole to look outside.

"Oops," said Oliver. He hated to admit it, but Celia was right. Things just got worse.

As the boat rose to the top of a swell, they saw, less than fifty yards away, a giant cruise ship covered with growths of algae and rust. Oliver realized that the "Princess" he'd heard the pirates talking about wasn't a person. It was their pirate ship. They had taken over a Princess cruise ship, except where the logo of the fun-loving cruise company should have been grinned a white skull on a black background with bones crossed below it, the universal sign of the pirate, sometimes known as the Jolly Roger.

Oliver's complexion changed from green to ashen.

"If we do have to duel," Celia told him, "I'm going to let you win."

"No way," said Oliver. "I'm your brother. I have to let you win."

"I'm older," said Celia.

"By three minutes!"

"And forty-two seconds."

"Well, you are not letting me win. I won't be a pirate without you."

"Well, I won't be a pirate without you."

"One of us has to protect Dad and Corey," Oliver said. "And you're better at that stuff."

Celia didn't answer him. She was trying to come up with a plan that would save them all. She wondered what her mother would do.

"Well, you landlubbers," Twitchy Bart said as he opened the door to their bunk, "we've reached our destination! I'm sure you'll enjoy all the fine amenities aboard our fair ship. We've got a swimming pool and a waterslide, a spa run by the finest wenches you'll ever meet, and satellite television in every cabin." He picked his nose and flicked what he found toward the twins, cackling when they flinched. "Of course, only one of you will get to enjoy it! Now come on deck, Big Bart wants to see you."

As they followed Twitchy Bart on deck, Celia noticed that the bunk where Corey and her father had been held was open and empty.

"Where's our dad?" she demanded. "And where's Corey?"

"Relax," said Twitchy Bart. "They're on their way over already." He pointed to the dinghy, which was speeding away toward the pirates' cruise ship, being driven by a rough-looking man in a bandanna and camouflage pants. Both Corey and Dr. Navel had their hands tied behind their backs and gags in their mouths. Their father was looking back at the sailboat, trying to see the twins. Corey was looking forward at the cruise ship, his hair blowing in the wind.

Oliver thought it looked just like a scene from *Agent Zero*.

"Well, children!" Big Bart called to them. "The moment has arrived! Soon you'll be aboard your first pirate ship. What do you think of that?"

"It doesn't look so great," Celia said, sticking out her chin defiantly.

"None of them look like pirates are supposed to," Oliver said.

"Oh, I like you kids." Big Bart laughed. "You're natural fighters!"

"Are we, like, dueling right now?" Celia asked. She hoped not. She didn't have a plan yet, and she really wasn't so sure Oliver would be okay without her after she let him win.

"Of course you're not dueling right now!" said Big Bart. "Don't be ridiculous. We'll need to introduce you to the crew and let them get to know you."

"Why do they need to get to know us?" Oliver asked.

"So they can place their bets on which of you will win! I think we'll have a banquet in your honor. We have a whole collection of dresses and tuxedos on board, from cruise ship weddings and the like. It'll be a real banquet. Properly formal."

"A formal banquet?" Oliver complained. "We hate those. Couldn't you just let us get this over with?"

"Get it over with?" Big Bart threw his hands in the air. "Oliver! We're leaving that attitude behind. On my ship, we never miss a chance for a banquet!"

"Pirates are just like explorers," Celia declared with disappointment.

22

WE'RE ALL DRESSED UP

THE BANQUET WAS laid out in what had been the grand ballroom of the cruise ship. A glass chandelier in the center of the room made tinkling noises as the large ship swayed slightly on the water. Pirates mingled and joked with each other, all of them dressed up in what was certainly their most formal attire. For some that meant cutoff shorts and flip-flops with a new coat of polish on their guns. For others, it meant shiny suits or out-dated tuxedos. Everyone carried weapons.

"None of them look like pirates," Oliver complained. He tugged at his collar, where his bow tie was too tight. "And why can't I ever have a tuxedo that fits?"

"At least you don't have to wear a dress," said Celia, who kept pulling on the puffy sleeves of the ball gown they had forced her to put on. The gown had probably never been in style, and it was certainly much older than Celia. It smelled like it too.

She held on to their backpack filled with the snack cakes and the wet suits, and their old Pocketed Pants. The pirates let the twins keep the backpack as a prize for whoever won. Oliver managed to keep the remote control in his pocket when he changed. He had to admit that he really missed wearing Corey Brandt's Pocketed Pants.

As the banquet wore on, the pirates munched on cheese and crackers, stale bread, pickled vegetables, and smoked fish. They guzzled rum and whiskey and told each other crude jokes about Blackbeard and a jaguar in a hot tub. They also kept coming over to Oliver and Celia to inspect them.

"Scrawny muscles," one said, squeezing Oliver's arm and shaking his head.

"*Belacan*," another said, provoking loud guffaws from his colleagues.

"What was that?" Oliver wondered.

"I'm sure it wasn't nice," said Celia.

"It means shrimp paste." Another pirate wandered up and gave the twins a long look. "I think he was being too nice . . . I wouldn't bet on either of you surviving." He walked away shaking his head.

For over an hour it went like that. The twins stood off to the side of the ballroom, trying not to be noticed and being noticed by everyone.

"This is just like at the Explorers Club," said Oliver.

"Except there, no one was placing bets on which one of us would live," said Celia.

"Are you sure about that?" Oliver smirked.

Celia laughed. Oliver laughed too. It actually felt good to laugh together in the face of certain death.

The doors to the ballroom burst open and their father came in. He was flanked by scar-faced pirates, who had all manner of frightening tattoos peeking out from their clothes. They held knives and guns in their hands and sneers and scowls on their faces. They spoke to each other in half a dozen languages.

"Oliver, Celia." Their father bent down and hugged them. "I'm so glad you're okay. Don't be afraid. I'll take care of all this."

"You don't know yet, do you?" asked Celia.

"Know what?" said their father, pushing his glasses back up on his nose. They were bent out of shape from his fall onto the deck of their boat and they slid down again immediately.

"We have to duel each other to see who gets to become a pirate and who gets thrown overboard," Oliver explained. "But it's okay, because I'm going to let Celia win."

"Are not. I'm going to let Oliver win," said Celia.

"Are not," said Oliver.

"Am too," said Celia.

"Are not," said Oliver.

"Am too," said Celia.

"No one is dueling anyone," their father said. "Not while I'm around. I've dealt with worse than mere pirates before. Wait here." He stood tall and strolled into the middle of the room, put his fingers to his lips and blew a loud, piercing whistle.

"I demand to speak to the captain!" he yelled. "Under the articles of piracy set down in olden days, I demand parley!"

Murmurs passed around the room as his demand was translated from English to French to Russian to Malay to Creole to Dutch to Chinese to Somali to Swahili and back into English, completely mangled.

"Why does he say he wants to dance with a parrot?" one of the scar-faced pirates whispered to Celia.

Celia didn't have a chance to answer, because just then Twitchy Bart came into the room holding Corey Brandt by the arm and pressing a knife to his throat. New murmurs passed around the room, but all of them were in English this time.

"*Agent Zero*," the pirates said, and "*Sunset High*," and "Lauren."

Corey smiled meekly, out of instinct, and gave a nervous wave with his tied-up hands. One of the pirates giggled and waved back at him. A few took pictures with what must have been stolen cell phones. One pirate shrieked and passed out where he stood. Corey Brandt had that effect on people.

"Greetings, my friends!" Big Bart shouted, striding into the room with a grand gesture. He wore a red velvet coat and starched white shirt, with black breeches and black leather boots. He had an ornate sword tucked into his belt and a wide-brimmed hat perched on his giant head, just above a heavy black eye patch over his left eye. A huge feather billowed from the brim of his hat, and Dennis clucked into the room behind him wearing a tiny version the same hat, feather and all.

"Is this better, Oliver?" Big Bart asked, removing his hat and making an elaborate bow. "Do I look piratical enough for you?"

"Will you say *arrr*?" Oliver asked.

"No," said Big Bart.

"What's with the eye patch?" asked Celia.

"It's not easy putting a hat on a chicken," said Big Bart.

"Rooster," corrected Celia, with a sarcastic smile.

Big Bart snorted and put his hat back on. He strolled up onto the stage at the front of the ballroom, gesturing for Twitchy Bart to bring Corey up behind him.

"My brothers from around the world!" Big Bart shouted, raising his arms in the air.

"Don't forget sisters!" someone in the crowd shouted.

Big Bart dropped his arms to his side and nodded gravely. "Unfortunately, our dear Bonnie did not make it back from our latest adventure."

"What happened?" another pirate shouted.

"Did one of the weaklings get her?" someone else called out.

"Maybe they bored her to death!" Everyone laughed.

"She had the idea that I was not fit to be captain," he said, moving his head from side to side, scanning the room. "I wonder if anyone else shares that particular sentiment?"

Silence. There was an uncomfortable cough. Big Bart raised one eyebrow.

"No, no!" said the offending cougher. "It's just my sinuses . . . I didn't mean nothing by it!"

Big Bart nodded at one of the scar-faced pirates, who grabbed the man and dragged him screaming from the room. His screams echoed down the hallway even after they'd closed the door again.

"Moving on to new business!" Big Bart continued.

"I can't believe this," Oliver whispered to Celia. "Even pirates make speeches at these parties."

"Our hostages!" said Big Bart, and the room burst into cheers.

"We love you, Corey!" a motley group of Samoan mercenaries shouted from the corner. Celia couldn't believe how much these bloodthirsty pirates were like her sixth-grade classmates.

"I'm happy to introduce a young man who really needs no introduction," Big Bart continued.

"Then why introduce him?" Oliver muttered.

"At only sixteen, he has starred as a student superspy on *Agent Zero* and a love-struck vampire on *Sunset High*, and he created the award-winning reality show *The Celebrity Adventurist*. And I'm thrilled to tell you all that, in hijacking his boat, we have also captured enough pairs of his trademarked Corey Brandt's Pocketed Pants for everyone!"

Whoops and hollers swept around the room. Corey actually smiled, even though he had a knife to his throat. He just couldn't help it.

"I'm glad you like them, guys!" he said. "Please don't kill me."

The pirates laughed.

"Charming as ever, Mr. Brandt!" Big Bart patted him on the back. "We should get a fine, fine ransom for you. Or a good price from the organ harvesters." The color left Corey Brandt's face. "As to our other hostages, we have Dr. Ogden Navel and his two lovely children, Oliver and Celia!"

Every eye turned to look at them as if they were pieces of meat in a butcher's shop. One of the pirates even licked his lips.

"We've all had a chance, I hope, to eat a little bit and to get to know our special guests," Big Bart continued. "Before we make our demands known to Hollywood on behalf of Mr. Brandt, I suggest we make our way to the aft deck, where the young Navels will give us some spirited entertainment. I for one cannot wait to see who will join our crew, and who will walk the plank!"

The room cheered.

"I thought pirates didn't really make you walk the plank," Oliver gasped.

"I guess they do," said Celia. She turned to her brother as Big Bart stepped down from the stage. "Follow my lead!" she said quickly.

"What about my parley?" Dr. Navel demanded of Big Bart as he passed. "The Pirates' Code is very clear that when parley is requested, the captain must promise the safety of—"

Big Bart waved his hand in the air, and two of the scar-faced pirates grabbed Dr. Navel and gagged him with an oily cloth. He squirmed and struggled. One of the pirates flashed his big knife and Dr.

Navel slumped where he stood. The pirates had to hold him up. He'd passed out again.

"Really, Dad?" Celia sighed.

"Are you ready to duel?" Big Bart asked the twins. "I am so excited for one of you to join my crew. I promise it will be wonderful. All the junk food you can eat, your own television in your cabin, murder and mayhem whenever you want it." He leaned in to whisper to them. "And, of course, if you happen to lead me to this island you've been searching for, well, maybe I will spare your father's life."

"I thought you lost the vote," said Oliver. "Your crew didn't want to look for the island."

Big Bart's eyes narrowed at him. "Sometimes my crew doesn't know what's in their best interests."

"We have one condition," said Celia.

"A condition?" Big Bart turned to her. "You are a feisty one, Celia! Perhaps I'll be rooting for you instead of your brother."

Oliver was too nervous to be offended.

"Whoever wins," said Celia, "takes responsibility for our father. He doesn't get thrown overboard no matter what."

"That is very sweet," said Big Bart. "But I don't know. We were going to shoot him out of a big slingshot. The boys really were looking forward to it."

"If we don't duel, then your boys don't get a show," Celia said. "And I'd hate to be the captain of a ship filled with bored pirates."

Big Bart's eyebrows smashed together on his forehead as he considered the little girl in front of him. For a second, Celia thought he might smash her with his giant fists.

"Fine," he said. "I would never have thought you were such a daddy's girl. Now come on. You two have to pick your weapons! The show's about to begin!"

He ushered Oliver and Celia, dressed in their ill-fitting formal wear, out of the ballroom toward the glaring sunlight and the chanting of a hundred pirates who wanted some bloody entertainment.

"How will we lead him to the island?" Oliver wondered. "We don't know where it is."

"I do," said Celia. She slipped the compass from her pocket and showed it to Oliver.

"So you have to win then," Oliver said. "You'll be able to save Dad."

"No." Celia dropped the compass back into her pocket. "We're all going together. I have a plan."

"You do?"

"Just think," Celia told her brother. "What would Mom do?"

"Oh no," groaned Oliver, because he had some idea what their mother would do if she were here. And it wasn't going to be pretty.

23

WE DO THE DUEL

"NOW, I WANT A GOOD, dirty, unfair fight," said Twitchy Bart. "Is that clear?"

Celia nodded.

Oliver nodded.

They stood across from each other on a large stage at the back of the ship. Corey and Dr. Navel were being held just off to the side of the stage, where everyone could watch them watching the battle. The sea sprayed and roared ten stories below them as the cruise ship sped through the waves. The twins faced the crowd of pirates.

They couldn't see much in front of them because of the blinding lights, but if they shielded their eyes they could make out arena-style seating in a semicircle around the stage, which rose high above them. Hundreds of scarred faces and malevolent eyes glowered down at the twins.

"Better not to look," whispered Celia.

Oliver nodded. His palms sweated on the grip of the heavy baseball bat they'd given him for bludgeoning his sister.

She held a metal golf club for smashing his brains in.

"Here are the rules," said Twitchy Bart. "When Big Bart says go, you hit each other until one of you loses."

"Loses what?" asked Oliver.

"Your life!" Twitchy Bart smiled.

"That's the only rule?" Oliver gulped.

"We're pirates." Twitchy Bart shrugged. "We don't have too many rules."

"My fine gentlemen!" Big Bart strolled onto the stage in his full pirate regalia, which is just a fancy way of saying costume. Dennis clucked at his side. "I won't waste words with long speeches and grandiose proclamations!"

"Yeah, right," said Celia.

"Whoever survives this ordeal shall be our newest crew member, joining the great tradition of the piratical life. I know he doesn't look like much, but perhaps this young lad here with the skinny arms and the glum expression is the next

Barbarossa! Perhaps this young lady, though she be not so pretty and not so smart, will grow into the next Anne Bonny!"

"Hey," Celia objected, but Big Bart kept his back to her.

"Either one will lead us to a treasure greater than old Captain Flint's pieces of eight, greater than Sir Walter Raleigh's El Dorado."

"Been there, not so great," muttered Oliver.

"Unlimited gold!" declared Big Bart. "Jewels and rubies! Wealth beyond compare!"

"Now he's just making stuff up," whispered Celia.

"What if all we find is giant squid?" Oliver whispered back.

"He'll be mad," whispered Celia. "But we'll be out of here long before then."

"And all that treasure shall be ours!" Big Bart yelled.

The crowd roared. They gave him a standing ovation, which he, ever the showman, encouraged.

"Didn't you and Bonnie vote against that?" Oliver whispered to Twitchy Bart. "You know, before he threw her overboard . . . what happened to your pirate code?"

"Hush up, you," said Twitchy Bart, scratching nervously at the back of his neck. "The captain knows what he's doing."

"Who says the winner will help him?" Celia prodded. "What if he or she doesn't know where that island is?"

"Well, he or she better figure it out," said Twitchy Bart. "Or the crew'll tear he or she apart, right along with Big Bart. Pirates is fickle folk."

"Fickle?" Oliver wondered.

"Easily changing their loyalty," said Celia.

"I guess I should have known that one," said Oliver, raising his eyebrows at his sister and glancing at Corey.

"That is so unfair," said Celia.

"Hey, kids!" said Twitchy Bart. "Stop fighting."

"Hey, kids!" Big Bart turned to them, dropped his arms, and backed to the side of the stage. "Start fighting!" he shouted.

They stood facing each other. Celia glanced back at her father and Corey. They both had knives to their necks. Big Bart nodded toward them and dragged his index finger across his throat, making it quite clear what would happen if the twins didn't give his crew a good show. Celia shuddered to think of Bonnie, drowned at the bottom of the ocean.

"I have a plan," she whispered through clenched teeth to her brother. "Take a swing at me."

"What?" said Oliver. "I can't take a swing at you!"

"Do it!" she said.

"I can't hit you with a bat!"

"You know you've always wanted to!"

"Thinking it is different than doing it!"

"Just think about how I treated you!"

"I forgave you already!"

"Well, unforgive me!"

"Do something!" a man yelled from the crowd.

"I'm bored!" yelled another.

"This is worse than the news!" yelled a third.

"If you don't swing at me, I'll swing at you," said Celia.

"Don't you dare," said Oliver.

"I have to," said Celia. "Just jump left when I swing."

"Wait, your left or mine? Or stage left? Which way is tha—AH!"

Celia swung at Oliver. He jumped backward and felt the breeze as the golf club whizzed just in front his nose. The crowd roared.

"Now swing at me!" Celia commanded.

Oliver closed his eyes, wound up, and swung the bat. It was a lot like playing baseball at the playground. He never opened his eyes when he swung then either. And just like at the playground, his swing caught nothing but air.

"Somebody hit somebody!" pirates jeered.

"Boooring!" others yelled, and it turned into a chant. "Boooring! Boooring! Boooring!"

Big Bart looked furious, his jaw clenched and his fists balled.

"I command you two to fight each other!" he yelled. "Or I will feed you, your father, and even Corey Brandt to the sharks."

"We are fighting!" yelled Celia.

"We're just no good at it," said Oliver. "It's like gym class!"

"You want us to fight?" Celia yelled, and tightened her grip on the golf club. "Fine!"

She stretched the golf club out in front of her and started spinning faster and faster, getting as much momentum as she could. If she hit Oliver like that, it'd be lights out for good. He backed away one step at a time, wondering what his sister was up to.

As she spun, Celia tried to wink at Oliver, to send him a signal that it was time for her plan, but she couldn't tell if he was getting it. She decided that winking wasn't clear enough, so she tried nodding her head and shrugging while she spun, but still Oliver was backing away. She added a kick to her spin.

"Why are you dancing?" Big Bart bellowed. "Attack!"

And with that, Celia let go of her golf club, sending it flying right into the men holding Corey and her father. The men ducked and fell away.

"Now!" said Celia. "Run to the back!" She staggered, dizzy, over to pick up their backpack and get to her father. Big Bart charged after her and Oliver rushed between the pirate captain and his stumbling sister, swinging his bat the only way he knew how: wildly.

The pirate crowd roared with rage. In seconds they were on their feet. They charged the stage.

"I'll get you for this!" said Big Bart. "You'll never get off this ship alive."

"Come on!" Dr. Navel called out as he pulled the gag out of his mouth and grabbed his daughter by the hand. Oliver kept swinging his bat and backing away as Big Bart stepped slowly forward. Dennis charged at Oliver's feet, pecking and clucking.

"Ow!" Oliver yelped and kicked. "Ow, ow, ow! Stop it!"

"Hold on," Celia told her father, and pulled away, running back toward Oliver. With one bold dive, she tackled Dennis and squeezed him to her chest.

"Now back off!" she said. "Or this time the chicken gets it for real!"

Big Bart stopped. He stuttered. He turned red. He looked, in a word, nonplussed, but he raised his arms for the onslaught of enraged pirates to stop.

He exhaled slowly to regain his composure. Then he roared, "He's! A! Rooster!"

The other pirates yelled and waved their weapons in the air, not because they had strong feelings about the chicken versus rooster debate, but because they really liked yelling and waving their weapons. They were pirates, after all. Most days they just sat around watching television while they waited for wealthy ships to come by. This was a particularly exciting day for them. They had to get all the yelling and weapon waving done that they could. Who knew when they'd have another chance?

Corey and the Navel family backed away to the stairs and rushed down belowdecks to hide in the labyrinth of looted shopping plazas, empty casinos, and luxury spas the cruise ship would never offer to happy vacationers again.

"That was wonderful," said Dr. Navel. "You guys performed the Romanian Ruse flawlessly! Your mother would be so proud."

"It was Celia's idea," said Oliver. He smiled at his sister. She had saved them from the duel, just like she said she would. As far as annoying twin sisters went, he guessed she was the best one he could have. Celia shrugged. She didn't know throwing a golf club at some pirates was a plan with name. It was just the first idea that came to her.

"What now?" Corey panted.

"We'll get to a lifeboat and get off the ship," said Dr. Navel. "Celia, don't let go of that chicken. He's our life insurance policy."

"Life insurance," Oliver groaned. "Only Dad

could make a daring escape from pirates sound boring."

Corey laughed. He thought Oliver was funny. Oliver started to think that maybe the star wasn't such a jerk after all.

"Bwak," Dennis squawked as they ran through the maze of corridors inside the rusted pirate cruise ship.

24

WE GET SOME STATIC

THEY RAN THROUGH the shopping mall on the ship, although all the store windows were smashed and all the merchandise was gone. They rushed through wide hallways, across balconies, past movie theaters and arcades. They saw piles of fake designer bags and illegally recorded movies stacked in corners and along hallways.

"Pirates," muttered Dr. Navel. "There's nothing they won't steal."

Corey Brandt's smiling face watched over them from a billboard as they rushed into the Tween-Zone. Someone had scrawled graffiti across his forehead in Mandarin Chinese. Luckily, only Dr. Navel could read what it said and he was not about to repeat those words in front of his children.

"I can't believe they defaced my poster," Corey lamented.

"They were going to hold you for ransom and kill us," panted Oliver. "And that billboard upsets you?"

Corey shrugged. They ran through an emergency door and found themselves running through narrow service hallways. Someone had taken down all the signs. They didn't know if they were running toward the sides or the middle of the ship. Every time they heard a noise in front of them, they would turn and run the other way.

"Dad," Celia asked. "Do you know where we're going?"

"I've never been on a cruise ship before," said their father. "I always thought the experience was artificial."

"Corey?" Celia tried.

"I've just done private yachts. Never anything like this."

"Celia," Oliver said. "What about *Love at 30,000 Feet*?"

"It takes place on an airplane."

"Remember that season that was all the Duchess in Business Class's dream? *Love at 30 Knots*?"

"Oh, right!" said Celia. "They were all on a

cruise ship, and it sank at the end of the season and the duchess woke up."

"So," Oliver asked. "Where did they find the lifeboats?"

Celia thought for a bit. "They didn't."

"Oh," said Oliver. *Love at 30,000 Feet* had gotten them out of so much trouble before, he never imagined it would let them down. He felt his hopes sinking.

"Television does not have all the answers, children," said Dr. Navel. "Sometimes you have to use your brains and your senses. You'd be amazed what you can figure out if you just look and listen to the world around you."

"Ugh," said Oliver. "Another explorer lecture."

"It's not a lecture. I'm just saying that sometimes the answer you're looking for is out in the world, not on the television. You have to—"

"Wait!" said Celia. "Listen! Do you hear that?"

They listened.

"That's television static," said Oliver.

"Guys," Corey said. "I kind of agree with your father. Now might not be the time for TV."

"This way!" said Celia, and she raced down a

side corridor with Oliver close on her heels. Corey and Dr. Navel followed and they found themselves suddenly on an open deck filled with lifeboats attached to cranes and beyond them, the roar of the ocean.

"How did you figure that out?" asked Dr. Navel.

"Television static!" said Celia. "I listened for a sound like the static on our broken television. The TV static always sounded like the ocean, so I figured the ocean would sound like TV static."

Oliver gave her a high five. Dr. Navel cocked his head to the side and opened his mouth, but he couldn't think of anything to say.

"I think Dad's nonplussed," whispered Oliver, who was glad he hadn't forgotten that word.

"No," said Dr. Navel. "I'm not baffled. I'm impressed. Good job!" He hugged both his kids. "Now climb into this boat," he said, pulling the cover off of one of the boats. "I'll work the crane to get you out and then I'll jump aboard when it starts lowering toward the ocean. Put on the life jackets. They should be in there."

"Maybe I should work the crane, Dr. N," Corey suggested. "You should stay with your children."

"Corey." Dr. Navel put his hand on the teen star's shoulder. "You're a good kid, but I am the adult here, and you need to get on the boat. Your parents and your agents and your managers would kill me if you came to any harm."

"But the pirates could kill you first." Corey's shoulders slumped. He liked to be the hero and didn't like to be reminded that he was still a teenager.

"Don't worry," said Dr. Navel. "I'll hop right on. I need you to look after Oliver and Celia. They're the most important ones here, okay? I trust you."

"Okay," Corey agreed. He liked being trusted by a famous explorer.

He climbed aboard and Dr. Navel hit the button on the control box. The lifeboat lifted up off the deck and swung outward, hanging over the side of the cruise ship at least fifteen stories above the ocean. Water churned and sprayed off the ship's side. Foam and mist rose nearly as high as the lifeboat, like they were floating on a cloud. Dr. Navel hit the button to release the raft.

Nothing happened.

He hit it again.

Still nothing.

"It's stuck," said Corey.

"Okay," said Dr. Navel. "Just hang on a second. I'll fix it."

"Stop right there!" Big Bart shouted, bursting onto the lifeboat deck. A mass of pirates rushed onto the deck behind him, armed to the teeth. Some of them had even sharpened their teeth.

Big Bart had shed his red velvet coat and gotten rid of his ceremonial sword. Now he held a machete in one hand and a very modern semiautomatic handgun in the other. He no longer looked like a pirate from a movie. He looked like a warlord from the news.

"No, you stop right there!" Dr. Navel turned to the pirates. Oliver and Celia weren't sure that yelling at a bloodthirsty warlord was the best idea at the moment. "Celia, show this man his chicken."

"Rooster," whispered Oliver.

"You'll never see your rooster again if you don't let us leave." Dr. Navel puffed his chest out.

Celia lifted Dennis up above her head as she

and Oliver and Corey ducked low in the boat. The bird squirmed and flapped, but Celia was not going to let Dennis get away.

Big Bart scratched the stubble on his cheek with the blade of his machete as he thought. Finally, he nodded.

"Fine," he said. "You leave me no choice." The other pirates looked disappointed. A few of them pouted. "I'll have to get a new chicken."

"Bwak!" Dennis squawked.

The pirates cheered.

Dennis stopped squirming. His wings settled against his side and his head hung down. Until that moment, neither Oliver nor Celia could have pictured a heartbroken chicken, but now it appeared that they were the proud owners of one. At least for the last few moments they would be alive.

"Now I'm going to gut each and every one of you from gizzard to gullet!"

"What does that even mean?" Oliver called out.

"Cut you wide open," Big Bart explained. Then he charged forward with a tidal wave of salty thugs behind him.

Dr. Navel turned to his children in the boat

and nodded. Oliver and Celia shook their heads vigorously.

"Oliver, Celia. I love you," Dr. Navel said. And then he kicked the lifeboat, tipping it over and dumping his children and Corey Brandt off the side of the cruise ship.

25

WE TAKE A SHORT SWIM

"AHHHH!" THEY SCREAMED as they plummeted toward the churning water. They only caught a glimpse of their father as the pirates swarmed him. He was struggling to push his glasses back up his nose while the pirates tackled him.

The twins fell past cabin windows where other pirates lounged watching TV, past on-board playgrounds and restaurants, past emergency doors and fire hatches, until they hit the ocean with a bone-crunching crash.

Walls of water erupted around them. Celia lost her grip on Dennis, who flapped his useless wings a moment before settling back down on the surface of the water like a duck.

They felt themselves spinning and turning and churning beneath the salty sea, knocked around in the wake of the cruise ship. First Celia, then

Oliver, then Corey burst through the surface of the ocean gasping for air.

"Everyone okay?" Corey shouted.

"I guess so," Oliver panted.

"Everyone . . . except Dad," said Celia.

As the cruise ship sped off, they looked up at Big Bart leaning out from the lifeboat deck, waving his machete in the air, and the pirates on the other decks shouting and throwing garbage into the water. The ship sounded its horn, which was loud enough to rattle their bones, but it kept speeding away, growing smaller and smaller on the horizon with their father on board, his fate unknown.

"Dad," said Celia, treading water. "He . . . he sacrificed himself for us."

"He could be . . . you know . . . okay?" Oliver said.

"Your father is a great man," said Corey. "He saved our lives."

"Sort of," said Celia. "But for how long?"

They looked around. They were alone on the open ocean, bobbing up and down in the waves. The backpack was still on Celia's back, getting waterlogged and heavy. She was struggling to keep her head above water.

"Ah!" Oliver shouted.

"What?" Celia yelled.

"Something brushed my leg!"

"A shark?"

"No." Oliver relaxed. "It was just my other leg. Sorry. False alarm."

"We shouldn't stay out here too long," said Corey. "The sharks will eventually come."

"Great," said Celia. "So what do we do?"

"Swim?" suggested Corey.

"To where?"

"How about that way?" Oliver pointed.

"Why?" Celia asked. "Is there land that way?"

"No," Oliver told her. "There's a boat."

Celia and Corey turned and saw a small wooden boat heading their way, and on board Celia saw the boy from the Orang Laut, Jabir, waving at them with a grin.

"You have taken your chicken for a swim?" Jabir laughed as he helped Corey and the Navel twins on board his boat.

"He's a rooster," said Oliver. "Are you an Orange Lord?"

"Orang Laut," said Jabir. "It means Sea People."

"It's good to see you again, Jabir," said Celia.

Jabir blushed. Corey and Oliver raised their eyebrows, and Celia punched her brother's arm.

"Where to?" said Jabir.

"We have to save your father," said Corey.

"I think we'll need to pay his ransom," said Celia, pulling the old brass compass from her pocket. "And I have an idea how."

26

WE HAVE SOME FOLLOWERS

"**THEY'VE BEEN PICKED** up by some fishermen at sea," Janice said as she watched the twins board the small fishing canoe through her binoculars.

"What should we do?" Ernest wondered. "Follow them or the cruise ship with their father on it?"

"We'll keep following them. The fishermen might take them to the island," Janice said.

"And when we get there, I'll get my revenge," said a wet and weary-looking Bonnie. "Big Bart wants that island and he'll have to go through me to get it."

"That island doesn't belong to you," Janice snapped at her. "We rescued you from the sea. We can toss you back in again."

"I'd like to see you try it," said Bonnie.

"Make me," said Janice, who was quickly

discovering that pirates did not make good guests aboard a small boat.

"Ladies," Ernest interrupted. He was quickly discovering that it wasn't easy sailing with a grave robber and a pirate. "Should we call Sir Edmund and let him know what's happening?"

"Not yet," said Janice. "We'll let the twins lead us to the island first. Once we know where it is, we'll call Edmund and get our reward."

"And then I'll get my revenge," said Bonnie. "With Sir Edmund's reward money, I can buy off Big Bart's whole crew and send him to the bottom of the Pacific, just like he tried to do to me."

"You aren't a very forgiving person," said Janice. "I like that."

She trimmed the sails and they continued following the small boat.

27

WE ARE NOT GOING ALL GOOGLY

JABIR'S BOAT HAD two small sails at the front and back and moved low in the water. It wouldn't be much use in a storm and wasn't really made for traveling in the open ocean.

"We don't usually go this far from land," said Jabir. "But I thought you guys might be in some trouble when I saw you sailing in circles."

"Your mother seemed angry when I left," said Celia.

"She wasn't happy that I made up all that initiation stuff," he said. "She still doesn't know that I gave you that compass. I think I will probably get in big trouble. But it is worth it to help you."

"You're doing all this for *her*?" Oliver scoffed. "Really?"

"For all of you," said Jabir, not making eye contact with anyone.

"Ha!" Oliver exclaimed. "You're going all googly for my sister!"

"I am not," said Jabir.

"You are!"

"I am not," he repeated.

"You are!"

"He is not!" Celia interrupted.

"Thanks for coming to the rescue, Jabir," Corey said, cutting the argument off. "I don't know what we would have done without you."

"I am your number one fan!" Jabir smiled.

"Oh great, now he's googly for Corey," Oliver groaned. All three of them gave Oliver a long stare. He burst out laughing and shook his head. "I was kidding . . . sheesh."

They sailed all day and all night. They took turns sleeping and steering and watching out for giant killer squid as they got closer to the island. Oliver and Celia couldn't really sleep. Every shadow beneath the waves made their blood run cold; every strange noise made them shudder with fear. Their imaginations conjured all sorts of sea monsters from the depths, but the night passed without see-ing one.

The next morning, land appeared in the dis-tance, a green volcanic island ringed with a white sand beach. They couldn't believe the boy had found his way there on the open ocean with just the broken needle of an old compass to guide him.

"I read the waves and the birds and the clouds." He shrugged. "They tell me where to go better than some little piece of brass."

He dropped the sails and rowed them to the shore.

"I will have to go back to my mother," he said. "She will worry if I do not come home soon. I have to bring her some fish or she won't eat today. You understand?"

"Family," Oliver said. "We get it."

"Thank you, Jabir." Celia took his hand and held it for a moment.

After a long silence, Jabir climbed back into his boat, raised the sails, and sailed away.

"Totally googly for you," Oliver told his sister. She didn't argue. "So what are we supposed to do now?" he asked.

"Bwak," Dennis said, running free up and down the beach, happy to be where chickens were meant to be: dry land.

They watched Jabir's boat vanish over the horizon.

"So this is the mysterious island," observed Corey. "We didn't see any giant squid on the way here."

"I told you the kraken isn't real. *Beast Busters* is never wrong," said Oliver. "So, you think Mom's here?"

"I dunno," said Celia. "But I guess we better start looking."

28

WE'RE MAROONED AND BLUE

THE TWINS SLUMPED down on the sand. They had spent an hour walking up and down the beach calling their mother's name. They received no reply. They needed a rest. They looked up at the sky.

"It looks like a yak," said Oliver.

"No it doesn't," said Celia, shading her eyes with her hands.

"Well, it changed." Oliver squinted up at the sky. "It used to look like a yak."

"No," his sister said. "It didn't."

Being three minutes and forty-two seconds older than Oliver meant that Celia was closer to being a teenager than he was, which meant the she was the expert on exactly what shapes the clouds were, and it was very irritating that Oliver would disagree.

"It looks like a herd of something," she told him.

"Yaks!" Oliver dug his toes underneath the mushy wet sand and kicked blobs of it into the surf. "A herd of yaks!"

"Chickens," said Celia definitively. "It looks like a herd of chickens."

"Chickens don't go in herds. They go in flocks."

"Well, it's gone now." She tossed a clump of seaweed into the breaking surf. On the beach behind them Dennis hopped by, pecking uselessly at the sand. The sun burned white-hot above them. The last puffs of cloud disappeared beyond the horizon, ruining Oliver and Celia's argument. There was nothing left to watch, just blue in all directions.

The water was blue.

The sky was blue.

They were feeling pretty blue.

"So we're marooned, huh?" said Oliver. He rested his cheeks on his knees and locked his hands under his legs. He exhaled slowly.

"Yeah," said Celia, scanning the horizon for any sign of Jabir's boat coming back or the pirate ship or the small sailboat that had been following them. "We're marooned."

"This stinks," Oliver said. He pulled the untied

bow tie out of his collar and threw it onto the beach next to him. His tuxedo shirt was filthy; his tuxedo pants were ripped at the knees. His shiny black shoes were long gone, and his tuxedo jacket was stretched out on a rock to dry. Oliver was learning what many an explorer before him had discovered: a tuxedo is a terrible outfit in which to be marooned on a desert island.

"It's not so bad." Celia had ripped the frilly, lacy part of her ball gown off so she was just wearing a long skirt and a T-shirt. She looked almost comfortable. She glanced back toward the low bushes and palm trees at the edge of the beach, where Corey was setting up a small shelter out of washed-up garbage and palm tree leaves.

"It's not so bad?" Oliver stood. "It's not so bad? How can you say that? We should be at home right now! We should be sitting on the couch watching *Sharkapalooza*, or *The Squid Whisperer*, or *Beast Busters*! But instead, I'm dressed in fancy clothes, stranded on a desert island in the middle of the Pacific Ocean because some Orange Lord was making googly eyes at my sister! And all my sister can do is make googly eyes at Corey Brandt!"

"I do not make googly eyes at Corey Brandt!"

"You do too!"

"I do not!"

"Do too!"

"Do not!"

"Do too!"

"Do n—"

"Please Remember What's First!" Corey called out, interrupting them. "It's a helpful mnemonic!"

The twins stared blankly at him.

"A mnemonic . . . a trick to remember something. *Please* for *Protection, Remember* for *Rescue, What's* for *Water, First* for *Food*. If you remember *Please Remember What's First*, you'll remember what to do when you're marooned on a desert island. I'm building us some protection!"

"Did you come up with that yourself?" Oliver asked.

"I am the Celebrity Adventurist," said Corey, which didn't really answer Oliver's question. Corey went back to building. He had his tuxedo shirt tied around his head like a bandanna with the bow tie to hold it in place. Somehow, the little wisp of hair that came out under it was still perfect.

Celia sighed. Oliver rolled his eyes.

"See. Googly," he said.

Just then, they heard a deep rumble in the distance. Both children looked toward the center of the island. Corey Brandt froze, broken plastic bucket and palm leaf in hand. Dennis stopped pecking at the sand.

In the hazy sky beyond the palm trees, the jagged black rock of a volcano jutted into the sky. Its flat top was tilted just a little and one spike of rock poked out from the rest, like a bad haircut. Oliver named it Mount Haircut. It rumbled again and belched a cloud of black smoke, then fell silent.

"Not good," said Oliver.

"Hey, guys." Corey trotted over to the twins. "So I, like, think we're okay for now."

"You do?" asked Oliver.

"When I was filming *Agent Zero* in Iceland, we had this, like, crazy volcano erupt. No one could pronounce the name of it, so when you tried to find out what was going on, people just acted like nothing was happening so they didn't have to talk about it. Everyone ignored all the black smoke and ash and just, you know, did their thing. Like shopping or whatever."

"That must have been so scary," said Celia. She could feel Oliver's eyes boring into the side of her head.

"It wasn't so bad . . . I was just stuck in my hotel room for a few days eating pickled shark meat."

Celia couldn't stop her face from wrinkling. She was relieved when Corey laughed.

"It was, like, delicious. Sort of salty and wet with a hint of—"

"Um." Oliver stopped him. "What about the volcano?"

"Right," said Corey. "So there were all these earthquakes, like, for days before the volcano erupted. I think we're okay here because there haven't been any earthquakes yet."

"Yet," repeated Oliver.

"Don't worry, bro." Corey patted him on the back. "Everything's gonna be C-O-O-L, cool."

"Yeah," agreed Celia, squeezing Oliver's shoulder to show how reassuring and big sisterly she could be. "See? We're gonna be fine." She smiled.

"Whatever," snapped Oliver. He stomped off down the beach. He hated when Celia acted like she was older than he was. Three minutes and forty-two seconds didn't count, not really.

"Don't go too far!" she called out as Oliver headed for the trees.

"I'm just going to look for some coconuts," he yelled back. "So you two can have your privacy!"

Celia blushed bright red. "I don't know what he's talking about."

Corey Brandt just shrugged. He was a teen superstar, so he was used to kids acting weird around him. Adults too. Pretty much everybody acted weird around him. The Navels were actually the most normal kids he knew.

"Eyjafjallajökull!" he yelled after Oliver.

"What?" Oliver turned.

"Eyjafjallajökull," he said. "That was the name of the volcano in Iceland." Oliver shook his head and kept walking, so Corey turned to Celia and flashed his smile. "I took lessons so I could pronounce it. Anyway, want to help me build this thing?" He pointed to the pile of garbage. Celia wasn't sure how that pile of garbage would become a shelter, but she figured it was better than walking up the beach calling her mother's name, so she started to help.

As Oliver wandered into the shady trees beyond the beach, he glanced back at Corey and his sister setting to work on a little hut. He felt kind of left out and wished he hadn't stomped off so dramatically. But he didn't want to be a castaway on a desert island in the middle of the Pacific Ocean, looking for his mother with his sister and Corey Brandt. He wanted to be at home watching Corey Brandt on TV and eating cheese puffs and snack cakes and waiting for their mother to return like she had promised she would.

It used to be that Celia wanted the same thing Oliver did. Even if they couldn't agree on what to watch on TV, they were still inseparable while watching it. There were Oliver- and Celia-shaped lumps in their couch, which now sat empty, like the ruins of a lost civilization.

All he ever wanted was to go nowhere, do nothing, and have no one bother him. He didn't want to get bitten by lizards, thrown out of airplanes, chased through jungles, marooned at sea, or hide from wedgies in the second-floor boys' bathroom. Why was all of that so hard?

Oliver was muttering to himself and stomping through the trees when he saw something weird in his path. It was a really big statue, at least four times his size. And there was another one next to it. And one next to that.

The statues were all arranged in a circle and, from what Oliver could see, they were all statues of giant men. They were made out of big, heavy stones, not even the same color as the other rocks he'd seen on the island, like someone had brought them from somewhere else. But who would carry giant stone statues to an island in the middle of nowhere?

Oliver stepped closer and pulled a vine down off the nearest one. The face wasn't the face of a man. It was a bug-eyed squid head on top of human shoulders. Its tentacles hung down like a beard. Oliver stepped around to see the other statues and it looked like they all had these weird squid faces.

In the center of the circle of the statues there was a watery hole, too big and too deep to be a puddle. It looked like it went down forever. Oliver had a churning feeling in his stomach, the kind of feeling he always had just before he did something exciting, or just after he ate his father's famous beet and beetle chili. He decided to turn back to the beach.

As he turned, he heard a snap under his foot. He froze. There was a quick whooshing sound. Leaves shook and branches broke.

"Uh-oh," said Oliver.

He couldn't move in time. A looped vine clamped around his ankle and a bent palm tree whipped straight up, scooping him into the air. As the tree settled, Oliver swung back and forth upside down, hanging fifteen feet above the weird statues and the strange blue hole. The remote control, which he'd been carrying in his pocket, slipped out and crashed down into the hole, vanishing below the water.

"Oh great," he groaned. Now he would have to explain to Celia that he'd lost their remote control. The watery cave below looked a lot deeper than the space between the couch cushions where he usually lost the remote. And a lot more dangerous.

29

WE SACRIFICE A SNACK CAKE

CELIA LOOKED BACK at the line of trees on the edge of the beach, wondering where Oliver had gone.

The volcano had been quiet for hours now and it was peaceful on their little desert island. The sun dunked itself into the horizon. Inky streaks of red, orange, and yellow oozed across the ocean. It was a beautiful sight. She was annoyed that her brother was missing it. It was just the sort of moment he would like.

She couldn't believe Oliver was still angry at her. She thought they had made up. Boys could be so fickle, she thought.

"Where do you think he could be?" she asked.

"Guys need to be alone sometimes," said Corey. "Maybe he's off collecting his thoughts."

"He doesn't have that many thoughts," Celia

said. "It's been hours. What if a wild animal got him? What if the volcano erupts and he's all alone? What if our mom shows up and he's not here?"

"Oliver can take care of himself. He's a tough kid."

"No," said Celia. "He's not!" She stood up and brushed the sand off her dress. "He's my brother. I know when something's wrong. I just know it."

"Okay," Corey said, standing. "Let's go look for him. We can't do any more work on . . . that today." He looked over at their sorry excuse for a shelter. It looked more like a pile of garbage than the garbage had before Corey piled it. Celia nodded.

As they walked off into the scraggly forest, calling Oliver's name, night settled over the island. The moon came out, bright and full, guiding them through the trees.

"Over here!" they heard Oliver call. They rushed toward the sound of his voice and stopped, startled, in front of a giant statue of a squid-headed man.

"What is that?" Celia asked.

"Look—there are more. They're huge," said Corey. "Who could have built these things?"

"Uh, guys?" Oliver called from above. They looked up and saw him hanging upside down by his ankle from a snare in one of the trees. "Little help?"

"What are you doing up there?" Celia called.

"Oh, you know, just sightseeing," Oliver snapped. "I got stuck! What do you think? It was a trap!"

"We'll get you down!" Corey called, rushing between the statues to reach the tree where Oliver's trap had been tied.

"Don't go that way!" Oliver warned a moment too late. There was a quick whooshing sound. Leaves shook and branches broke.

"Uh-oh," said Corey.

He couldn't move in time. A looped vine clamped around his ankle and a bent palm tree whipped straight up, scooping him into the air. As the tree settled, Corey swung back and forth upside down, fifteen feet above the row of weird statues, right next to Oliver.

"Oops," said Corey. "Hey, look at that weird puddle! It's like the entrance to an underwater cave or something."

Celia's shoulders slumped. Now she had to rescue both of the boys by herself. Why were boys always rushing into things? There was obviously more going on here than giant statues of squid

men and a deep puddle. Someone had put the statues here for a reason and someone had built traps next to them for a reason.

She glanced nervously around her. Suddenly every noise in the dark seemed filled with danger; every buzzing bug or rustling leaf was an enemy about to attack.

It was not unreasonable.

Every time Celia and Oliver had been alone in a remote wilderness, they'd been attacked by something. *The Daytime Doctor* always said "the best evidence for future behavior is past behavior."

It was that idea that told Celia that every time she wandered into a forest filled with booby traps and old statues, she would be attacked by mysterious and ancient forces. That was what always happened.

She didn't dare step any closer to the statues, in case there were more traps. She thought for a moment.

"I have an idea," she said. "Wait right there!"

"What else would we do?" Oliver wondered.

Celia disappeared back toward the beach. The boys hung quietly upside down, waiting for Celia to return.

"I didn't mean to come between you and your sister," said Corey.

"It's cool, whatever," said Oliver, like it was no big deal.

Thankfully, Celia came back at that moment. Oddly, she held the chicken under her arm. In the other hand, she held a snack cake. She set the chicken down and smashed the cake in her hands, tossing the pieces around the rope.

"Hey, that was our last cake!" Oliver objected, but the chicken ran, squawking after the sweet rubbery mush of Velma Sue's Strawberry Surprise. Its head bobbed up and down as it pecked at the ground.

"Come on . . . ," Celia murmured. "Come on. You can do it. Be a good chicken."

After a few more pecks, the sharp beak caught the vine that held Oliver in the air. A few quick pecks around it and the fibers started to snap.

"Hey, Oliver," Celia called up. "You might want to brace yourself."

The vine snapped and Oliver fell straight down, landing with a thud on the top of one of the statues, then sliding down the side. He wasn't hurt, but what was left of his tuxedo looked like it had been torn apart by wild animals.

"Chickens to the rescue!" Corey Brandt laughed. "It's, like, so—" He didn't get to finish saying what it was so like, because the chicken pecked through his vine and he fell, just missing the top of the statue and landing with a hard smack on the ground, next to the watery hole.

"You okay?" the twins called out, not daring yet to rush toward him in case there was another trap.

"I'm okay." Corey stood up slowly, catching his breath. "I've had worse accidents on set. I once fell into the orchestra pit during a rehearsal of *Sunset High: The Musical*."

"There was never a musical of *Sunset High*," said Celia.

"We never opened." Corey brushed himself off. "I landed on an oboe player during my 'Vampire Blues' song. He sued to shut down the show." Corey looked around at the statues that towered over them, casting heavy shadows in the moonlight. "So, I guess we should figure out what this place is?"

"This is the place we're looking for," said Celia.

"Why do you think that?" wondered Oliver.

"Because of this," she said, bending down next to the hole and picking up a small brass plate from the ground. Two letters were engraved in the brass, just like on the compass Jabir had given her: *P.F.*

The chicken pecked at the ground around the hole, clucking quietly.

"Does that mean—?" Corey began to ask. "Could this be—could this hole lead to . . . the Lost Library?"

Celia shrugged and gazed into the dark blue water.

"Celia?" said Oliver. "How do we always discover this stuff by accident? I mean, I just walked off. It doesn't really seem, you know, possible that we'd end up in the exact right place. Do you think it's, like, destiny? Like the oracle in Tibet said?"

"No," said Celia. "There's no such thing as destiny. It's just luck. Really, really bad luck."

Just then, the leaves next to one of the statues rustled and shook. Corey stepped in front of Oliver and Celia. The chicken clucked.

"I wouldn't call it really bad luck," said their mother, Dr. Claire Navel, stepping from behind one of the squid men. Her hair was a mess of matted leaves and the wet suit she wore was torn and frayed. "In fact, I couldn't be happier to see you guys! I count this as my lucky day!"

Oliver's and Celia's mouths hung open and they stood frozen and mute.

Nonplussed.

30

WE LEARN THE PLURAL OF *NEMESIS*

"MRS.—I MEAN, DR. NAVEL!" Corey rushed forward to shake her hand. "It's an honor to meet you."

"Please, call me Claire," she said.

"Mom!" Oliver finally spoke. "Mom?"

She rushed forward to give Oliver a big hug. "I am so glad you made it here. I knew you would. I just knew you would find a way."

"You've been here this whole time?" Celia scolded her mother.

"I could at least get a hello, Celia," her mother scolded her back.

Celia just grunted. Mothers should not disappear and reappear like this, she thought. It wasn't fair.

"I came here with a group of Orang Laut, but they wouldn't stay," Dr. Navel explained. "They marooned me here because they were afraid of the kraken—that's a giant squid."

"We know," said the twins.

"I've been stranded here for a few weeks now. I knew Chris Stickles would contact you if I didn't return. I just hoped you would be able to persuade the Orang Laut to lead you here."

"One of them is all googly for Celia," Oliver explained. Celia elbowed him.

"Where's your father?" their mother asked.

Oliver looked at his feet. Celia frowned.

"He, like, sacrificed himself," said Corey. "To some pirates. For us."

"We need to find Plato's map," Celia told her mother. "We need to try to ransom him from the pirates."

"We can't do that," said Claire Navel.

"What?" Oliver objected. "But . . . it's for Dad!"

"Ollie, honey, your father would not want anyone else getting their hands on Plato's map."

"But it's just some dumb old artifact!" Oliver stomped his foot. "The Explorers Club is full of dumb old artifacts!"

"This one is different," she told her son. "This one cannot fall into the wrong hands."

"Why not? Who cares? This is about Dad!"

"This map will lead to Atlantis, where the Lost Library is hidden."

"So what?" Celia demanded, agreeing with her brother.

"There is a reason the library was hidden in the lost city of Atlantis," she told her children. "It is something like locking the key to a safe inside the safe."

"If you lock a key to a safe inside the safe, no one can get in," Oliver said.

"Duh," Celia added.

"Exactly," said their mother. "You see, inside the Lost Library there are the greatest and most powerful books of all time. Including a sort of instruction manual."

"All this is about, like, an instruction manual?" Corey scratched his head.

"An instructional manual to bring Atlantis back from the depths," said Claire Navel. "An instruction manual to return the empire of Atlantis to its former glory and to conquer the world."

"Oh," said Corey, because what else can you say to something like that?

"We have to do something to help Dad," said Celia.

"That's only one of our problems," Corey said, pointing at Mount Haircut. Clouds of thick black ash billowed upward into the clear blue sky. "When Eyjafjallajökull erupted, it looked just like that," Corey said.

"You pronounced *Eyjafjallajökull* really well," said Claire with a smile. "Not everyone can do that."

"Thanks." Corey blushed. "I took lessons."

"They were worth it," she said. "Icelandic is a very hard language and your accent is lovely, almost like a young Hilmir Snær Guðnason."

"Mom." Celia rolled her eyes. "Maybe we should save the language lesson until after we get off this island?"

"We aren't going anywhere," she answered.

"But what about Dad?" Celia wondered.

"I think the pirates will be bringing your father here soon enough. Sir Edmund will probably be right behind," she said.

"How will they find us?" Celia demanded.

"You're eleven years old, Celia," said her mother. "You aren't that hard to follow."

"Eleven and a half," Celia corrected.

"So what are we going to do?" Corey asked.

"They will certainly attack," said Claire Navel. "And when they attack, we'll be ready. I don't know which of our nemeses will attack first, but we'll have to be prepared."

"That's it," said Celia.

"What's it?" Her mother turned to her.

"The plural of *nemesis*—an implacable enemy bent on our destruction," said Celia. "It's *nemeses*!"

"You and your words," groaned Oliver.

Their mother smiled. "It's from the ancient Greek."

"Yep," said Oliver. "Just like Plato's map and the Lost Library. All our problems come from some ancient Greeks."

31

WE LOOK BEHIND
THE BOOKSHELF

SIR EDMUND did not like the odds.

"It's too much of a coincidence," he said, gazing across the top of his big brandy snifter at Janice the grave robber, Ernest the celebrity impersonator, and a rough-looking woman in brightly colored pants with too many pockets who said her name was Bonnie. "They are plucked from the sea and taken to the very island we've been looking for. I don't like the odds of that one bit. It feels like a setup."

"How could it possibly be a setup?" Janice asked. "No one knew where this island was. That's why everyone was looking for it in the first place! And you said yourself you wanted them to find it first."

Sir Edmund snorted and didn't answer. He stood and paced across the thick carpet on the floor of his cabin. He studied a large wall map and twirled the end of his mustache with one hand, swirling the brandy in his glass with the other. Ernest and Janice waited patiently for him to finish his thoughts. Bonnie, however, did not.

"So when do I get my revenge on Big Bart?" she asked. "I want to board his ship, toss him into the sea, and take command."

Sir Edmund turned to her. "Soon," he said. "When we seize the island and I get what I'm after, you'll be paid. These two"—he pointed at Janice and Ernest—"work for me already. You don't. You have to earn your keep by bringing the Navels to me."

"Or what?" Bonnie did not like taking orders. Big Bart may have tried to kill her, but he never bossed her around. After all, pirate ships were a democracy. The captain was elected and could be removed by a vote. Or by violence.

"Or I will feed you to my kraken," Sir Edmund told her.

"There's no such thing as a kraken." Bonnie

laughed. "Your empty threats don't frighten me. I—" Her voice caught in her throat as Sir Edmund pressed a button on the wall.

An ornate mahogany bookshelf slid to the side, revealing a giant saltwater tank and, in it, a giant saltwater squid with huge coiled tentacles covered in hundreds of large pink suckers. Shining black hooks, like the claws of a tiger, glistened inside each of the suckers and the squid's intelligent yellow eyes blazed through the glass as it gazed into Sir Edmund's cabin.

"I caught it not far from here, with this very ship," said Sir Edmund. "There aren't any other ones in captivity in the world. So you see, it would be quite an honor to be eaten by this one."

Bonnie's face drained of color. There were countless pirate legends about the kraken devouring entire ships. She hadn't believed any of them until now.

Sir Edmund made a quick gesture with his hands, opening and closing his palm, and the kraken responded by spreading wide its tentacles, rearing back and showing its gaping mouth, ringed with rows of teeth like a shark's jaw, and beyond the teeth a rough black tongue and a darkness from which nothing could escape. Sir Edmund gestured again and the kraken relaxed.

"They are quite intelligent beasts," he said. "This one is just a baby, but already it knows who to call its master."

Janice and Ernest stood frozen in place. In their fright, they had grabbed each other by the hand. Once the bookshelves slid shut again, they looked at each other, blushed, and let go. Janice wiped her hand on her shirt.

"That's not possible," Bonnie muttered. "The legends say that only the rulers of Atlantis itself could command the kraken of the deep."

"Is that so?" Sir Edmund polished the medal on his chest, the symbol of a scroll wrapped in chains, and he shrugged.

"Who are you?" Bonnie exclaimed.

"I am a simple explorer and businessman, founder of the Gentlemen's Adventuring Society and a keeper of exotic animals," said Sir Edmund.

"So how do you control the kraken?" Bonnie asked, still backing away from the tank.

"Well, I also happen to be a descendant of the original rulers of Atlantis. There are thirty of us alive today, as there are always thirty of us through-out history."

"That's your Council," Janice whispered. "That's who you are!"

"What did you think? We just got together to play bingo?"

Janice nodded a little.

"My Council of Thirty will stop at nothing to raise Atlantis from the depths and restore its glory to the world. Unfortunately, Claire Navel's stupid library contains the instructions for how to do it."

"I thought that P.F. hid the Lost Library in Atlantis," said Janice. "I thought that's why we were looking for it."

"He did hide it there, the devil," said Sir Ed-mund. "It was like locking a key inside a safe. The only way to get to it would be with an expert safe-cracker. And that is what the Navels are. They are my safecrackers."

"Those brats?" Janice asked. "No!"

"I am as baffled as you are," said Sir Edmund. "But a prophecy is a prophecy and I have seen enough movies to know better than to question a prophecy."

"What about Corey Brandt?" Ernest wondered. "Is he, you know, part of a prophecy?"

"He's just a celebrity," said Sir Edmund. "If we capture him alive, you can do with him what you like."

Ernest smiled.

"And when we're finished?" Bonnie wondered. "Then you'll, what? Bring Atlantis up from the depths and rule the world?"

"I'll rule what's left of it." Sir Edmund smiled. "I imagine that the process of raising Atlantis from the sea will be a little, shall we say, disruptive. It's a lost continent, you see. It vanished from the earth in a single day some ten thousand years ago. Some things will have to be moved around as it rises. Cataclysm, I believe, is the word. Earthquakes, tidal waves, volcanic eruptions. Bad television reception."

"Where?" Janice asked. "Where will there be a cataclysm?"

"Oh, you know." Sir Edmund waved his hand dismissively. "Europe, the Americas, Africa, Asia, Australia." He nodded in thought. "Antarctica will stay where it is, I suppose. The survivors will flock to us for safety and security. They will crave order, and my Council will give it to them."

"You're a madman," said Bonnie. "Your whole plan is based on a fairy tale! A fantasy! Atlantis isn't even real!"

"Is that kraken a fantasy?" asked Sir Edmund. "Is this island we're approaching a fantasy? Perhaps destiny is at work right now. Perhaps you are playing a role in this prophecy yourself?"

"You're nuts," Bonnie said. "But I'll help you get those twins, as long as I get Big Bart. At least I know he's real."

"Good," said Sir Edmund, checking his watch. "We should reach the island by daybreak."

"And then what?" Ernest wondered.

"Haven't you been listening?" Janice snapped at him.

"We get the twins," said Sir Edmund. "And we find P.F. He has a map to Atlantis."

"And we get Big Bart's ship for me," Bonnie added. "Don't forget."

"Right, the pirates," agreed Sir Edmund. "We'll fight your silly pirates."

32

WE'RE WEDGIED TO A WAR COUNCIL

BIG BART LIKED THE ODDS.

"Two children, a teenage actor, and my old chicken alone on an island," he said. "I like those odds."

He took a big sip of rum through a long pink curly straw in his pink plastic Princess Cruise Lines novelty cup. He had scrawled "Big Bart" across the cup in black marker so none of the other pirates would take it.

"How do we know they're alone?" asked Twitchy Bart. He sat next to Big Bart at the round table in the banquet hall, holding a smaller pink plastic Princess Cruise Lines cup with a less curly straw.

"Who could they have run into on an uninhabited island?" Big Bart laughed. "I'll bet they are all crying for their mommies right now. Maybe they'll thank us for kidnapping them again."

The other scar-faced buccaneers huddled around the table laughed and sipped rum from their own pink plastic cups through their own pink plastic straws and eyed the luxurious curls of Big Bart's straw enviously. If he weren't so big they might be tempted to fight him for it, but Bonnie had always been the toughest among them, and she was gone.

"Rmpf bttr ut ffrubrbgur," Dr. Navel groaned through the oily rag they'd stuffed in his mouth again. All the pirates looked up.

The explorer's arms were tied behind his back and he was hanging from the crystal chandelier by his pants with the worst wedgie he'd ever experienced in his many years of exploration.

While we must understand that wedgies are to be expected in the explorer's line of work—there are always Stone Age funeral monuments or tangled mangrove roots on which to snag one's jockey shorts—a pirate-induced wedgie on the ballroom chandelier of a luxury cruise ship is not a circumstance for which one can adequately prepare.

Dr. Navel's nostrils flared, and, to add even greater discomfort to his indignity, his glasses

slipped down his nose and he could do nothing about pushing them up again.

"RRRHUMRPFLAH!" he shouted. The pirates below laughed heartily.

Dr. Navel had thought the pirates would throw him overboard right when they first caught him, but Big Bart was determined to follow the twins to the island, so they had hung him from the chandelier and called together this war council.

"Here's the plan, brothers," Big Bart told them. "We'll get to this lousy island, find those Navel brats and their celebrity friend, and hold them for ransom again."

"What about the kraken? Didn't they tell you this island was guarded by giant squid?" one of the pirates asked.

"You afraid of some fairy tale?" Big Bart sneered. "Piracy ain't no hobby for me. I want to get paid! And the only way we get paid is if we capture that Corey Brandt again."

One of the pirates raised his hand. Big Bart nodded at him to speak. "I really think that at the end of *Sunset High*, Corey Brandt should have ended up with Laur—" Big Bart cut him off with a punch square across the jaw.

"No more talk about *Sunset High*," he told his crew. "I'm tired of hearing about teenage vampires. Now, who's with me?"

"About the vampires?" Twitchy Bart wondered.

"About the island!" Big Bart roared. "We attack at dawn! We take the Navels. We take the teenager. And we take whatever treasure we can find!"

"You really think there'll be treasure?" Twitchy Bart asked. The whole crew leaned in to hear the answer. As a general rule, pirates are quite fond of treasure.

"There's always treasure!" Big Bart roared. "And this time it's ours for the taking! Now who's with me?"

The pirates jumped to their feet, clapping and whistling and cheering for their captain, who sat back in his chair and smiled. He laced his fingers together behind his head and gazed up at the ceiling, looking Dr. Navel right in the eyes. As the wedgied explorer squirmed, dancing in the air over the ballroom, Big Bart gave him a friendly wink and dismissed his war council so they could go get ready for battle and maybe use the old waterslide a few times before it was time for mayhem.

Once they left, Big Bart stood. "Good night,

Doctor," he said, and flipped the lights off, leaving Dr. Navel hanging in the dark of the old ballroom.

"Mrmffff," groaned Dr. Navel. He wiggled furiously, trying to loosen the rope around his hands. He had to get free and try to stop the pirates somehow.

His fingers found the zipper on his pair of Corey Brandt's Pocketed Pants. He felt the sharp edge and realized he might be able to use it to cut his hands loose. Then he would have to figure out how to get down to the floor below without cracking his head open or causing too much noise. But first, he would have to escape from the anguish of his underwear.

He sawed his hands free with the jagged zipper edge and then reached up to the chandelier. He lifted himself up to relieve the pressure of his wedgie and sighed with glorious relief. He tried to wriggle the pants free from where they were snared, but he had to hold on to the chandelier with both hands to keep from falling. He couldn't get free. Corey had said the Pocketed Pants had special wedgie protection built into them for life-or-death wedgies. He must have had a defective pair. Dr. Navel decided that he would write a strongly worded letter to the manufacturer, just as soon as he escaped and saved his family.

He thought about the sadhus of India, some of whom could hold their bodies in impossible positions, endure great pain and discomfort, and become free of the limits of the physical realm. He tried thinking like them, bending and flexing and twisting to lift himself out of his underwear and descend peacefully to the floor.

It didn't work.

"Ow!" He grimaced as his wedgie worsened.

Then he remembered something else about the sadhus of India. He realized what he would have to do to escape.

The sadhus of India were often stark naked.

He sighed a sigh worthy of his children at their most annoyed and wriggled himself right out of his pants, leaving them hanging on the chandelier as he dropped down onto a table below.

As they ran to and fro preparing for battle, none of the pirates noticed Dr. Navel—who was wearing a tablecloth like a toga—creeping about, hiding in doorways, and slipping through narrow passageways belowdecks, searching for a way to escape.

And for some new pants.

33

WE DON'T GET A MONTAGE

OLIVER, CELIA, their mother, and Corey spent much of the night preparing for battle. They had changed back into Corey Brandt's Pocketed Pants, leaving their formal wear behind. It made working a lot easier, and there was plenty of work to do.

They reset the snares by the large statues that had caught Oliver and Corey. They gathered rocks onto high hilltops to tumble down on intruders. They dug pits and covered them with leaves.

It was hard, physical labor and most of it was tedious and dull. Oliver spent hours digging the same pit. Every time he got deep enough, water would flood up from below and cave in the walls and he'd climb out gasping and muddy.

Celia spent hours tying rope snares. Just when she got one attached, the volcano would rumble, the earth would shake, and the snare would snap and she had to do it all over again.

"If this were on TV, there'd just be a bunch of scenes of us building different traps while music played," Oliver said. "And funny little things would happen, like Corey getting stuck in a net, and we'd help him down and we'd all laugh. And then by the time the song was over, we'd be done."

"It's called a montage," said Celia.

"Yeah," said Oliver. "That's what we need. A montage. We'd get this done faster if it was a montage."

"Well, this isn't television," said Celia. "So keep digging that hole."

The sun was starting to peek over the horizon by the time their mother said they were done. Mount Haircut rumbled and belched smoke.

"I'll bet we've only got a few hours before it blows," said Corey.

Their mother shimmied down from a treetop.

"That's plenty of time," she said. "Sir Edmund's ship is just offshore and the pirates are close behind. Both of them will launch their dinghies any minute now."

"*Dinghy* is such a dumb word," said Oliver. "It doesn't sound like something to be afraid of."

"These dinghies will be filled with Sir Edmund's thugs and groups of bloodthirsty pirates," his mother answered.

"That sounds scarier," said Oliver.

"Don't be afraid," his mother told him. "We want them to come. We need to get off this island somehow."

"So we're going with Sir Edmund?" Celia was incredulous.

"Or the pirates?" Oliver was equally shocked.

"Bwak-bwak-bwak," Dennis clucked, which almost certainly had nothing to do with the conversation. He was, after all, just a rooster.

Corey, however, still had fresh memories of the pirates threatening to sell his hair. He shifted uncomfortably on his feet.

"Well, that depends," the twins' mother answered.

"Depends on what, Dr. Nav—?" Corey started. "I mean, Claire."

"It depends on whose ship is easier to hijack." She smiled.

"You mean, like, steal?" Oliver asked. "Like pirates do?"

His mother nodded.

"That's crazy," said Celia.

"Don't worry." Her mother squeezed her shoulder. "I have a plan. I'll keep you safe."

"How will you do that?" Celia stomped her foot in the sand. She had been working all night and was pretty hungry, which made her grumpy. She also got grumpy when she was about to be attacked by Sir Edmund's thugs and bloodthirsty pirates. *The Daytime Doctor* might call it a "psychological coping mechanism." Celia thought it was perfectly reasonable to be grumpy at times like this.

"You couldn't keep us safe from Sir Edmund or from those pirates! You couldn't keep Dad safe and now he's gone! You can't keep anyone safe! You never have! All you do is leave!"

Celia had tears running down her cheeks and, realizing that Corey and brother were staring at her, she blushed and bit her lip. She turned her back on all of them.

"We'll need to be brave for a bit," Claire Navel told her daughter. "My plan needs all of us to work together. Once it's done, we'll save your father and get out of here."

"What about Plato's map?" Celia sniffled. "You'd just leave off looking for it?"

Her mother smiled, but it wasn't a happy smile. It was a mask to cover a sadness. "I need to make sure you and your father are safe."

"That's not an answer. You mean you'll go right back to looking for it," Oliver said. "Right back down that hole." He pointed to the watery cave surrounded by strange statues. "You'll leave us again."

Their mother's lips had just begun to form an answer when the high-pitched buzz of a small boat engine cut through the tense air among the Navels. Corey darted away to the trees and rushed back again.

"That's Sir Edmund," he said. "He's got Janice and Ernest and even that pirate Bonnie with him. And a few thugs."

"What's Bonnie doing with them?" Celia wondered.

"They must have rescued her from the ocean after Big Bart threw her overboard," said Corey.

"I'll bet she's mad," said Oliver, which really didn't need to be said.

"They don't know I'm on this island," their mother said. "That is our advantage. We have the element of surprise."

"What do we do?" Corey asked.

Claire Navel spelled out their plan. It was dangerous and crazy and if it worked they would save themselves and their father. They'd also put an end to the pirates once and for all.

If the plan failed, Oliver and Celia would never have to give that report to the whole school about what they learned while they were absent. There's an old pirate saying that goes "dead men tell no tales."

They don't give school reports either.

34

WE'VE LAID OUR PLANS

"I WANT PARLEY!" Sir Edmund shouted, standing on the beach with his arms in the air. "Come on out and parley with me!"

"That's the same thing your dad was shouting about on the pirate ship," said Corey as he and Oliver and Celia squatted behind a tree watching Sir Edmund unload his men and weapons onto the beach. "What's parley?"

Celia shrugged.

"You don't know?" Oliver smirked. It felt good to know something that Corey and his sister didn't know.

"Don't get that look," said Celia. "Just tell us."

"It's from the Pirates' Code," said Oliver. "When someone demands the right of parley, they get to talk to the leader of the enemy ship and they can't be harmed until the parley is over. It's from the French word for 'talk,' which is, uh . . ."

"Whatever." Celia cut her brother off. "If Mom's dumb plan is going to work, we have to go talk to Sir Edmund now."

"Your mother's plan isn't dumb, Celia," Corey told her. "You really should be nice to her. She's a brilliant woman."

"She ditched us to explore the world, then got us thrown out of an airplane, lost in the Amazon, and now stranded on a desert island," said Celia. "You can be nice to her. I'll be how I want to her. Now let's do this." She looked at Oliver. "You go first."

"What? Why do I have to go first?"

"That's the plan."

"You always make me go first; it's not fair."

"None of this is fair," said Celia. "Just go."

"Don't worry, Ollie, we've got your back." Corey winked.

"Don't call me Ollie," Oliver grumbled at him as he stood up with his arms in the air and walked across the beach toward Sir Edmund. "Parley!" he shouted out. "We give you . . . uh . . . parley! So no, uh, sneak attacks!"

Celia and Corey watched from the bushes at the edge of the beach.

"Sneak attacks? Me?" Sir Edmund acted outraged. "I am an honest explorer leading a mission of research and discovery! It is you who are sneaky, Oliver Navel. I don't know how you managed to find this place, but I am sure you want to get home very badly. Perhaps your mother is there waiting for you now."

Oliver scrunched his toes in the sand and tried not to look like he was hiding something. It didn't really work.

"I see," said Sir Edmund. "So your mother is here?"

"No," said Oliver.

"Don't lie to me, Oliver. I have known you since you were a child. I know when you are telling lies."

"I'm not lying," he lied. "And I'm still a child."

"Well." Sir Edmund stroked his mustache. "It doesn't matter. Your father is certainly not here. My friend over there"—he pointed at Bonnie—"tells me that a pirate named Big Bart has your father."

"So?" said Oliver, sticking his chin up defiantly.

"So how about I help you get him back?"

"Help us? Why would you do that?"

"Because you are going to help me too, boy."

"I am?"

"You and your sister are going to find Plato's map for me. I know it's on this island. All you have to do is lead me to it."

"What if we don't know where it is?"

"You'll figure it out," he said. "You always do."

"Not this time," said Oliver. "We're not helping you with anything."

"You want to get off this island, don't you?" said Sir Edmund. "There's a volcano erupting."

"Maybe we like it here." Oliver shrugged, acting like he didn't care about the volcano. "If that's it, I guess we're done parleying."

"I suppose we are." Sir Edmund smirked. "You know what that means, don't you, boy?" His men inched forward, ready to pounce on Oliver.

"I do," said Oliver. "It means there's no truce and you are going to attack."

"That's right," said Sir Edmund.

Sir Edmund nodded and two of his men rushed forward to seize Oliver. He jumped backward and the two men stepped after him. Suddenly, there was a snap and then a whooshing sound as ropes snared around their ankles. They tripped forward and the ropes grew tight. Just like when Oliver and Corey set the traps off by the statues, bent trees whipped upright and the men were thrown into the air.

"See?" said Oliver. "We can attack too!" He turned and ran back to the tree line and into the bushes.

"After him!" shouted Sir Edmund. "And find the rest of his family and that teenager."

Sir Edmund said the word *teenager* the way you might say "vomit sandwich."

Bonnie and Janice and Ernest raced off with three more of Sir Edmund's men, leaving only one man on the beach with Sir Edmund. Watching through binoculars from a treetop, Claire Navel smiled at how well her son had done.

So far, everything was going according to plan. Her children might just become great explorers after all.

35

WE GO AWRY

OLIVER RAN PAST THE TREE where his sister and Corey were crouched, leaping at the last moment. Janice and one of Sir Edmund's thugs were right behind him.

"No use leaping like a gazelle, Oliver!" Janice called out. "You're too slow!"

After Oliver passed by, Corey and Celia, who were crouched low to avoid being seen, pulled a vine off the ground, holding it tight. Janice tripped over the vine and the thug tripped over her, and they both crashed forward through a layer of big green banana leaves into a shallow pit, thick with gloopy mud.

Corey and Celia were up on their feet in a flash. They gave each other a quick high five and ran off in opposite directions.

Celia charged through the underbrush, heading

toward the rising edge of the volcano. She could hear someone chasing her, but she stayed low so it wouldn't be easy for the adults to see which way she went. She ducked and weaved her way to the exact spot her mother told her to stop and then she stopped. She turned.

"You . . . have . . . nowhere . . . to . . . run," Bonnie panted. Pirates didn't do all that much running and she wasn't used to it. But the rather intimidating man behind her was used to it. He rushed forward.

Celia smirked. The man looked up just in time to see a pile of rocks crash down on him from above. Bonnie flew into a rage before Celia could react. She leaped right onto the rock pile, climbing over the unfortunate soul beneath, and dove onto Celia, holding a big bowie knife. Celia crumpled underneath her and felt the woman's knees press down on her chest, pushing her back into the hard dirt and black rock on the slope of the volcano.

"Good thing you're just a child." Bonnie slapped away Celia's arms as they struggled to grab her. "You won't bleed as much as a grown-up."

"I'm not a child." Celia bucked like a bronco underneath a rodeo rider. "I'm. A. Tween!" She wriggled out from underneath Bonnie and slid forward to grab a rock.

Bonnie dove onto Celia's back, grabbing her by the hair and lifting her up from the ground. She held her knife up to Celia's neck.

"I never did understand what a tween is supposed to be," Bonnie whispered in her ear. "Does it mean you're too young for Corey Brandt to care about you but too old to cry for your mommy when I gut you like a fish?"

Celia shuddered. She felt the cold metal against the soft flesh of her throat. Then she heard a loud *thunk* and the knife fell to the ground beside her. Bonnie fell to the ground beside her too. Celia turned and saw her mother standing with a heavy piece of driftwood from Corey's failed attempt at making a shelter.

"You never have to cry for me," her mother said. "I'll always be there. I promise."

"Touching." Sir Edmund appeared behind her. "But predictable."

One of his men stepped out on the other side of Celia.

"You really should have seen this coming," said Sir Edmund as his man raised a blowgun to his lips and shot a dart right into Claire Navel's arm. "Although I do suppose it's your husband I usually poison, isn't it? Too bad he's not available at the moment."

"You won't get—" Claire Navel stepped toward him with her driftwood, stumbled once, staggered, and then fell flat on her face.

"The best-laid plans of mice and men often go awry," Sir Edmund muttered to himself. Celia didn't know what he was talking about, and she didn't care to.

She charged at Sir Edmund, fists raised, ready to punch the cruel little billionaire right in his big red mustache, but as she threw her punch she came up short and swung wide. She felt herself yanked backward by the waistband of her pants and lifted into the air by Sir Edmund's goon.

"Celia Navel," said Sir Edmund. "Are you ready to help your old friend Edmund change the world forever?"

It was hard to tell, but underneath his mustache Sir Edmund was wearing a very big grin.

36

WE GO EVEN MORE AWRY

OLIVER DIDN'T STOP RUNNING until he got to the other side of the island, right where his mother told him to go. He was out of breath, but he knew more of Sir Edmund's thugs would be right behind him. Ernest too. That was part of the plan.

He and Corey would distract them for long enough that his mom and Celia could get across the island, spring the trap on Ernest, and save the day. Then they'd all go steal Sir Edmund's dinghy and use it to take Dad from the pirate ship while the pirates were still searching the island for Oliver and Corey and Celia.

After that, they'd take whichever ship they wanted and go home, leaving the pirates and Sir Edmund marooned as the volcano erupted. It wasn't a very nice plan, but they were up against some not very nice people.

Their mother had named the plan "the Island Intrigue." Explorers loved naming things.

Oliver felt a pang of doubt as he heard crashing branches and the cruel oaths of Ernest and one of Sir Edmund's goons from the Gentlemen's Adventuring Society racing toward him.

"You!" Ernest yelled, stopping in his tracks when he saw Oliver. He motioned for the goon not to step any closer.

Oliver saw Corey sneaking off to the side, holding a rock at the ready, but he couldn't see his mother lurking in any of the high treetops. It would probably take her a minute to get over here. She and Celia had to trap Bonnie first, and they'd probably need a second to rest, and Celia could be really slow sometimes. He and Corey would have to stall for time. His mother would be here soon. Oliver was sure of it. She would come. She had to.

"You sure you don't want to come get me?" Oliver taunted.

"Don't go any closer. There could be booby traps," Ernest warned. "And I'm no booby."

"You look like two big boobies to me!" Oliver stuck out his tongue.

Ernest seethed, but he didn't move. He pulled out a pistol from his belt.

Oliver put his tongue back in his mouth. He got that seasick feeling again, even though he wasn't on a boat. He felt strangely like taking a nap. It was amazing how much fear could feel like sleepiness. His whole world shrank around him. The barrel of the gun looked much larger than it could possibly have been. The trees and the sky all seemed smaller. Even the rumbling volcano in the distance lost its importance. All that mattered was Ernest and that gun.

"You, uh, you wouldn't shoot an eleven-year-old," Oliver said, losing his confidence. He thought about his sister. "Eleven and a half," he corrected himself.

He managed a glance toward Corey. Why wasn't he throwing the rock yet? The teenager crouched in the bushes, unmoving. Seeing him brought Oliver back to his senses. He couldn't just give up. He couldn't let Ernest win. He had to stall. His mother and his sister and his father were all counting on him. He had to get Corey to throw that rock.

Oliver flared his nostrils and bugged his eyes, trying silently to signal Corey. Still the teenager didn't throw his rock. He tried waving his arms and moving his legs, hoping Corey would understand that he was trying to tell him to throw the stupid rock at Ernest before he got shot! This wasn't television! He wasn't secretly wearing a bulletproof vest that he hadn't told anyone about.

"Why are you dancing around like that?" Ernest asked. "Is that supposed to make me pity you for being wrong in the head?"

Oliver stopped dancing. He looked over at Corey one last time, still frozen with the rock in his hand, motionless.

Of course Corey Brandt would let him down, Oliver thought. Of course Corey Brandt would betray him.

First he came between Oliver and his sister and now he was getting Oliver killed. In all his eleven and a half years, meeting Corey Brandt was the biggest disappointment he had ever experienced. And thanks also to Corey Brandt, it was going to be the last disappointment he would ever experience. He exhaled and let his shoulders slump, preparing for the end.

If he hadn't been so focused on the barrel of Ernest's gun, however, he might have noticed that Corey wasn't throwing his rock because there was a pirate hiding just behind him with a knife to his back whispering for him not to move unless he wanted a hole where his heart should be.

"I guess you can shoot me now," Oliver said, shrugging. What was the point of fighting? It dawned on Oliver that his mother wasn't coming to the rescue. She'd let him down too. She'd vanished. Like always.

He wasn't even twelve years old yet and he'd lost his father to pirates, his mother had abandoned him, his sister had betrayed him, and his onetime hero was about to let him get shot. Even the chicken he'd kidnapped was nowhere in sight. He felt more lonesome than he ever had before.

"I'll shoot you when I'm ready, Oliver Navel," said Ernest. "I want to enjoy this." Ernest's hand caressed the handle of his gun, then his arm straightened and his eyes widened. His mouth opened. He stepped slightly backward.

Oliver thought it curious that Ernest would be the one who looked suddenly afraid, when Oliver was the one who was about to meet his maker, but in a flash he understood.

A band of pirates burst out from behind the trees, whooping and hollering.

"I'd drop that weapon now if I were you," said Big Bart, stepping in front of Oliver without the slightest fear of the pistol pointed his way. "Unless you want my friends to make you drop it."

Ernest dropped the pistol. Corey was dragged to his feet by the pirate who'd caught him.

"Sorry, Oliver," Corey said. "The guy, like, totally surprised me."

Oliver glanced at the surly group of buccaneers around him. He recognized two of the scar-faced men and one of the Malay-speaking pirates who had laughed at him at the banquet. He tried to look into the bushes and trees beyond them, scanning for Celia and his mother, but he still couldn't see them.

"Tie those two up," said Big Bart, hooking his thumb toward Ernest and the goon. "And let's get these kids back the ship. We'll get our ransom after all!"

He bent down in front of Oliver and smiled a

crooked smile. "It's good to see you again, Oliver. You're a brave lad. I'm almost sorry to have to take you hostage again."

"So don't," Oliver suggested.

Big Bart guffawed and patted him on the back so hard he thought his eyes might pop out. "Oh, you're a funny one! Maybe you'll join my crew after all! Now tell me, where's Dennis?"

Oliver looked down at his feet and shrugged.

"You didn't eat him, did you?" Big Bart's face turned red.

"No!" said Oliver. "But I don't know where he is."

Big Bart nodded. He told three of his pirates to stay on the island and search for his rooster.

"Your what, boss?" one of them asked.

"My rooster, Dennis!" he repeated. The men cocked their heads at him and furrowed their brows. "My chicken!"

"Oh, right!" The pirates nodded. "The chicken." They set off to scour the island.

The volcano rumbled suddenly and a plume of ash and smoke rose into the sky. The earth shook.

"And be quick about it!" Big Bart called after his men.

As the others led Ernest and Sir Edmund's thug and Corey away toward the beach, Big Bart whispered to Oliver.

"Don't look so blue," he said. "At least you'll get to see your father again."

"He's alive?" Oliver felt some relief.

"Oh yes." Big Bart laughed. "When we left him he was just kind of . . . hanging out."

Oliver didn't know what was so funny about his father "hanging out."

And Big Bart didn't know that Dr. Navel was, at that very moment, storming the bridge of the cruise ship wearing a bright-pink bathrobe stitched with the logo of Princess Cruise Lines.

WE BOTHER BLOBFISH

BONNIE HAD A BIG LUMP on her head and a sour expression on her face as she helped Sir Edmund's henchman carry Claire Navel toward the pool of water by the old squid-headed statues. Sir Edmund and Celia walked side by side in front of them.

"No way," said Celia, after Sir Edmund explained what he wanted her to do. Her mother's plan had fallen apart, and now she had fallen into his clutches.

"You don't have a choice, Celia," he answered her. "Not if you want to save your mother from the same fate as her old friend Chris Stickles. There's no hospital for her around here. That poison will drive her completely crazy soon."

"She was completely crazy before." Celia acted tough. "So your threat doesn't scare me."

"I could, of course, just feed her to my kraken." He shrugged.

"You don't have a kraken," said Celia. "They aren't even real."

"Oh, mine is quite real," said Sir Edmund. "And he is quite ornery. That means bad tempered."

"I know what *ornery* means," Celia snapped at him.

"Of course you do." He clasped his hands behind his back.

"The kraken," Claire Navel muttered. "Call the kraken . . ." She started whistling to herself.

"See, your mother is already going insane. She's whistling to a giant squid."

Celia watched her mother whistling. Her eyes were glassy and her head lolled around limp on her neck.

"So will you cooperate?" Sir Edmund demanded.

"I'm too young to scuba dive," said Celia.

"As you so kindly remind us all the time, you are almost twelve years old," said Sir Edmund. "That is exactly the right age to start."

"What if I can't find what you're after?"

"Well, in that case," Sir Edmund sighed, "I would hate to be you."

Just then, the island rumbled with a violent earthquake. They struggled to stay on their feet. The volcano belched a cloud of thick black ash and the island fell quiet again. The last of the seabirds took flight and disappeared into the sky.

"Fine," said Celia, realizing that she had no choice. The whole plan was in shambles. She didn't know what had happened to Oliver and Corey, but she and her mother were prisoners and they had no way to help her father. But if she got Plato's map for Sir Edmund, maybe he would help them.

They reached the hole in the ground between the weird squid-headed statues. It looked like little more than a deep puddle.

One of Sir Edmund's men was already there waiting for them. He had scuba gear set up and ready for Celia to put on. She dipped her toe in the water and realized why her mother had sent those wet suits long ago. Even though they were in the hot Pacific Ocean, the water was cold.

She pulled her wet suit out of the backpack and squeezed into it over her clothes. Next she put on her flippers and the big vest with the heavy air tank attached. Sir Edmund's man had to hold her upright. She felt like a penguin waddling around. Last, she put on the big face mask with a microphone in it and a headlamp on top. The tank on her back was pulling her over in the wrong direction. The heavy weights on her belt, to keep her from floating up too high, pressed uncomfortably on her hips. She couldn't believe that people actually went scuba diving for fun. Just getting dressed in the equipment felt like medieval torture.

"You look almost like a real explorer," Sir Edmund said. "I am sure your parents would be so proud if they could see you. Too bad they can't."

Celia's words were muffled by the sound of her air tank turning on and the thick seal of the mask, but Sir Edmund understood well enough what she said. We won't repeat it here.

"Don't you dare come back empty-handed," Sir Edmund told her as he gave her a watertight bag to tuck into her vest and helped her sit on the edge of the hole, dangling her legs into the water.

"I also suggest that you stay near the edge as you go down."

Celia shrugged to signal that she didn't understand why. The edge looked dark and craggy with black volcanic rock. The center of the pool was calm and blue and clear. You could see all the way down to a soft sandy bottom.

Sir Edmund stooped and picked up a rock. He threw it into the center of the water. It sank slowly. For a second, everything looked fine. Suddenly a column of bubbles burst out from the middle of the sand at the bottom of the pool, surrounding the stone and rising, sizzling, to the surface. In just a few seconds the bubbles stopped and the stone was gone.

"It's connected to the volcano," Sir Edmund said. "It would melt a little girl even faster than a stone."

Celia nodded that she understood.

"Enjoy your dive!" Bonnie laughed as she shoved Celia off the edge with her heel and Celia slid into the water. She turned in the water, gripping the wall to stay close, and gave Bonnie one long glare before she sank below the surface.

The heavy, dry air from her tank filled her mask and she found that she could almost breathe normally. Water trickled into her wet suit with a cold gurgle, soaking her completely, but quickly warming with her body heat. She sank slowly with her belly pressed against the side wall to stay as far from the center of the pool as possible. Her light bounced off the jagged black rocks in front of her, and as she got deeper she felt her ears popping with the pressure. The wall smoothed as she got lower, and in under a minute, she was on the soft sand at the bottom, looking directly into the open mouth of a low, dark cave.

The bubbles that came out every time she exhaled tickled her ears, and she stood still for a while, listening to the hiss of air filling her face mask when she inhaled and the roar of bubbles escaping when she exhaled. This felt a lot different than the dive she did with Jabir, when she only had on goggles and had to hold her breath. This time she felt more like an astronaut on another world than a swimmer.

As her fins kicked up the loose sand along the bottom, she saw a universal remote control, just like the one they'd brought with them. She bent down to pick it up and saw that it wasn't just like their remote control. It was their remote control. She recognized the orange stains from cheese puff dust, which not even salt water could wash away.

She rolled her eyes. Oliver must have dropped it

down here while he was off wandering the island and getting stuck in that trap. He was so clumsy that way. He'd probably been too embarrassed to tell her. She shoved the remote into the pocket of her dive vest.

"Are you still alive?" Sir Edmund's voice blasted through a speaker by her ear.

"Yes," she said, surprised that she could talk almost normally with the mask on. This reminded her of the time in Peru when Sir Edmund made them go into the ruins at Machu Picchu. Back then, her brother was with her. Back then, he could go first.

Not this time. She hoped he was okay. She hoped he'd be okay if she didn't make it out of this cave. He wouldn't make a very good only child.

"I'm going in," she said.

She exhaled and kicked forward into the long cave, gliding deeper into the darkness with every stroke of her fins. She turned her head from side to side, scanning the walls with her light. So far, all she saw was smooth black rock. She caught a glimpse of a long green eel with razor-sharp teeth, floating like a ribbon in the breeze, but the moment her light caught it, it darted away into a small hole in the wall and was gone. As she swam past its hole, her light glistened red off the two watchful eyes of the lurking eel.

Her breathing quickened, but she told herself to stay calm. Her family's fate was in her hands. At least if she lived through this, Corey would be impressed. He couldn't possibly think of her as a little kid then.

The long cave opened up into a big chamber, so big she couldn't even see the walls in any direction. The beam of light from her headlamp shot out into the dark and faded to nothing. She spun around and looked up and down and side to side. It was like she wasn't even in water. It felt more like flying.

She kicked her way forward through the dark and saw something strange down below her. She realized that it was easier to rise up when she inhaled because her lungs were full of air, and easier to go down when she exhaled because her lungs were empty. So she breathed out and kicked down toward the strange shapes looming on the edge of the darkness—they were a line of those same statues of squid men. Beside them were the petrified trunks of trees, their leaves long gone, but she could clearly see by their branches that they had once been palm trees, as if this whole cave had once been above water.

Strange translucent fish and spiny crabs scuttled out of the path of her light. Her fin kicks disturbed a lazy blobfish, drifting just above the floor. It seemed to ooze away backward into the darkness.

Celia looked up into the grim face of the squid men, now towering above her in the dark. Her light cast strange shadows as she swam between two rows of them toward an opening into another chamber. She felt like a knight entering a castle in one of Oliver's sword-fighting movies. Out of the corner of her eye shapes darted between the statues, vanishing as soon as her light hit them. She imagined sharks and eels and giant squid lurking just beyond the beam of her light.

She thought she saw a giant tentacle wrapping around the base of one of the statues, but when she flashed her light on it, there was nothing there. A giant shadow moved in the dark behind her. She whipped her light around, but again there was nothing to see.

She suddenly felt more like a girl in a horror

movie wandering through a haunted house in her pajamas. Everyone watching knew she was doomed, but she kept going anyway, driven by that horror movie rule that says, "No matter how bad an idea it is, you have to go into the creepiest and darkest room possible."

She felt suddenly colder, but not because the temperature had changed. She missed her brother. She felt safe when he was around, when they were a team. She regretted how she'd treated him, just to impress Corey Brandt. He'd acted like a baby, but it was no excuse. She was older by three minutes and forty-two seconds. She was supposed to be more mature. She vowed to apologize to him for real if she ever saw him again.

"Where are you?" Sir Edmund's voice blasted in her ear. "You better not have drowned."

"I'm here," Celia said. "I'm going through a big stone archway."

She swam forward, leaving the statues behind and entering a new room. Her light hit a black wall of volcanic rock a few feet in front of her. She looked up and saw her bubbles rising in a long column, up, up, and up until they broke on the surface.

The surface.

She swam gently upward, hoping with every kick that she wasn't about to set off a booby trap or wake a sleeping sea monster.

Her head broke through into a large cavern with a roof of rock and spiky stalactites. Crushed up against the rock on the far side of the cave, she saw a sight that took her breath away: a grand wooden ship lying on its side, its sails torn and tattered, its hull broken open.

She swam over to it and hoisted herself onto its tilted deck. She sat along the rail, what sailors called the gunwale, and pulled her fins off.

"I found a ship," she said into her mask. "I'm getting out of the water."

"Keep your microphone on!" Sir Edmund spluttered, but Celia took the mask off and couldn't hear him anymore. She wriggled out of her vest and left all her scuba equipment on the deck. Then, in a chilly wet suit, she climbed up toward the bridge of the ship where the captain would have sat, hoping she'd find what Sir Edmund was after.

Hoping she could save her family with it.

When she reached the captain's chair, she gasped.

She turned and ran back down again, grabbed her mask, and panted into the microphone without putting it back on.

"I found him," she said. "I found P.F."

"Does he have it?" Sir Edmund sounded gleeful even through the static of the wet speaker. "Does he have Plato's map?"

"I didn't look," Celia said.

"Well, get up there and look for it, right now!"

Celia dropped the mask again and trudged back up to the chair, dreading what she would see: a skeleton in a ragged khaki outfit and pith helmet, like old-time explorers wore, clutching a leather journal to his chest.

He was surrounded by old tools and empty cans of food. His feet rested against a wooden steamer trunk. Celia didn't need to look at the brass plate on the top of it to know that it belonged to P.F., the explorer who had found the Lost Library before anyone else and then vanished. This was his final resting place.

38

WE GO TO WEDGIE WAR

"SOMETHING'S WRONG," Big Bart said as he stepped onto the forward deck of the Princess cruise ship. "I left the Somali guy and the Norwegian guy out here."

"I'm the Somali guy!" one of the scar-faced pirates complained. "My name's Yusef! We've sailed together for five years!"

"And there is no Norwegian guy," said the other scar-faced pirate. "He's Swedish."

"I can't keep track of all of your countries," Big Bart groaned. "I'm not the United Nations."

The Malaysian said something in Malaysian and all the pirates but Big Bart laughed.

"Oh, if you think Twitch would be a better captain, by all means, say so," Big Bart bellowed, grabbing the handle of his knife. The other pirates stopped laughing. "I thought so," said Big Bart. He turned to Oliver and Corey and bent down.

"The pirate's life is no pleasure cruise," he said gravely. "There are a lot of languages to learn."

Big Bart's men dumped Ernest and Sir Edmund's henchman, both bound and gagged, onto the deck with two loud thuds. The pirate named Yusef bent down and snatched the plastic parrot off Ernest's shoulder, then he knocked Ernest's fancy hat into the ocean.

"Hey," Ernest whined, but Yusef put his boot on Ernest's neck. "I didn't want to dress like a pirate anymore anyway," he wheezed from underneath the boot.

Big Bart stood back up and called out for Twitchy Bart. He called out for the Swede. There was no answer. In fact, the ship was silent. Oliver noticed Big Bart's lips pursing in alarm.

For those of you who have never been on a pirate ship, I can assure you that they are not usually quiet places. Parties go all night with loud music and singing and shouting. Shouting often turns to yelling. Yelling often turns to fighting. And fighting sometimes turns to singing again. Everyone turns their televisions up too loud.

"Let Oliver go!" someone shouted from above. Oliver looked up to see his father standing outside the door to the bridge, where the captain and his officers steered the ship. He was holding Twitchy Bart in front of him by the elastic band on the pirate's underpants.

"Ow!" said Twitchy Bart.

Dr. Navel gave his wedgie a tug. "Hurts, doesn't it?"

Oliver wondered why his father was wearing a fuzzy pink robe, but he was so happy to see him again that he didn't make any sarcastic comments.

"Hey, Dr. Navel!" Corey called out.

"Hi, Corey!" Dr. Navel called back. "Release Corey too, or I'll give your friend the Tiger Wedgie of Doom."

"No one can perform the Tiger Wedgie of Doom!" Big Bart shouted.

"I learned it from the Shaolin monks in China," said Dr. Navel. "They performed it on me almost every day."

The other pirates gasped.

"You kidnap my chicken, you escape, and now you wedgie my first mate!" Big Bart said. "I am very fed up with the Navel family."

He snatched Oliver by the back of his pants and lifted him off the ground with one hand. The wedgie was instantaneous.

"Ow! Leggo!" Oliver kicked and squirmed, but Big Bart didn't so much as bend his arm.

"I could toss Oliver overboard this second," Big Bart called to Dr. Navel. "I don't imagine he could survive the fall."

"Why is everyone always trying to kill me?" Oliver yelled. "I just want to be left alone and watch TV!"

"Don't worry, Oliver," his father shouted. "I'll get you home!"

"Let go of Twitch," said Big Bart, "and I might spare your son."

"Let go of Oliver first," said Dr. Navel.

"Do it, Cap'n," said Twitchy Bart. "I can't take much more o' this wedgie!"

"It looks like we've got a Bulgarian standoff," said Big Bart. "Wedgie to wedgie."

"Guess so," said Dr. Navel.

"Where's the rest of my crew?"

"They're hanging out in the banquet hall," said Dr. Navel. "Just like you left me."

"How did you—" Big Bart was astonished.

"I learned a lot from those Shaolin monks," said Dr. Navel. "In between wedgies they taught me martial arts."

Oliver was impressed with his father for maybe the first time ever. Or at least he would have been impressed if he didn't feel like his underwear was climbing into his lungs.

"You have one problem, Dr. Navel," said Big Bart.

"What's that?" Dr. Navel called.

"I don't care if you wedgie Twitchy Bart right off this ship. I'm not giving up my hostages."

"Hey!" Twitchy Bart objected. "No! How could you?"

"Sorry, Twitch," said Big Bart. "It's just business."

"That ain't right, Captain," one of the men behind Big Bart said.

The Malaysian said something in Malaysian. The others agreed.

"Now, fellas, just a second." Big Bart sounded shaken. "Don't get crazy . . . I'd never let him do that to any of you . . . you guys are my favorites!" He started to reach for the knife in his belt with his free hand, but the Somali caught him tightly by the wrist and stopped him.

"What's my name?" he asked.

"Why . . . it's . . . I know it . . . just hold on." Big Bart stammered as he struggled to free his wrist.

"It's Yusef!" Oliver called out. "Your name is Yusef! And Big Bart would throw you overboard too, just like he did to Bonnie. Don't trust him!"

"Why you little—" Big Bart started to yank Oliver's wedgie, but the waistband broke away and Oliver crashed onto the deck just as the other pirates pounced on Big Bart.

"My wedgie-proof pants worked!" Corey was thrilled. He helped Oliver up and they climbed the metal ladder to Dr. Navel on the bridge while the pirates were fighting each other.

Dr. Navel hooked Twitchy Bart's underpants on the railing hanging over the side of the ship and bent down to embrace his son.

"Don't leave me like this, Navel!" Twitchy Bart yelled. "I swear I'll get you if you leave me like this."

"Thank you, Corey," Dr. Navel said, without letting go of Oliver. "I thought I might never see him again."

"No problem, Dr. Navel," said Corey.

"Please, call me Ogden," said Dr. Navel. He looked down and saw Big Bart holding one of the pirates in a headlock and keeping the others at bay with a knife. Yusef was trying to sneak up behind Big Bart with a big metal pipe. Ernest and Sir Edmund's henchman were watching the scene wide-eyed, trying not to get stepped on in the scuffle. Dr. Navel looked toward land and saw the black smoke belching from the volcano. "We have to get back to that island and find Celia."

"And Mom," said Oliver.

"You found your mother?" Dr. Navel's face flushed. "She was really on that island?"

"Yeah," said Oliver. "She was waiting for us to come and rescue her, I guess."

"She's not . . . behind all this, is she?" Dr. Navel grimaced.

"Not this time," said Oliver. "And I think she might be in trouble. She and Celia were supposed to save me and Corey from Sir Edmund's thugs. They never showed up."

"All right," said Dr. Navel. "We'll take the dinghy and leave these pirates to their fight."

"Dad?" Oliver suggested. "Maybe you should get some clothes first."

Dr. Navel nodded and looked back over at Twitchy Bart.

"Oh no!" said Twitchy Bart. "No way!"

Minutes later, Oliver, Corey, and Dr. Navel, who was now dressed in Twitchy Bart's shirt and Pocketed Pants, crept along the deck, past the waterslide and the swimming pool. Big Bart was chasing the Malaysian on the other side of the deck with a knife in each hand, and Yusef was chasing Big Bart with his big metal pipe swinging.

As Oliver climbed onto the dinghy, he saw Ernest spit his gag out.

"Don't leave us here," he called out from where he was tied up. "Don't you leave us here!"

"You tried to kill me!" Oliver yelled, and hopped into the boat.

Dr. Navel hit the button that lowered the dinghy slowly into the water and he jumped aboard.

"I'm happy you could come with us this time," Oliver told his dad.

"Thanks for coming back to rescue me," said Dr. Navel.

"But we didn't," Oliver answered. "They kidnapped us . . . it was an accident that we rescued you."

"Shh." Dr. Navel put his fingers to his lips and smiled. "That's not how I remember it. I remember you being a hero."

Oliver looked at Corey. Corey nodded. "H-E-R-O," he said.

The boat settled in the water; Dr. Navel unhooked its chain and started the motor. They sped back toward the island, where the volcano rumbled and spat red-hot lava.

"Look," said Oliver. "It's erupting! Everyone's running away."

Sir Edmund's men were rushing from the brush, sprinting across the beach, and clamoring onto their boats to flee. Janice, covered in mud, kicked one of the men out of the way as she flopped onto one of the boats.

Oliver didn't see Sir Edmund, Bonnie, his mother, or Celia anywhere.

39

WE SCOLD A SKELETON

CELIA MOVED CLOSER to the explorer's skeleton one squishy-wet footstep at a time. Even though his eye sockets were dark and empty, he looked like he was watching her approach, and grinning at her because she was afraid.

She thought about her brother and Corey and her mother in need of rescue and her father aboard the pirate ship. She didn't want any of them to end up like this skeleton. She had to be brave. She took another squishy step.

"You're not so scary," she told the skeleton, trying to trick herself into being brave. "You look ridiculous in that hat."

She marched right up to the skeleton and leaned in to look it right in the eyes. Or at least right where its eyes used to be.

"You hear that?" she said. "I'm not afraid of you.

Now you have to help me save my family. Where's Plato's map?"

Celia pursed her lips and waited. Of course nothing happened; she knew nothing would happen. In fact, she felt pretty dumb scolding a skeleton the way she scolded Oliver. But feeling pretty dumb was better than feeling pretty terrified, so she stood up straight and slid the leather notebook out of the skeleton's hand. Sometimes doing something silly could conquer being afraid.

"Excuse me," she told the skeleton. "I suppose you don't need this anymore."

She opened it carefully, knowing from what her parents always told her that old books fell apart easily. The pages of this one were brittle and faded, but she could make out the writing in ink on the first page.

"Property of Colonel Percy H. Fawcett," she read. *"If found, destroy without reading."* Celia raised her eyebrow at him. "Sorry, Colonel Fawcett," she said. "I don't want to read it any more than you want me to. But I have as much choice as you do."

His bone-faced grin smiled back at her. She guessed he was beyond caring.

She turned the pages. The writing was hard to make out in the light from her headlamp. She saw drawings of South American towns and of native tribes. She even recognized some of the plants and animals from her own trip into the Amazon.

And then she was startled to see detailed drawings of the temples at El Dorado, the very place she and her brother had been last summer, where they were supposed to find the Lost Library. His pencil writing all over the drawing was hard to make out; there were letters she knew to be ancient Greek and there was the symbol of the key from her mother's secret society, and there was Sir Edmund's Council's scroll in chains. On the back of the page with the drawing, she read what Colonel Percy H. Fawcett had written.

"I do not regret what I've done. Though it cost me my son and his friend along with him, I bear this burden alone. Only my thoughts in this diary keep me company on this lonely outpost. Even the builders of this once great civilization are gone. I am alone on an island I know not where, just as I planned. For I did not escape the far reaches of the Amazon with my treasure only to turn it over to philistines."

Celia didn't know what a philistine was, but it didn't sound like a good thing to be. She added it to her list of words to use against people she didn't like.

"These memory keepers would make fools of the ancient sages and this council would bring destruction to all. It cannot fall into either hands. So I locked it in on itself; the Lost Library of Alexandria. Secure in Atlantis. And Atlantis secure within the Lost Library. Only the old Greek's map will tell. And that shall perish with me."

She couldn't believe it. This old explorer had left the Amazon, where everyone thought he had vanished forever, only to hide the Lost Library and then come to this island and vanish forever.

And what was that about the memory keepers? Could he have meant the Mnemones? A mnemonic was a way to remember something. Did that mean he was hiding the Lost Library from the Mnemones and from Sir Edmund's Council? Why? What difference would it make if someone made fools of the ancient sages?

From what Celia could tell, they did just fine making fools of themselves. If they were so sagey, why'd they lose their library in the first place? And how could the Council use the library to "bring destruction"?

It seemed like every time she discovered anything, it only led to more questions.

She stomped her foot, and the island rumbled in answer. Dust crumbled from the ceiling. Black chunks of rock crashed into the water. Then the cave shook from side to side, knocking Celia off her feet. She pulled herself up again using the old wheel of the ship. She tracked a droplet falling from the ceiling. Another followed it. When they hit the deck of the boat, they sizzled with steam and cut a perfect hole in the wood.

Lava was leaking through the roof.

Celia needed to find Plato's map and get out of there, and fast!

She flung open the explorer's trunk and saw all kinds of empty tins of food and strange instruments and odd devices. There was no diving gear, of course. Percy Fawcett vanished long before scuba diving was invented. He must have come to this place to hide when it was still aboveground, before the last volcanic eruption.

If she didn't find Plato's map soon, she would be entombed here too.

She tossed supplies out around her as she rummaged, muttering apologies to the old skeleton, to whom she'd already gotten used to talking, the way some people talked to pets or dolls or little brothers. She didn't expect him to respond.

"Where is it?" she muttered. "Where's that map?"

The trunk was empty. There was no papyrus scroll. No ancient Greek writing. No Plato's map.

She ran around the ship, tearing open every nook and cranny. It was empty. Percy Fawcett had traveled here alone and traveled without much luggage. There was nowhere else to hide it.

She looked back at the skeleton and groaned.

"I'm glad Oliver's not here," she told the bones of the old explorer as she rummaged through his pockets. "He would flip out. He's such a wuss. He'd be helpless without me, you know?"

She tugged and pulled at the old clothes, which seemed to come apart in her hands. All he had in his pockets was a worn-down pencil nub, a rusty compass that had lost its needle, and a faded black-and-white photograph of two young boys and a sad-faced woman. That must have been P.F.'s family.

"Ugh!" She yelled in frustration and threw the

photo at him. "I am going to lose my family if I don't find this map!"

The island rumbled. The water around the temple gurgled and bubbled. A giant stalactite broke from the ceiling and crashed into the water. She looked back at the old skeleton, deeply annoyed by his dumb skeleton smile. But that feeling—that annoyed feeling and that dumb smile—made her think of Oliver and she knew where to look.

"Gross!" She groaned. "Boys!"

She reached around behind him to the waistband of his pants, just where you'd grab to give the old skeleton a wedgie, and sure enough, she found a roll of old cloth tucked into the back of his pants. She pulled it out and unrolled it.

She knew it immediately. There was the ancient Greek writing, there was the drawing of the world with all the continents in the wrong places, and, strangely, there was the symbol of Sir Edmund's Council, a scroll locked in chains.

But Plato's map was older than the Lost Library, thought Celia. Why would his Council have existed before it did?

"This council would bring destruction to all,"

Percy Fawcett had written. A library couldn't bring destruction to all . . . but maybe Atlantis could. Celia found herself getting that seasick feeling.

If Sir Edmund got this map, he would "bring destruction to all."

But if he didn't get the map, he would definitely bring destruction to Celia's family and to Corey Brandt.

"Oh man!" she said out loud, with big roll of her eyes. She didn't know how she was going to do it yet, but she had no choice. She had to figure out how to save her family and then save the world.

She shined her light upward and saw steaming hot drops falling from cracks in the ceiling, like lava was fighting its way in from above. It was time to go.

"Good-bye, Colonel," she told the bones of Percy Fawcett. "If I can, I'll tell your family what happened to you."

The skeleton stared back at her, unmoving and unmoved.

The room shook and another great chunk of black rock fell into the water with a splash.

Celia shoved Plato's map and the leather diary

into the plastic bag Sir Edmund had given her and tucked it into her wet suit. Then she struggled back into her scuba gear and slipped into the water.

"I'm coming back!" she said into the microphone as she sank below the surface, giving one last good-bye wave to poor, dead Percy Fawcett.

"It's about time!" Sir Edmund's voice crackled. "Bonnie was ready to leave you and your mother for dead. This whole island is going to blow!"

"I'm swimming as fast as I can!"

"Did you find it?" Sir Edmund said. "Did you find Plato's map?"

"Affirmative," said Celia, because that's how people answered that sort of thing on TV.

"Did you find anything else down there?"

"Negative," said Celia, thinking of how she would hide the journal before Sir Edmund saw it, because that's what heroes do on TV, and Celia guessed it was time to be a hero.

Though no one but the blobfish and whatever else lurked in the shadows of the deep was there to see it, a heavy stream of bubbles rose from Celia's mask, which proved that, indeed, it was possible to sigh underwater.

You see, Celia really didn't feel like being a hero.

40

WE FOLLOW THE CHICKEN

THE LITTLE BOAT HADN'T even hit the beach when Oliver threw himself over the side and splashed through the low breakers, calling out for Celia. Waves piled on, knocking him over with every new step he took. He spat out salt water and seaweed, pulled himself up, and kept stumbling on through the surf.

"Celia!" he yelled. "Mom!"

The last of Sir Edmund's men, ignoring Oliver completely, leaped into their own boats and sped off toward their ship.

The dinghy slid onto the sand behind Oliver. Dr. Navel lifted the motor so it didn't get stuck, and he and Corey jumped off.

"Everyone's, like, gone," Corey said.

"No." Oliver pointed. "There's one boat left. That has to be Sir Edmund's."

The ground shook and knocked all of them off their feet. Trees toppled and a cloud of black ash blotted out the sky.

"We have to find them!" Oliver said as he stood back up and pulled seaweed out of his ears. "We'll need to split up."

"No," Dr. Navel told him. "I almost lost you once. I am not doing that again. We stick together."

"We don't have a lot of time," said Corey. "We don't even know where they are."

"This way!" Oliver ran, not even looking to see if they were following him. They rushed through the tangled tropical forest until they reached the giant statues of the squid-headed men. One of them had cracked and another was leaning perilously to the side, like a pirate after too much rum. Below it was the watery entrance to the cave. Dennis pecked and clucked around the edge in a state of high anxiety.

"Bwak-bwak-bwak," he said when he saw Oliver.

"They were here." Oliver rushed over to the edge of the hole.

"Did the chicken tell you that?" his father

asked, surprised that his son could speak to poultry.

"No," said Oliver. "And he's a rooster."

Oliver bent down and picked the old remote control out of the grass.

"I dropped this into the water," he said. "And now it's here. And it's still wet. Celia must have left it here so I'd find it."

"So where did she go?" Corey wondered.

They looked around, searching for footprints or trampled grass, any clues at all.

"Ow," Oliver said as Dennis pecked at his feet. He swatted at the bird. The volcano rumbled.

"Watch out!" Dr. Navel tackled Oliver just as one of the statues snapped at the base and collapsed onto the hole, blocking its entrance.

"I hope no one's still down there," Corey said.

"Bwak," said Dennis, flapping his useless wings.

Dr. Navel helped Oliver up.

"Bwak!" Dennis said again.

Oliver looked at Dennis and then at Corey; Corey looked at Dennis and then back at Oliver.

"Chicken to the rescue?" Corey said.

Oliver nodded.

"What?" asked Dr. Navel.

"Dad," said Oliver. "We've got to follow the bird."

With that, Dennis took off through the bushes. Dr. Navel, Oliver, and Corey Brandt chased after him, hoping he would lead them to Celia and Claire Navel.

They ducked branches and leaped over logs. When the bird weaved to the left, they weaved to the left. When it hopped to the right, they hopped to the right. Soon they were back on the beach, panting. They'd run in a big circle.

"That was a wild-goose chase." Dr. Navel rested his hands on his knees.

"Chicken," said Corey.

"Rooster," corrected Oliver.

"A wild-rooster chase," said Dr. Navel. "The meaning is the same. We didn't find anything."

"Bwak!" said Dennis, kicking his yellow claws into the foamy surf and running away as the waves crashed, only to run forward again when the water went back out. "Bwak," he repeated with every charge toward the sea.

"There!" Oliver pointed just offshore, where they saw the last motorboat speeding away from the island with Sir Edmund and one of his henchmen holding Celia hostage. Their mother was next to her, half draped over the side of the boat like a sack of wet clothes. Oliver swallowed hard, hoping she was knocked out and not, well . . . he didn't even want to think it.

"Where's Bonnie?" Corey wondered. "I didn't, like, see her in any of the boats."

They heard a chuckle from behind them. "I'll be taking your boat back, I think," she said. She was leaning on a palm tree and she wasn't taking any chances. She had a gun pointed at them.

"You're going to kidnap us again?" asked Dr. Navel.

"Not this time," said Bonnie. "Sir Edmund got what he was after from your daughter, so the Navels are worthless to me now." She smiled at Corey, although it didn't look like a happy smile. It was more like a wolf baring its teeth. "But the Hollywood brat and the chicken will still do me some good with Big Bart's crew."

"You're too late," said Dr. Navel. "The ones I

didn't knock out are at each other's throats. There will be nothing left of that ship or that crew by the time you get there."

Bonnie shrugged. "I'll take my chances. I'm sure my odds are much better than yours. Stay where you are and I'll let you fend for yourselves as the volcano erupts. Try to chase me and I'll shoot you." She nodded at Corey. "You! Grab the bird and come with me."

"I'll never leave my friends!" said Corey.

"Then I'll have to shoot them right here." She raised her gun.

Corey looked at Oliver and Dr. Navel with wide wet eyes. He didn't know what to do.

"Go," said Dr. Navel. "We'll be all right. You go and I promise we'll come for you, just like you did for me."

Corey hugged Dr. Navel and bent down to Oliver.

"I'm sorry I came between you and your sister," he said. "I never meant to upset either of you. I think you guys are, like, amazing."

"You gonna spell that?" Oliver smiled.

Corey laughed and hugged him. "Take care of your dad."

"Don't worry," said Oliver. "We'll see you again soon. Like, S-O-O-N."

"Touching," said Bonnie. "Now bring that dumb chicken and get on the boat."

"It's a roost—," Oliver started, but Bonnie gave him a look that told him not even to think about correcting her.

She made Dr. Navel push the dinghy off the beach while Corey started the motor. Bonnie shouted orders and waved her gun around.

Dr. Navel and Oliver watched from the beach as Dennis and Corey sped away toward the pirate ship in the distance. Sir Edmund's dinghy was back at his own ship. Both of them, it seemed, would be gone soon, and Dr. Navel and Oliver would be alone under the volcano.

"Remember all that sailing stuff I taught you?" Dr. Navel asked.

"Yeah," said Oliver.

"Well, it's time to use it. We're getting off this island."

"How?" Oliver wondered.

"Let's grab that pile of garbage over there." He pointed to the shelter Corey had started to build. "We're making a raft."

"You know how to do that?" asked Oliver.

"Son," Dr. Navel said, "I may not be on television, but your old dad can still do one or two cool things."

"Like build a raft out of garbage to save us from an erupting volcano and rescue Celia and Mom from an evil explorer?"

"Exactly that."

"That's pretty cool, I guess." Oliver shrugged.

Dr. Navel couldn't help but smile. The island rumbled and another dark plume of smoke burst into the air. Red-hot lava began to flow down the side of the mountain. Gray dust fell from the sky like snow, coating the trees and the beach in ash. Within seconds it was falling like a blizzard.

"We have to build fast!" said Dr. Navel. "Grab anything that floats and drag it over here!"

Oliver ran up and down the beach, covering his mouth and nose with his sleeve so he didn't breathe in ash. His hair and clothes and face were all gray and ghostly, but he worked as quickly as he could. He found driftwood and plastic bottles, empty gas cans and more plastic bags than he could count. He found the shredded remains of an inflatable airplane emergency raft that struck him as quite familiar. He dragged his haul back down the beach to his father, who was working on the raft that Corey had begun.

"Why's there all this garbage here?" Oliver choked out the question through the blizzard of volcanic ash.

"Everything has to go somewhere. Did you know that all the plastic ever made still exists on earth in some form? Litter goes into rivers and oceans and catches the current and eventually washes ashore."

"Dad?" said Oliver. "Now might not be a good time for a lecture. Let's just be happy that so many people throw away things that float!"

Dr. Navel nodded and Oliver helped him tie a driftwood beam in place for a mast. The island rumbled and a sheet of sizzling hot rocks crashed down the side of the volcano, racing toward the beach.

"We need to go faster," Oliver said. He ran off to collect more plastic.

On board the research vessel *Serenity*, Janice and Sir Edmund scanned the island through their binoculars but couldn't see much through the falling ash.

They could just barely make out Oliver hauling an armful of water bottles through the breaking surf.

"It looks like Bonnie chose to leave your son and husband to the tender mercies of nature." Sir Edmund turned to Celia and her mother.

"You're a lucky winner!" said Claire Navel. "Thousands in cash and prizes!" Her head lolled back and forth and her eyes were glassy, distant. She drooled.

"You made her crazy!" Celia shouted.

Sir Edmund raised his eyebrows at Celia.

"Crazier than she was, anyway," added Celia.

"She'll be fine in a few hours," said Sir Edmund. "We gave her the antidote, just like we promised."

"You said you'd let us go!"

"You should be happy that we didn't let you go," Janice told her. "We could have left you for dead along with the rest of your family. Now you'll get the thrill of being an only child!" Janice laughed.

"Now, Janice, be nice," said Sir Edmund. "That is no way to treat the young lady who has brought us this." He held up the papyrus scroll of Plato's map. His mustache twitched with glee. He turned to one of his crew. "Take the prisoners belowdecks. I want Claire Navel contained before the poison is out of her system. And then get us under way. We have a map to follow, a Lost Library to discover, an ancient civilization to restore to glory!"

"What about Bonnie?" Janice asked, lifting her binoculars again to watch Bonnie and her hostages speeding toward the pirate cruise ship.

"She knows too much," said Sir Edmund. "We'll let the kraken take care of her."

"But Ernest is still on that pirate ship," said Janice. "He's an idiot, but he's been loyal."

"If we were to rescue him, you would have to split the money I'm paying you," said Sir Edmund, raising his eyebrow.

Janice looked toward the pirate ship again, then she shrugged.

"I thought so." Sir Edmund nodded. He called down to one of his crew on the lower deck. "Release the kraken!"

"What was that, sir?" the crewman called up.

"I said"—Sir Edmund cleared his throat—"Release! The! Kraken!"

"What?" The crewman looked over his shoulder. No one was there. "You mean me?"

"Yes! You! You idiot!" Sir Edmund stomped his foot. "Release it now!"

"Release what, sir?" the man shouted back.

"The kraken!" Sir Edmund's face had turned red with rage. "The giant tooth-clawed squid we've been driving around the Pacific Ocean! Release it now!"

"Oh, that squid thing?" the man said. "It gives me the creeps."

"Just release it! Now!"

"I'll have to find one of the engineers to open the tank, sir. I'm not sure how."

"Do that then!"

"Yes, sir!" The man rushed below to find somebody who could tell him how exactly one went about releasing the kraken.

Sir Edmund sighed and turned to Janice. "These things always seem so much easier in the movies."

41

WE HEAR A FAMILIAR HISS

CELIA HEARD a great commotion on the deck above the tiny metal room where they'd locked her with her mother. Men were running and shouting and barking orders at each other. Something dramatic was going on, but Celia couldn't really focus on that because her mother was singing in the corner.

"Fifteen men on the dead man's chest . . . Yo-ho-ho, and a bottle of rum!"

"Mom, shh. Stop singing pirate songs." Celia tried to calm her. "It'll be okay. You just have to rest for a while."

"Drink and the devil had done with the rest," her mother crooned.

Celia slumped against the wall, rubbing her

eyes, exhausted. Beneath her wet suit, the journal of Percy Fawcett was digging into her back. The pages were soaked, but at least she managed to keep it hidden from Sir Edmund.

She had put on quite a fit to keep her wet suit on. She learned long ago that no one, not even Sir Edmund, could stand to watch a little girl cry if they could help it. So when she got out of that water, she cried and whined and threw a tantrum to keep her wet suit on. Sir Edmund must have thought that letting her wear the wet suit was a small price to pay for peace and quiet. Luckily.

"Psst," someone whispered from right next to her. "Psst."

Celia listened carefully and tracked the sound to a vent by her feet. She crouched down and pressed her ear against it.

"Hello?" she said.

"Claire?" the voice whispered. It belonged to a man. "Is that you?"

"I'm her daughter, Celia. Who's this?"

"Celia!" The voice nearly shouted, so she had to turn her ear away quickly. "Celia, how can it be you? How did you get here?"

"Who is this?"

"It's Professor Rasmali-Greenberg," the man said.

"Professor!" Celia recognized the voice of the Explorers Club president now. It was more hoarse than she'd ever heard it, but it was him.

"I was abducted just after you left the Explorers Club with Corey Brandt. They lured me to a conference on the hermeneutics of the later cults of Poseidon and snatched me from my hotel room."

Celia had no idea what hermeneutics were but she knew that Poseidon was the Greek god of the sea, so that probably meant it had something to do with Atlantis.

"I fear Sir Edmund has something terrible planned," he went on.

"I know he does," said Celia. "He's got Plato's map."

"He does! How?"

"I gave it to him," said Celia, burning with shame. "I had to. He was going to kill Mom."

"But you . . . ," the professor stammered. "How did you find it?"

"I had to scuba dive through a cave and take it out of Percy Fawcett's underpants," she told him, like it was just another dull day of sixth grade.

"Oh," he said.

"We have to get out of here," said Celia. "We have to find Dad and Oliver and Corey Brandt."

"Do you know where they are?"

"I saw them on the island, but there's a volcano erupting. Corey got taken to the pirate ship."

Just then they heard a ferocious, inhuman shriek, followed by very human shouts of fright and confusion.

"I fear that pirate ship is in the gravest of dangers," the professor said.

"I heard Sir Edmund say something about a kraken," Celia told him.

"He is abusing the poor creature from his zoo," said the professor. "Escape is going to be rather a challenge with a giant squid on the loose."

"But how will we even get out of these cells?" Celia asked, just as her door swung open.

Patrick the monkey screeched happily at her and rushed into the cell, slobbering kisses all over Celia's face, and then leaped onto her mother to do the same.

"Ogden," she said. "You need to shave, but I love your new cologne."

"That's the monkey, Mom." Celia helped her mother stand.

The professor came into the little cell with Beverly the lizard at his side. He was wearing a filthy white linen suit with no tie. It was the first time Celia had ever seen him without a tie on. He noticed her glance at his neck.

"They took my tie when they abducted me." He sighed. "It was a beautiful mallard on a golden background. I loved that tie."

"But what are *they* doing here?" She gestured at the animals.

"Stowaways," he said. "I took them to the conference with me to make sure they were looked after while you were gone. They followed me when I was kidnapped and have been running around stealing food on this ship ever since."

"Why didn't you tell them to help you escape before I got here?" asked Celia. "You could have stopped all this from happening!"

"Oh, I tried," he said. "They are stubborn creatures. They showed no interest in escape until they heard your voice a few minutes ago. I think they were waiting for you."

"So what now?" Celia asked.

"We need to stop Sir Edmund," said the professor.

"I don't care about him right now," said Celia. "I want to rescue my family and go home and watch TV and get through middle school alive."

Professor Rasmali-Greenberg shuddered. "I can think of no worse fate than middle school. The wedgies I suffered . . ." He hugged himself. Celia didn't ask him to explain. "Anyway, we'll have to stop Sir Edmund in order to escape and save your brother and father."

"Okay, so how do we do that?" Celia asked.

"I hadn't thought that far ahead," the professor told her.

"Hey there!" one of the crewmen shouted, discovering that the prisoners had gotten out of their cells. Patrick screeched and Beverly, quick as lightning, darted over to the man and hissed.

"Don't hiss at me!" He raised his foot to stomp on the lizard, and she sprang up and bit him on the toe.

"Ow!" he yelled. Within seconds he fell against the wall, pale and sweating.

"Beverly!" Celia cried. "I think she just killed that man."

"No," said the professor. "A bite that quick won't kill him. It might make him wish he were dead, but after a few days of painful misery and discomfort, he'll be as good as new. And, for some reason science has never fully explained, lima beans will taste better."

"Hmm," said Celia, who really didn't like lima beans.

The crewman slumped to the floor, whimpering. Celia felt bad for him until she remembered that he didn't seem to have a problem serving on Sir Edmund's crew, leaving her father and brother behind as the volcano erupted, or holding her mom and Professor Rasmali-Greenberg prisoner.

Celia, Beverly, and Patrick slipped past the groaning crewman. The professor helped Celia's mother follow along the gangway. She was still out of her wits.

"Yo-ho-ho," Claire Navel sang as they crept along.

Celia rushed along the narrow passageway that stretched down the center of the ship. She heard the crew shouting above and froze every few feet to make sure the coast was clear. When they came to an intersection, she stopped.

"Which way do we go?" she wondered aloud.

"Right! Right!" Celia's mother called from the back of the group. "The right is right!"

"Your mother says to go right," the professor repeated.

"But she's crazy," said Celia.

"But she's right," said the professor.

"How do you know?"

"Because madness often leads to inspiration," he said. "Also, there's a sign."

He pointed to a sign at the corner just above Celia's head. It had a map of the ship on it. The rafts were clearly labeled. This was much easier than aboard the pirates' cruise ship.

Moments later, they found themselves creeping toward a stairway that led above deck.

"Well, no going back now," said Celia.

She stepped onto the deck and her heart sank when she saw an empty space where the life rafts should have been.

"Sir Edmund is breaking the law," the professor observed. "He is not supposed to travel without life rafts."

None of the crew had noticed the escaped prisoners yet. They were all looking off the left—what sailors call the port—side of the ship.

Celia followed their gaze and saw the mysterious island engulfed in flame and ash and steam. The whole thing was crumbling into the sea.

"Oh no," she whimpered, afraid that her father and brother and Corey were lost forever.

But then, a shadow formed in the haze. It grew clearer with every second. It was a raft with big sails cutting through the water toward them, a raft made of garbage. She could only make out two forms on board, but the way the littler one slouched as it moved about and the way the taller one pointed and gestured wildly made her feel sure that it was her brother and father.

"Where's Corey?" she wondered.

"And what is that?" The professor pointed at a huge shadow, twice the size of the raft, racing toward it just below the surface of the water.

"The kraken," whispered Celia's mother. She grabbed Celia's shoulder.

The shadow was charging right for the raft.

42

WE SAIL THE SQUIDDY SEA

"TRIM THE MAINSAIL!" Dr. Navel called out, and Oliver yanked the tangled bit of rope they'd attached to the big sail on their garbage raft. The raft rose slightly on its side as it picked up speed away from the island. Oliver couldn't believe his father had managed to build a raft out of garbage in such a short time.

Its hull was a pile of driftwood lashed together with vines and torn plastic bags. Underneath, they'd attached an old fisherman's net and filled it with empty plastic water bottles to make it float better. They had two masts made out of the hollow plastic pipes that one sometimes sees on construction sites, and two sails made from the yellow plastic of the ruined airline emergency raft.

Oliver almost felt hopeful as the wind blew

through his hair, the salt spray splashed his face, and they raced after Sir Edmund's ship. Behind them, the island burned and cracked apart, vanishing into roiling sea and thick smoke as they fled. Glancing back at it as they left, Oliver truly understood the meaning of the word *cataclysm*. If that's what had happened to Atlantis ten thousand years ago, it was no wonder no one had found it since.

"Your mother will be so proud!" Dr. Navel called out from his position on the rudder, which was made out of a broken paddle tied to the rusty propeller of an old airplane. "We'll call this raft the *Trash-Tiki!*"

"What's that?" Oliver asked, not even embarrassed to show his father that he was curious. It was the first time he could remember ever actually being impressed with his dad.

"After the *Kon-Tiki.*" His father smiled. "The famous raft Thor Heyerdahl used to cross the Pacific in 1947. He was an amazing explorer. We almost named you after him!"

Oliver didn't feel much like a Thor, so he was glad his parents had decided against that name. The kids at school would have mocked him ruthlessly if he was named Thor Navel.

"So what do we do when we catch up with Sir Edmund's ship?" Oliver asked.

"I'm not sure we can," said his father. "The best we can do is follow them for now, and make sure they don't get away with your mother and your sister."

"And what about Corey?"

"He'll be okay for a while," said Dr. Navel. "The pirates will want to ransom him, so they won't hurt him."

It wasn't exactly a comfort, but Oliver figured they could only follow one ship at a time. As they raced after Sir Edmund's big whaling ship, the pirate cruise ship got farther and farther away. Somehow, though, Sir Edmund's ship wasn't getting farther away from their raft. It was getting closer.

"Look!" Oliver pointed. "Sir Edmund's ship has stopped. We're gaining on them!"

"We are!" Dr. Navel smiled. "We might just catch up with them yet!"

"We'll need a plan," said Oliver, walking back to where his father was steering the *Trash-Tiki*. "We can't just storm the ship and demand they let Celia and Mom go, can we?"

"We could always try the Kathmandu Caper," said Dr. Navel.

"What's the Kathmandu Caper?" Oliver asked.

"Well, one of us will act like an angry goat while the other collects as many jellyfish as he can, and then—oh no!"

"What?" Oliver asked. His father pointed in the direction of Sir Edmund's ship.

Oliver saw a dark shape in the water racing from the ship toward the *Trash-Tiki*. It was bigger than any shark or whale Oliver had ever seen on TV. It was bigger than their entire raft and it was moving much faster.

"Coming about!" Dr. Navel yelled. "Evasive maneuvers!"

Oliver ran to the forward sail and let the rope go free as Dr. Navel tried to turn the raft and get some speed in a different direction from whatever was coming at them. There was no time. The shadow was on them in seconds, an inky splotch in the ocean, blossoming beneath them with eight impossibly long arms. It hung for a moment in the water.

"The kraken," Dr. Navel gulped.

"But *Beast Busters* said there was no such thing," Oliver objected, just as the tentacles came alive, snapping tight and breaking the surface with slimy suckers glistening. As the tentacles rose into the sunlight and towered over their raft, sharp black fangs, each bigger than one of Oliver's fists, unsheathed themselves from the suckers along the undersides of the tentacles.

"You can't believe everything you see on TV," said Dr. Navel as the first tentacle slashed the mainmast clean off. The rope attached to it whipped into the air and he dove to knock Oliver out of the way. Oliver hit the deck when his father pushed him, but another tentacle slapped down between them and coiled itself like a boa constrictor around his father, hoisting Dr. Navel toward the sky.

Oliver screamed. He tried to stand and catch his father's foot, but the raft lurched violently to the side. One tentacle had wrapped around the back and the other around the front. The kraken pulled itself up halfway on the deck, its weight tearing the raft in two.

"I have an idea," yelled Oliver, grabbing one of the old ropes they'd used to build the raft. "We have to give this squid a wedgie!"

"How do we give a squid a wedgie?" his father yelled, wriggling to free his arms from the giant tentacle.

"Catch the other end of the rope!" Oliver tossed the rope to his father. "Now pull!"

Oliver pulled his end and Dr. Navel pulled his end, and the rope tightened underneath the squid.

"It's working!" Oliver called as the rope wedged itself into the monster's underside.

Oliver, however, was hardly an ichthyologist, and failed to understand the basics of squid science. The underside was where the giant squid had its mouth, and the kraken, being the most fearsome of giant squid, had a mouth filled with fangs. Its jaw snapped shut and the rope snapped in two. Then the monster sucked the rope into its mouth the way one might suck in two strands of spaghetti. The slurping sounds echoed for miles across the ocean.

Oliver fell backward and the monster dunked Dr. Navel underwater and scooped him up again in a violent flurry of tentacles.

"I fear the kraken is wedgie proof!" his father spluttered, spitting seawater.

Oliver grabbed the forward mast and clung to it

as the enraged kraken lifted the whole *Trash-Tiki* out of the water. Its terrible face rose from the frothy foam—two heavy-lidded yellow eyes on either side of its head and a giant round mouth with rows and rows of pointed teeth. One leftover bit of rope was stuck between two of its fangs like a piece of floss. Water splashed in all directions. The tentacles flailed, so one second Oliver and his father were close enough to touch and in the next Oliver and the raft slammed into the water and his father was flung toward the sky again.

"Hold on, Ollie!" Dr. Navel yelled.

"AHH!" yelled Oliver back, shutting his eyes, too terrified to watch his dad shoved into the terrible jaws of the sea monster. He didn't even object to being called Ollie.

And then, with a splash, all was quiet. Oliver was lying on his back on the deck of the *Trash-Tiki*. His father, panting, hung off the side, pulling himself out of the water. The giant squid was gone.

"What happened?" Oliver choked out.

"He just dropped me," said Dr. Navel. "He just let go and vanished underwater again."

Oliver pulled himself up onto his knees and

looked at the water below their broken raft. There was no inky shadow to be seen.

But then he heard shouts from Sir Edmund's ship and looked up to see the giant black form speeding toward it. There on deck, now close enough to see, were Celia and their mother and Professor Rasmali-Greenberg and Beverly and Patrick, huddling together in terror.

There wasn't just the one kraken around Sir Edmund's ship, there were five, and they were all bigger than the one racing back toward them. As soon as it arrived, the pod of giant squid broke the surface of the water together to wage a new attack. This time on the research vessel *Serenity*.

43

WE KIBITZ WITH THE KRAKEN

CELIA WATCHED as the first massive tentacle burst from the sea and, with one swipe, smashed the mainmast clean off of her father's little raft. Another thick tentacle rose from the frothy water and wrapped itself around the back of the raft, a third whipped up and circled around her father, and even with the distance between them, Celia could hear her brother scream.

"Stop it!" Celia yelled. "Stop it!"

Sir Edmund looked down on her from the bridge.

"I'm afraid the kraken knows no mercy," he said. "Now, what are you all doing out of your cells?"

Celia looked back toward the water, seeing her father hoisted high in the air and the gaping, fanged mouth of the giant squid rising from the water. Oliver was clinging to the half-shattered raft as it was tossed back and forth by another of the giant squid's arms.

Celia felt a tugging at her stomach, and the bitter taste of adrenaline rose at the back of her mouth. She had to do something. She heard her brother's screams across the water. She thought of those hours of *The Squid Whisperer* he'd made her watch. She had no idea how to get a squid's attention, but she put her fingers to her lips and blew out as loud and as long of a whistle as she could.

"What did you hope that would do?" Sir Edmund laughed. He was about to order his crew to surround the escaped prisoners when the words froze on his lips.

The kraken dropped Dr. Navel and vanished beneath the surface. Celia relaxed as she saw her father hoisting himself back onto the wreck of his raft. Celia noticed that it appeared to have been made entirely out of garbage. No wonder the giant squid ripped it apart so easily.

"How did you do that?" Professor Rasmali-Greenberg asked.

"I don't know," Celia told him. "I just panicked and whistling seemed like the thing to do. I didn't have a bagpipe."

The professor lowered his eyebrows, wondering what a bagpipe had to do with anything (he had never seen *The Squid Whisperer*). Then he pointed to the sea.

"I fear you've done more than you bargained for," he told Celia.

Giant shadows rose from the depths all around Sir Edmund's ship, their eight humongous arms spreading wide as they neared the surface.

"The baby's coming back!" one of the crewmen shouted and pointed at the water, where indeed the kraken was racing back toward their ship.

"That one was a baby?" said Celia. "You kidnapped a baby kraken!" she yelled at Sir Edmund. He shrugged. It wasn't the first time he had kidnapped a baby mythical creature. It was kind of his hobby.

"They're attacking!" Janice yelled as the whole family of giant squid raised their tentacles from the sea.

We should not be surprised to note that Sir Edmund did not pay his crew nearly well enough for calm and discipline to prevail under attack from a pod of mythical sea creatures. A lone kraken had been known to drag ships down to the bottom of the sea for the sheer joy of it. There was no telling what a family of kraken bent on revenge would do. Sir Edmund's crew were neither explorers awed by the majesty of the sea nor warriors daring to face the beast and conquer it like heroes from storybooks.

To put it more bluntly, as the krakens' dark shapes blossomed underneath the research vessel *Serenity*, everyone went crazy.

Members of the crew scrambled, bumping into each other and climbing over each other and punching each other in the nose to get to safety. All thoughts of locking the escaped prisoners up again were quickly forgotten.

Sir Edmund stood with Janice by his side, his mouth agape, watching the sea creatures lay siege to his boat.

"We have to do something!" cried Janice. "Call them off! Don't they obey you?"

Sir Edmund didn't answer her. His mouth hung open, his arms hung limp at his sides. His plans were falling apart.

He was, in a word, nonplussed.

The first of the creatures' tentacles wrapped around the bow of the ship and yanked it down toward the water. Sir Edmund grabbed the railing, ignoring the shrieks of his crew as kraken snatched them up with other tentacles. As one long, slimy, tooth-encrusted tentacle reared above him, he broke out of his stupor and dove to the side. The tentacle smashed the railing where he'd been standing and ripped it right off the boat.

"AHH!" his first mate screamed, hauled into the air in a coil of the monster's arm. Another kraken had begun tearing apart the back of the boat, opening a huge hole in the side, where water rushed in.

"Impossible!" Sir Edmund shouted, getting to his feet again. He pointed at Celia with eyes ablaze. "Only an heir to Atlantis can command the kraken! And the Council are the only rightful heirs! Tell me how you did that!"

Celia shrugged.

As tentacles ensnared crewmen right and left, it seemed that those around Celia were safe. All around, crewmen were being snatched from the

deck and sucked unceremoniously beneath the waves. Their screams didn't even have time to echo.

"You are not an heir to Atlantis!" Sir Edmund shouted, rushing down the stairs to the main deck and waving his finger at Celia, as if she were his greatest concern, not the monsters tearing his ship to shreds and eating his crew. "You are a Navel! And a lazy one at that! You watch too much television!"

"There's no such thing as too much television," shouted Celia.

"The kraken are mine! All of them!"

"It sure doesn't look that way to me," Celia answered, crossing her arms.

The ship tilted dangerously. The kraken had lined up along the starboard side and were slowly rolling the ship over. Their terrible mouths gaped and their cat-yellow eyes gazed up at the terrified crew. Sir Edmund turned and stood directly in front of the row of monsters, unafraid.

"I command you all back to the depths!" he yelled.

They didn't move.

"I will not stand here and kibitz with you!" he yelled. "Return to the deep!"

"Kibitz?" the professor wondered.

"It means chit-chat," said Celia. "And we don't have time for it! This boat is sinking!"

With all the chaos on the ship, one cannot be too certain what happened next, but it appeared that the baby giant squid spat a thick black loogie onto Sir Edmund, covering him from head to toe.

Janice pulled him out of the way just as one of the creature's tentacles slapped down where he had been standing, tearing into the metal deck with its clawed suckers.

"Trust me," Janice told Sir Edmund, pulling him along, "you don't want to stay and chat. Let's get out of here. Where are the life rafts?"

"There aren't any," said Sir Edmund.

"What?" Janice let him go.

"I will not lose my kraken and my ship on the same day!" Sir Edmund declared, wringing thick squid ink out of his mustache. "And I will not lose them because of Celia Navel. She's a child!"

"She's a tween," Janice corrected him.

"What does that even mean? It's not a real word!"

He didn't wait for Janice to answer. He ran to the harpoon gun.

Celia knew that the ship was sinking. They needed to get off fast.

But she didn't see Beverly the lizard and Patrick the monkey anywhere. Oliver would never forgive her if something happened to Beverly. And Patrick was practically a member of the family.

"We can't leave without the monkey and the lizard," she said.

"There!" The professor pointed.

Beverly was perched on the harpoon gun, hissing at Sir Edmund, and Patrick had jumped on Janice's back, clawing at her hair.

Celia whistled at them as loud as she could. She figured that if it worked on a kraken, it could work on a monkey and a lizard.

It didn't.

They ignored her.

The kraken, however, did not. Six pairs of giant eyes turned to look at her.

"Perhaps you shouldn't whistle at these monsters until you know what you are saying," suggested the professor.

"Too late," Celia squeaked. All six giant squid

dragged themselves along the side of the ship until they had come directly to Celia.

"Those are some big calamari," Celia's mother whispered.

"So, uh, what do I do?" Celia said, staring into the giant eyes of the kraken. The largest of the giant squid reached out with one of its great tentacles. It didn't whip it at Celia or encircle her. It simply extended it, stopping just in front of her face.

Celia thought of *Valerie-at-Large*. Even though Valerie would never really be friends with the mean girls in the Six Sisters Club, they shook hands with each other at the end, because they had an understanding. They couldn't change who they were, but they could change how they treated each other. Celia guessed maybe the kraken felt the same way.

She reached her hand out and touched the tip of its tentacle. It was wet and much harder and rougher than she'd thought it would be, but oddly gentle. It tickled her palm.

"This will teach you to disobey!" Sir Edmund shouted, pointing the harpoon gun right at the biggest sea monster. It looked his way and Celia was certain she could see its eyes widen with what had to be fear. Sir Edmund was about to fire when, instead, he screamed.

Beverly's jaws were clamped tight around his ankle.

"Beverly, you traitor!" He groaned as he slumped against the harpoon gun. Even his mustache sagged as her poison began to course through his veins. "I hate lima beans."

Janice tried to jump to the gun, but Beverly hissed at her and she stopped.

"Good lizard," she cooed. "Be a nice lizard, good lizard."

Beverly hissed again and Janice fainted.

"Go," Celia said to the giant squid. "Go . . . and . . . uh, don't sink any more ships, okay?"

The kraken looked to Celia, then back to Sir Edmund groaning in agony, and then back to Celia. It let go of the ship and slipped back into the ocean, vanishing with one stroke of its eight massive arms. The others followed.

"*Below the thunders of the upper deep; / Far, far beneath in the abysmal sea, / His ancient, dreamless, uninvaded sleep, / The Kraken sleepeth : faintest sunlights flee*," Celia's mother said.

....

"Great," said Celia. "Mom's crazier than ever."

"That was from the poet Alfred Tennyson," said the professor. "He wrote *The Kraken* in 1830."

"So are we just going to stand here and recite poetry now?" Celia wondered.

"We should get off this ship before Sir Edmund recovers from that bite," the professor said.

"Sounds good to me," said Celia. "But how?"

"Maybe your friend can help." The professor pointed to a small wooden fishing boat sailing up alongside the sinking ship, and Celia's friend Jabir standing on the bow with his mother, waving.

44

WE WON'T FORGET OUR FRIENDS

"NEED A LIFT?" Celia called out as their boat approached the floating pile of garbage where Oliver and Dr. Navel had watched the attack of the kraken unfold.

"Celia!" Dr. Navel clamored to his feet, so happy to see his daughter again that he lost his balance and fell into the water.

Jabir's mother used a long pole to pull him out again. Dr. Navel hugged Celia, and then he saw his wife.

"Claire!" He knelt in front of her. "Claire?"

"Ogden," she said dreamily. "Am I still crazy? Is that you or the monkey?"

"It's me!" he said, embracing and kissing her.

"Gross," Oliver muttered as he climbed aboard the fishing boat.

"Hi, Oliver," Jabir said to him.

"Hi," Oliver answered.

"You dropped our remote control," Celia told Oliver.

"You talked to a giant squid," Oliver told her.

"You okay?"

"Yeah. You?"

"Yeah."

They stared at each other for a while, both of them looking pretty bedraggled from their adventures, and then they hugged. As annoying as it could be to have a twin, they were pretty sure it was much worse not to have one.

"Where's Corey?" Celia asked, and Oliver shook his head sadly.

"The pirates," he said.

"Celia, Oliver," their mother called out. "You're all right! And you saved us!"

Oliver hugged his mother.

"Are you, like, still crazy?" Celia asked warily.

"I have a headache," she said. "But I'm feeling fine. The last thing I remember is you, Celia, standing up to Sir Edmund."

"It didn't really work, though," said Celia. "I had to give him Plato's map."

Her mother couldn't hide the worry sweeping across her face.

"I did keep this, though," Celia said, unzipping her wet suit and pulling out the soaked leather journal.

"You found Percy Fawcett!" Dr. Navel exclaimed.

"Yeah," said Celia. "I sort of had to."

Her father started flipping through the journal. It was hard to read because it had gotten very wet, but he nodded eagerly. "You might just be the greatest explorer in history!"

Oliver stuck his tongue out at her. Jabir smiled at her. Celia managed to scowl at her brother and blush at the same time.

"There are clues in here," her father said. "We can use this!"

"We?" Celia raised her eyebrows.

"Sixth grade will be there when you get back!" Dr. Navel smiled. "How would you like to find Atlantis instead?"

"Pass," said Celia.

"Pass," said Oliver.

"You'd be saving the world," their mother told them.

"No, thanks," said Celia and Oliver together.

"Well, we'll have to discuss that on the way," Dr. Navel told them.

"On the way to where?" Celia wondered, shooting her brother a nervous glance.

"On the way to find those pirates," said Dr. Navel. "And to rescue Corey Brandt."

"Oh," said Celia.

"And Dennis?" Oliver asked. "He's a pretty good rooster."

"And Dennis," Dr. Navel agreed. "Can we count on your help?" he asked Jabir.

"As long as those pirates are at sea, the Orang Laut will help you find them," Jabir said. His mother said something. "First we need to get something to eat," he translated. "And clean you guys up. You smell like kraken."

"I am so writing a letter to *Beast Busters*," said Oliver. Celia agreed.

They still didn't want to go off looking for Atlantis, but saving Corey Brandt, star of stage and screen, and their best friend in the world? Well, sometimes friendship had its price.

"I get to be first mate," said Celia.

"I want to be the bosun," said Oliver.

"You don't even know what a bosun is," said Celia.

"So?" Oliver told her. "Neither do you."

"I know the first mate is in charge of the bosun," she said.

"Then you can't be first mate! That's not fair!"

"I talked to a herd of giant squid!"

"Squid don't go in herds!" said Oliver. "They go in pods!"

"Who says?" said Celia. "I'm the one who talked to them!"

"I'll bet you didn't even do it on purpose. You were probably trying to tell them to eat me."

"Why would they eat you? You're gross!"

"Am not! I'll bet I'm delicious."

"Are not!"

"Am too!"

"Are not!"

Drs. Claire and Ogden Navel held hands and watched their children argue as the small boat sailed toward the nearest inhabited island. It would take time to find the pirates again, but it would also take time for Sir Edmund to wake up from Beverly's bite and repair his ship.

Together, conscious, and relatively safe for the first time in years, the Navel family was going on another adventure.

It was a good thing, too, because back at the Explorers Club, their television was still broken.

AUTHOR'S NOTE

BY NOW, of course you know that some of the stranger things found within this story are indeed true, from pirates and sea people to giant squid and Percy Fawcett.

In 1907, in his history of piracy, Colonel John Biddulph wrote, "There was no peace on the ocean. The sea was a vast No Man's domain, where every man might take his prey."

His words are as true today as they were a hundred years ago. There really are dangerous modern-day pirates who sail the seas looking to hijack ships and they really are a motley crew of international miscreants, just as they were in the old days of notorious pirates like Barbarossa in the Mediterranean or Blackbeard in the Caribbean. You would not want to come across them in your own travels.

The Orang Laut really are some of the last sea

nomads on earth, with a rich and complex culture that is often misunderstood and, like so many nomadic cultures, mistrusted. Pollution threatens their fishing habitats and, deprived of their traditional livelihood, many are forced to leave the sea behind and settle on land. They are one of the countless societies around the world whose power to determine their own future is threatened by forces beyond their control. Their understanding of and relationship to the sea could be of great benefit for all humanity, if they are able to survive the challenges of the twenty-first century.

As for the kraken, it is an old myth from Norway and Sweden. Some believe the myth was inspired by sailors seeing very real giant squid, which can grow up to fifty feet long. Some old accounts of the kraken aren't based on fish at all. The bubbles from the deep, rumbles in the ocean, and ships dragged down by sudden currents could all have been caused by volcanic eruptions under the sea near Iceland. Of course, the ocean is the last great unexplored region on earth, and scientists are only beginning to discover the wonders of its depths.

Percy Fawcett, the long-lost explorer, really did vanish in the Amazon. He really did have a strong interest in Atlantis and the mysteries of the occult. However, the real whereabouts of Percy Fawcett's remains are unknown. Perhaps he is in a cave on an island somewhere, waiting for a brave soul to come looking.

If you do find him, let us know by writing to:

C. Alexander London
Care of: Philomel Books
345 Hudson Street
New York, NY 10014 USA
Or visit http://www.calexanderlondon.com

KEEP READING FOR A SNEAK PEEK AT

OLIVER AND CELIA'S FINAL ADVENTURE

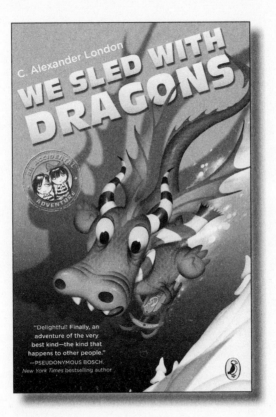

WE PLAN THE PLAN

"WHOSE BOOTY?" OLIVER Navel asked for the third time, as their small boat bobbed gently on the waves and lights twinkled on the shore.

"It's no one's booty!" His twin sister, Celia, groaned at him. "It's Djibouti! It's the name of the city. *Jib-boot-tee!* Djibouti."

"Huh?" Oliver grunted.

"Djibouti!" His sister jumped to her feet, waving her arms like a lunatic and rocking the boat back and forth. "Djibouti! Djibouti! Djibouti!"

Their parents, Dr. Claire Navel and Dr. Ogden Navel, ducked out of the way of Celia's flailing arms and steadied themselves on the sides of the boat. They were world-famous adventurers and the Explorers-in-Residence at the Explorers Club in New York City, and they had learned a few things in their travels, such as how to dodge a

wild boar attack and how to escape a hive of enraged killer bees. They found the same tactic
came in handy when dealing with their eleven-
and-a-half-year-old twins: get out of the way as
quickly as possible.

Oliver fell off his narrow bench, laughing at
his sister. He splashed into a puddle in the shallow hull of the boat, but he was laughing too hard
to care.

He knew, of course, that Djibouti was the city
whose lights were twinkling on the shore a short
distance away on the coast of North Africa. He'd
seen at least five episodes of his favorite spy TV
show, *Agent Zero*, that were set in Djibouti.

He probably knew more about Djibouti than
Celia did. He just liked hearing his sister yell it
over and over again.

"What is *so* funny about Djibouti?" Celia demanded. Oliver snickered and pulled himself
back up onto his bench.

Brothers can be so immature, she thought. She
was three minutes and forty-two seconds older
than Oliver, but sometimes it seemed like she
was three years older. Oliver was giggling like an
idiot just because Djibouti sounded like "booty."
She noticed her father was smirking too.

Celia looked at her mother and rolled her eyes. Boys never grew up.

"It's just the city's name." She blew a strand of hair out of her face. "Djibouti."

"Bwaaah!" Oliver exploded in laughter again. He leaned over the side of the boat, turning bright red and shaking. He held his hand up in the air. "Enough," he gasped. "No more . . . I can't . . . don't say it again . . ."

"Djibouti," said Celia.

"Bwaaah!" Oliver cried, convulsing with violent laughter.

"Djibouti," she said again.

Oliver was turning purple, doubled over, long past the point when laughing was fun but unable to stop. We all certainly know the feeling, which usually occurs at the least opportune moment, such as during study hall or when a famed astronomer is giving a lecture on the ice mountains of Uranus.

"Oliver, calm down," Dr. Claire Navel, Oliver and Celia's mother, said. She grabbed Oliver by the back of his T-shirt to keep him from laughing himself over the edge of the boat. "And Celia, stop harassing your brother."

"He asked for it," said Celia.

"Be that as it may"—their mother looked from Celia to Oliver and back again—"there is nothing funny about Djibouti."

Their father snickered, but his wife shot him a glance that could have melted the ice mountains on Uranus. He fixed his face into a serious expression and stayed silent.

"The city is a den of pirates, thieves, and tourists," their mother continued. "Who knows what they're doing to poor Corey Brandt in there?"

"Don't forget Dennis," said Oliver.

Dennis was a chicken. Technically, being a male chicken, he was a rooster, but we don't really need to be so persnickety, do we?

The important thing to know about Dennis is that he was a chicken who had proven himself intelligent and heroic, in spite of having once served as bird-in-residence aboard a pirate ship. He had belonged to the captain, a ferocious rogue named Big Bart, but Bonnie, another pirate on Big Bart's crew, took Dennis the chicken prisoner at the same time that she kidnapped Corey Brandt.

Corey Brandt, we should note, was not a chicken. He was an actor. He had, however, once dressed as a chicken for a discount mattress commercial. That was a long time ago, and he doesn't like to talk about it.

Currently, Corey Brandt was the most famous teenager in the world, star of hit television shows like *Agent Zero*, *The Celebrity Adventurist*, and the groundbreaking teen vampire drama *Sunset High*. He wasn't yet eighteen years old, but he earned more money in a day sitting in his trailer wearing vampire fangs than the entire population of Djibouti earned in a year.

It was no wonder pirates were holding him for ransom.

Corey was also Oliver and Celia's best friend in the world, like a cool older brother, and he had been kidnapped while trying to reunite the twins with their parents and find a map to the lost city of Atlantis. The Navels were happy to be reunited. It had been years since they had all been together, but they hadn't been able to keep the map to Atlantis from falling into the hands of an evil explorer or keep Corey from falling into the hands of a vicious pirate.

It had taken weeks to track the pirates from the Pacific Ocean, through the Strait of Malacca, across the Bay of Bengal, along the Kerala coast of India, and now across the Arabian Sea to

Djibouti, and the twins were not only missing most of sixth grade, which they didn't mind one bit, they were also missing the season finales of all their favorite TV shows, which they minded quite a lot.

"Are you sure this plan will work?" Celia asked her mother. "Because I'm missing the last episode of *Celebrity Fashion Crimes.*"

"And the new season of *World's Best Rodeo Clown,*" said Oliver.

"And *Love at 30,000 Feet,*" said Celia.

"And *Soup Wars,*" said Oliver.

"And *Bizarro Bandits,*" the twins said together.

They were missing a lot of television.

"We'll get you home soon," their mother told them with a sigh. She couldn't understand why they'd rather watch TV than plan a raid on a pirate stronghold in Djibouti. "The Prague Proposition is foolproof."

"But this isn't Prague," said Celia. "It's Djibouti."

"Bwah—" Oliver started to laugh, but Celia scowled at him. He clamped his hands over his mouth. Dr. Ogden Navel let out one high-pitched giggle.

....

"I've adapted the plan for this city," their mother said.

"So why not call it something else?" Oliver suggested. "Like the Djibouti Jinx?"

"Oh, that's good, Ollie! You're thinking like a real explorer now!" His mother licked her thumb and tried to press Oliver's stray hair flat against his head. He flinched and ducked away but couldn't help smirking just a little. He'd never admit it, but he liked that he'd impressed his mother.

"What'll happen to Corey if the Djbou—" Celia glanced at Oliver. "If the plan doesn't work?"

"You worry too much," she said. "The Prague—I mean, the Djibouti Jinx will work."

"It better." Celia glanced across the water at the city, which stuck out into the Gulf of Aden like a stray hair on Africa's head. "Or else we'll have missed all our shows for nothing."

"Trust me," their mother said, smiling at her family. She grabbed her husband's hand and squeezed it. "We're all together again. Nothing can possibly go wrong."

DON'T ACCIDENTALLY
MISS AN ADVENTURE!

**Follow the Navel twins at
www.calexanderlondon.com**